BUMBLE

LEGEND OF THE IR'INDICTI SERIES, BOOK ONE

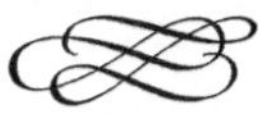

CONNIE SUTTLE

Print Second Edition (2018)
Print ISBN: 1-63478-058-2
Print ISBN-13: 978-1-63478-058-2
eBook ISBN: 1-939759-10-2
eBook ISBN-13: 978-1-939759-10-8

Published by:
SubtleDemon Publishing, LLC
PO Box 95696
Oklahoma City, OK 73143

Cover art by Renee Barratt @ The Cover Counts

To Walter, Joe, Larry, Lee, Dianne, Sarah and Mark.
Thank you.

ACKNOWLEDGMENTS

As always, this book is the result of collaboration. If it weren't for the support of my editor, my cover artist and my beta readers, it would be less than it is. All mistakes, as usual, are mine and no other's.

About the Author:
Connie Suttle lives in Oklahoma with her husband and a conglomerate of cats. They have finally banded together to make their demands, which has proven disconcerting to all humans involved.

You may find Connie in the following ways:
Facebook: Connie Suttle Author
Twitter: @subtledemon
Website and Blog: subtledemon.com

High Demon Series:

Demon Lost

Demon Revealed

Demon's King

Demon's Quest

Demon's Revenge

Demon's Dream

God Wars Series:

Blood Double

Blood Trouble

Blood Revolution

Blood Love

Blood Finale

Saa Thalarr Series:

Hope and Vengeance

Wyvern and Company

Observe and Protect*

First Ordinance Series:

Finder

Keeper

BlackWing

SpellBreaker

WhiteWing

Rose and Thorn

Black Rose Queen

Queen of Thorns and Roses

Future Wars Series

Buffer Zone

Black Zone*

Other Titles from SubtleDemon Publishing:

Malefactor

Transgressor

Underhanded*

by Joe Scholes

*Forthcoming

FOREWORD

A note about the locations in this series:

Cloud Chief, Oklahoma is a real ghost town, located near Cordell, Oklahoma. All of the land is now privately owned and the Cloud Chief community portrayed in this book is fictitious in nature.

CHAPTER 1

Preoccupied with approaching doom while snowflakes settled on his hair and sheepskin jacket, Ashe Evans walked right past the white buffalo standing in two inches of snow beside the road. A disgruntled snort disturbed the snow-muted morning as the buffalo, offended by Ashe's rudeness, thumped a hoof impatiently against frozen ground. Startled from his thoughts by the sudden noise, Ashe turned swiftly to locate its source.

"Good morning, Mr. Thompson." Ashe, his nose and ears red from the cold, breathed a relieved sigh and waved at the large bison, causing the heavy backpack he carried to slip from his shoulder. Mr. Thompson's breaths were misty white clouds in the late March snowfall as he blinked at Ashe in irritation.

Ashe Evans might have been any twelve-going-on-thirteen-year-old trudging toward a rural school in the snow. He wasn't. Cloud Chief might have been any small farming community in western Oklahoma. It wasn't. The buffalo might have been any buffalo still living in the Central Plains, but Amos Thompson would tell you himself (quite majestically, in fact) that he most certainly was not.

Protected by three vampires and a perimeter spell laid each year by an itinerant witch, Cloud Chief, Oklahoma, appeared to be a ghost town on maps and to passing non-residents. Inside the spell's boundary, werewolves, shapeshifters and vampires populated the small but thriving community.

"Sorry I didn't see you, Mr. Thompson," Ashe apologized. Snow had collected atop Mr. Thompson's woolly head, giving anyone with any imagination at all the idea that he wore a beret between short, curving horns. Ashe waited until he'd turned away to smile. Stamping his hoof again (Mr. Thompson had no patience for inattentive children) the buffalo trotted off to help neighbors check on spring lambs.

Hunching into his sheepskin jacket, Ashe hefted the backpack to a more comfortable position and continued on his way. Transformational Arts, his first class of the day was waiting, along with inevitable shame and eternal embarrassment.

Every seventh-grade student at Cloud Chief Combined was expected to take (and pass) Transformational Arts. With a vampire father and a shapeshifting mother, Ashe should be passing Transformational Arts easily. He wasn't. Ashe, no matter how hard he tried, couldn't produce a single scale, feather, talon or patch of fur. The school year was winding down too, with only six weeks of classes remaining. Struggling to fight off a recurring bout of misery, Ashe wondered if his parents ever imagined that he might turn out frustratingly ordinary.

"What happened to you?" Ashe, dumping his backpack beside a desk in Transformational Arts, stared at his best friend. Black-haired, dark-eyed and looking much like his werewolf Packmaster father, Salidar DeLuca frantically swiped at his left ear and hair, attempting to brush white chalk dust away before Mrs. Rocklin arrived.

"Dori hit me with an eraser," Sali growled, glaring accusingly at Dori and Wynn across the aisle. Dori Anderson, a shapeshifting ocelot and Wynn O'Neill, an extremely rare unicorn, glared right back. A feud simmered constantly between Sali, Wynn and Dori, with occasional eruptions of mild violence and adult language. Fed mostly by insults from Sali, the hostility showed no signs of ever letting up.

"Don't you know to duck?" Ashe wanted to snicker at Sali's predicament—the chalk dust wasn't easily removed from dark hair.

"It was a well-planned, two-prong attack," Sali replied, his nearly black eyes staring at the chalk dust that now covered his fingers.

"Ah, the ocelot-unicorn maneuver—surround your enemy and distract him," Ashe nodded respectfully at Dori and Wynn. Wynn, quite pretty with long white hair and pale-blue eyes, acknowledged the near-compliment with a return nod. Dori, wearing her curly, dark-blonde hair shorter, wasn't about to concede anything to the enemy camp. With green eyes flashing a warning at Sali and Ashe, Dori turned away with a disgruntled "hmmph."

"Mrs. Rocklin's coming," Ashe hissed, shutting down conversation inside the classroom as nine students scrambled for seats. Ashe heard their instructor walking down the hall from the opposite end of the building, giving his classmates plenty of time to slide into seats and innocently face the blackboard before Mrs. Rocklin arrived.

Exceptional hearing seemed to be Ashe's only gift. Better than the werewolves and his vampire father's, Ashe's ability to hear the tiniest sounds from a distance had the entire community scratching their heads in confusion. As Ashe hadn't managed to become anything other than himself, he wasn't about to boast of his auricular proficiency.

Mrs. Rocklin eyed Sali, who continued to surreptitiously brush chalk dust from his hair. Knowing without question that Sali had been up to something, Mrs. Rocklin called on him first. "Salidar," she said, lifting an eyebrow, "You will go first this morning. Try to get all your fur out on the initial attempt."

Reddening guiltily, Sali stood. Ashe knew Sali was self-conscious during his changes from human to wolf and at times his turns weren't a complete transformation under Mrs. Rocklin's watchful eye. Dori snickered, earning a nasty glare from Sali.

"You can do it," Ashe reassured his friend in a whisper so soft only Sali might hear. If Sali were alone or with Ashe, his turns were perfect. Whenever Sali transformed in front of his older brother

Marco, something always went wrong. Marco wasn't merciful when he teased Sali about the unsuccessful attempts, either.

Closing his eyes, Sali focused on changing. Before long, a furry, half-grown werewolf pup stood amid a puddle of Sali's clothing, with no missing patches of fur. Proud of his accomplishment, Sali sat on his haunches and grinned a wolfish grin, his pink tongue lolling mockingly.

"Showoff," Dori grumbled. Sali's wolf hearing caught Dori's words easily. Turning his head, he offered a sharp-toothed grin to her as well.

"Your ear is still covered with chalk dust," Wynn pointed out maliciously. Several classmates stifled laughter as Sali raised a paw to awkwardly swipe at his left ear.

"Very good, Salidar," Mrs. Rocklin acknowledged Sali's flawless transformation while ignoring chalk dust. "Ashe, would you please?" she gestured with a hand. Mrs. Rocklin no longer had to finish the sentence; Ashe understood what was expected. Without a word, Ashe rose and pulled Sali's clothing from beneath the wolf pup's feet. Following a tail-wagging Sali, Ashe carried jeans, T-shirt and sneakers to the changing cubicle at the back of their classroom.

Ashe performed clothing duty six times before Mrs. Rocklin called his name. Lowering his head to hide the flush that crept up his neck and threatened to become full-blown embarrassment, Ashe stood amid whispers from his classmates. *"He can't,"* competed with *"he's human."* For the first time, however, Ashe caught the worst insult any shapeshifter could level against another. *"Empty,"* echoed in his ears.

Blowing out a sigh and chanting "change," softly to himself, Ashe concentrated, focused and grunted, even. Nothing. Not a single thing happened. Head hanging and cheeks flaming, Ashe sat down again. It was no use; he had no talent.

Feeling anxious and a bit nauseous, Ashe sat miserably through two more classes before lunch. "Dude, you're trying too hard," Sali whispered as they walked toward the school cafeteria. Worried that he'd bungled a spelling test and then failed to hear when Mr. Dawkins called on him in Math, Ashe barely listened to Sali's attempt at reassurance. Mr. Dawkins, a werewolf, accused Ashe of daydreaming. Ashe wished it were daydreaming. Or spring break fever, which was affecting the other students.

"Hurry up; we'll miss seconds on dessert if you don't walk faster than that." Sali pushed Ashe to a quicker pace along the polished tile corridor that separated rows of classrooms. Filled with noise and students rushing toward the same goal, the hall was crowded but not impossible for Sali to negotiate. "Dude, lose that funk and let's eat, I'm starved," Sali declared as they stood in line to get their trays. "It's burger day," Sali added, craning his neck to see what was being served. "If you don't eat yours, I'll take it."

"You can have it," Ashe replied listlessly.

"Ashe, it's not something you can help," Dori's older sister, Cori, sat next to him at the cafeteria table he and Sali frequented. Sali traded his empty tray for Ashe's mostly full one.

Great, Ashe thought. *Dori's been talking already. Now it's all over school. They'll all call me empty before it's over.*

Eighty-six students attended Cloud Chief combined, with all twelve grades taught in the same building. Sometimes, Ashe watched the two tiny first graders and wondered if he'd ever been that small. After considering it for a moment, he supposed that he had. Ashe liked most of his classmates, but Dori and Wynn would never sit with him and Sali at lunch; there was the unspoken war between them, after all. The others moved in their own circles and seldom included Sali and Ashe.

Cori, a pretty blonde, was a high school junior and four years older than Ashe. She didn't mind talking to Ashe now and then. Cori and Dori's father, Nathan, was a good friend to Aedan, Ashe's father. Both of them vampires, they'd known one another for a long time— long before they'd married and had children.

Vampires weren't capable of having children in the normal sense. Aedan Evans had gone to scientists in the supernatural world and his and Adele Evans' DNA was combined in a fertilized, donor egg. Ashe was quite familiar with that particular knowledge; his parents explained it carefully to him when he was ten. It was the only way a vampire could have children, and those children could only be born to a shapeshifter mother. Human DNA failed to combine with that of any vampire to produce a child. Cori and Dori, both born in a similar fashion (although their mother, Lavonna, had supplied the egg), had no trouble shifting. Ashe's persistent failures were becoming fodder for school gossip.

"Cori, you're a panther. That's an amazing ability," Ashe acknowledged Cori's gift. "You don't know what it's like to have all of them staring and whispering when you can't do anything."

"Ashe, you're smart," Cori said. "You catch onto your lessons faster than the others. I know that may not sound important right now, but it is. And you can hear better than anyone else in the community. Everybody has a gift; you just have to figure out what yours is." Cori blinked green eyes at Ashe, smiled slightly and picked up her nearly empty tray before Sali could snatch anything off it. Flouncing away toward the tray drop, (mostly to taunt Sali) Cori walked out of the cafeteria without a backward glance.

"Everybody else always knows what I should be doing." Ashe rubbed his forehead.

"Dude, just forget it. Can we go into Cordell this afternoon and help your mom?" Sali gave Ashe a hopeful look.

Ashe's parents owned Cordell Feed and Seed. Sali's seventeen-year-old brother Marco could drive them; he had a car and welcomed any excuse to drive the short distance into Cordell to visit a human girl who worked at the Burger Hut. It was nearly spring break and Cordell Feed and Seed was busy—people were buying plants already. If Ashe and Sali came to help, Adele usually put them to watering trays of seedlings and sweeping the greenhouse.

"I guess," Ashe mumbled an answer to Sali's question. Sali jogged off to find his brother, who sat with a group of friends on the other side of the small cafeteria.

"He says he'll drop us off," Sali was back in no time. Ashe didn't answer; he merely nodded his head.

Ashe wasn't sure he'd live through his last three classes. He did, but barely. When Principal Billings sent for him during the final class of the day, Ashe became more worried. Was it because he hadn't been paying attention in class? His parents would certainly be upset over that.

Principal Benjamin Billings, PhD, werewolf, sat behind a desk too large for his small office, dressed in a three-piece suit and tie. With dark-brown hair that held no hint of gray and brown eyes capable of boring straight through any mischief-bent student, Principal Billings ruled Cloud Chief Combined with a growl and an iron will. If Ashe hadn't known he was werewolf when he turned, he may have guessed that Principal Billings was a bull. With a thick neck and compact, muscular body, Principal Billings evoked such an impression.

"Ashe, take this note to your parents," Principal Billings smiled as he handed the sealed envelope to Ashe. Satisfied over something Ashe couldn't immediately define, the old werewolf leaned back in his leather chair, causing it to creak annoyingly. "Make sure they get it," Principal Billings said with a wave of dismissal, sending Ashe back to class. Sali had an eyebrow lifted, asking the nonverbal question as soon as Ashe slouched into his seat in Social Studies. Shoving the envelope inside his book bag, Ashe pretended to pay attention to Miss Campbell and didn't look in Sali's direction once.

Later, Ashe was glad he was sitting by himself in the back seat of Marco's car on the way to Cordell. The snow had melted off as the day warmed up, leaving only a scattered, well-shaded patch here and there. Sali sat in the front passenger seat, restlessly turning his head this way and that to see everything as they drove past it. Ashe figured it was the wolf in him; Sali liked to poke his head out the window during warmer weather as long as his mother didn't catch him doing it. Just the thought of Denise DeLuca getting onto Sali for hanging his head out the car window made Ashe smile for a moment.

"Dude, you think your mom will have cookies?" Sali was now peering over the seat at Ashe.

"She might."

Adele Evans had a small kitchen at the back of the store and often baked cookies when Sali and Ashe came to help. When Ashe didn't say anything else, Sali mumbled, "I hope she made oatmeal raisin," before sliding down in his seat.

The familiar scents of fertilizer, chicken feed and live plants greeted Sali and Ashe as they stepped inside Cordell Feed and Seed. Rows of shelves stocked neatly with gardening and farming needs lined the store's polished, concrete floor. Just inside the door, Adele stood behind the register, helping two customers when both boys walked in. Noticing Ashe's slumped shoulders immediately, Adele frowned slightly as she closed the register drawer.

"Sali, there's a plate of cookies on the table in the back." As soon as her customers were gone, Adele sent Sali toward the rear of the store before stepping in front of Ashe. "Honey, what's wrong?" she touched Ashe's face briefly before taking her hand away. Tendrils of Adele's honey-blonde hair had escaped the clip she'd used to tie back her shoulder-length locks, telling Ashe the day had been a busy one; his mother hadn't had time to tidy up. Now her pretty, golden-brown eyes gazed worriedly at her son.

"Principal Billings sent this." Ashe pulled the sealed envelope from his book bag and handed it to his mother, stepping around her quickly to follow Sali. He didn't miss his mother's expression, however; Adele stared at the envelope in shock. Ashe joined Sali at the tiny kitchen table, and ate one cookie while Sali ate four. Ashe pushed Sali toward the greenhouse afterward to water tomato and pepper plants.

Flats of tomatoes and peppers were lined up neatly across slatted wooden tables. Sali loved to use the sprayer hose, sending a fine mist over the small, tender plants. Ashe left him alone; he'd already swept beneath the tables so Sali wouldn't create a river of mud when the water dripped down. While Ashe swept the rest of the greenhouse, he weighed his options. Perhaps he could do gardening or landscaping someday, since he didn't have any shapeshifting ability. He could certainly open a gardening shop somewhere. He'd worked with his mother since he was six—he'd learn everything about the business and support himself somehow. Sali, moving on to spray larger plants in pots at the back of the greenhouse, left Ashe alone to consider his probable human future.

❧

"Sali, your mother's here to pick you up," Adele stood in the greenhouse doorway an hour later with Denise DeLuca.

"But mo-om," Sali turned one syllable into two, his dark eyes pleading with his mother to leave him with Ashe.

"Sali, come along, I'm sure you have homework to do," Denise DeLuca held out a hand. Sali wasn't about to take it; he was too old for *that*. He waved at Ashe and walked out ahead of his mother, ducking away from the hand she placed on his shoulder. Ashe went to put away the broom.

"Ashe, we'll sit down and talk when your father wakes," Adele said. Face paling at her words, Ashe nervously chewed his lip as he studied his mother's frown. "Honey, don't look like that, you're not in trouble. Not that much, anyway," Adele said, giving Ashe a smile that didn't reach her eyes. Ashe attempted to school his face; he'd been depressed all day over Transformational Arts. "Come on, let's close the store."

Adele closed the store at six. Always. She might have made more money by staying open later, but she wanted to be home when Aedan woke every day. The store was closed every Sunday no matter what, giving Adele a day off. Ashe began counting out money from the register and adding up checks—he loved that part of closing down the store.

"Here, Mom. The deposit slip is filled out." Ashe handed the bank bag with the cash and checks inside to his mother. Smiling a genuine smile this time, Adele took the bag and slipped it in her purse. She made a stop at the bank every morning before opening the store for the day.

"At least the snow melted off," Adele observed as they climbed into her old and battered Ford truck. "But that's Oklahoma; freezing in the morning, hot by afternoon."

"Not hot," Ashe huddled into his sheepskin jacket.

"I know, baby. But it did get into the high forties." Adele put the truck in gear and pulled out of the tiny parking area behind the store.

Ashe and his mother kept a calendar in the kitchen that listed sunrise and sunset times, so they'd know when Aedan would wake. Thursday, March twenty-sixth listed sunset time as seven forty-six. They'd gotten home a quarter to seven and Adele set about making dinner for herself and Ashe—spaghetti with garlic bread and salad.

Ashe chuckled softly. The old myth that vampires were allergic to garlic was just that—a myth. He and his dad had laughed many times over the vampires portrayed in movies and on television. Still, he'd never seen his father's fangs. Or the claws. His dad always said someday, when Ashe was ready. Ashe guessed that twelve-going-on-thirteen wasn't ready.

Dinner was done at seven-thirty and Adele got Ashe seated at the table with a plate of spaghetti in front of him. "Go ahead and eat, Ashe. I'll get your father up." Ashe watched his mother as she unlocked the door into the lower level of the house and walked down the steps. The locked middle door was to protect his father while he slept during the day. Aedan was very strong and could punch right through the heavy steel door if necessary.

"Aedan?" Adele called softly before walking into her husband's steel and concrete bunker. Concealed below the underground portion of the house, the entrance to Aedan Evans' bunker was hidden beneath a cleverly designed trap door. Any bit of sunlight that hit Aedan's skin could cause it to blister and disintegrate within seconds. He, Nathan Anderson and Old Harold, who claimed no last name as his own, all had hidden rooms beneath their homes to protect them from sunlight. Aedan watched his wife carefully as she let herself down the ladder into his bunker.

"What's wrong?" Aedan asked, shrugging into a shirt. He knew something was; Adele never came down to the bunker, she always waited for him to come to the top floor of the house.

"That's exactly what I asked Ashe earlier," Adele held the envelope out to Aedan. Aedan's gray eyes flared briefly as he examined the handwritten address in near-darkness. Lifting the envelope from Adele's fingers, Aedan carefully opened the letter to read.

Mr. and Mrs. Evans, the note began, *I hesitate to place labels upon any child who studies in my school, but I cannot turn a blind eye to the status of your son. In no time during my lengthy tenure as an educator have I actually witnessed a child born of supernatural parents who had absolutely no ability. Children born to a human-supernatural mix, yes, but this—not until now. Ashe holds no ability. He has produced no sign of it during the entire year and my initial fears are now confirmed. I suggest you search for an alternative method to educate your child beginning with the fall semester, as he will not be allowed to continue at Cloud Chief Combined.*

Sincerely,

Benjamin Billings, PhD, Principal.

Adele backed out of the way while Aedan punched a hole through the black cinderblocks of the bunker, denting the sheet of thick steel behind.

～

"Son, why didn't you tell us you were having trouble?"

Ashe looked into his father's gray eyes as he spoke. He'd seen them go red at times if Aedan were angry. Aedan's eyes weren't red. Breathing a sigh of relief that his father surely heard, Ashe shrugged. "Son, I realize this is embarrassing for you, but you could have said something. The last grade card we received had satisfactory on it."

"But Dad, three of the others hadn't turned at that point. Now I'm the only one," Ashe slapped a hand over his mouth at the outburst.

"Ashe, will you keep trying? Please?" his mother sat next to him on the sofa, placing an arm around his shoulders. His father had settled on the coffee table, facing Ashe so they could have one of their man-to-mans, as Aedan called them.

"I always try," Ashe muttered, bowing his head. He was almost as embarrassed now as he was during Transformational Arts class. Rubbing a spot of smeared dirt on his jeans, Ashe couldn't meet his father's steady gaze.

Raking a hand through jet-black hair, Aedan watched his son carefully. Ashe was slight of build, although tall for his age, at five feet, four inches. Aedan was nearly six-four, so he wasn't surprised that Ashe was taller than normal. The boy would fill out in time.

Ashe had slightly curly, light-brown hair and inquisitive blue eyes that examined the world around him, eager to learn everything he could about it. His grades were always good and his bedroom was filled with shelf upon shelf of books; Ashe loved to read.

Aedan had decided quickly not to tell Ashe about the contents of the note and the possibility of his expulsion from Cloud Chief Combined. He had no desire to place more pressure on his son than he already bore. The summer months were coming and if Ashe failed to exhibit any ability by that time, he and Adele would talk to him then.

"Son, all we're asking is that you keep trying. Just relax, it'll come," Aedan quirked a smile. "Any homework?"

"No, Dad. But I think I flunked a spelling test today."

"Perhaps you should do a little studying anyway."

"All right." Ashe slid off the sofa and shuffled toward his room.

"Aedan, what if the fertilized eggs got mixed up? Sharon and Jonas O'Neill donated, but what if the clinic didn't use it?" Adele turned worried eyes on her vampire husband. "Ashe could be human, Aedan."

"There would be no child if the egg came from a human. You

should know my DNA will destroy any human element introduced into it."

"I don't know, Aedan. What if this is an exception? What if our child is human anyway?"

"We'll cross that bridge when we come to it," Aedan muttered. "We have a child. Most vampires don't ever get that. Will it matter if he isn't like us?"

"I'd like to think it wouldn't matter to anyone, but you know the community won't see it that way. Most of them, anyway."

"There's still time. Time for him to prove them wrong. Ashe is special. Smart. Persistent."

"There's a part of me that might be glad if he's human. You know the Council will come calling if he shows anything special."

"Stop worrying about that. If they follow the rules, he'll only be offered vampirism when he's older. Much older. And able to make that decision for himself. At least that's how it was explained to me when I was offered the chance to have a child. Only a few vampires were allowed to have children. Or to attempt it, at least."

"At least Nathan's girls are safe." Adele hugged herself and turned away from Aedan. "Girls don't turn. They die. So they don't attempt it."

"It would be foolish to do so," Aedan agreed softly. "There hasn't been a female vampire successfully turned in nearly seven hundred fifty years."

"But what if Ashe ever shows anything exceptional, Aedan? How would the Council look at him, then?"

"You know they have a different set of rules regarding enrichment of the vampire race. If they find someone that will benefit the race, they'll bring them in and make the turn, forcefully and early." Aedan looked away. Adele watched as a sadness she couldn't explain briefly crossed his features.

"Yes. I do know that. I wish Lavonna hadn't told me." Adele sighed. "Well, it looks like we won't have to worry about it anyway. Our son may be human, despite our DNA. And we'll have to deal with it."

"Ben didn't bother to tell me he was sending the note," Greta Rocklin's mouth tugged into a frown as she slammed the refrigerator door harder than warranted. "Ashe tries so hard and he never says a word about having to pick up and carry for his classmates. Aedan and Adele are probably going crazy. I would if I had to send my child off to Cordell Junior High in the fall." Greta was one of thirty-eight adult werewolves in Cloud Chief. They had their own Pack—Marcus DeLuca was Packmaster; Greta's husband Micah was Marcus' Second. Greta's hair was nearly black, her eyes deep brown, while her husband's hair and eyes were black. Both were tall and lean as most werewolves were. Usually in a sunny mood when her husband came home, Greta now vibrated with unhappiness.

"It's not werewolf business, it's shifter business," Micah reminded his wife. "Would you say anything if it were a human-shifter mix?"

"No, but they should realize what they're doing going in. That poor child. This will cause harm, Micah. Aedan is always the first there if someone needs help. Aedan, Nathan and Old Harold rebuilt the O'Neill's barn in four nights after the tornado last year."

"You're saying that Billings is letting his racism show. That's a serious charge, Greta."

"I didn't say that." Greta hugged herself and walked away from Micah.

"Good. If you didn't say it, I don't have to report it."

CHAPTER 2

"Ashe, you may go first today. Take your time; we're not in a hurry." Ashe jerked in his seat at Mrs. Rocklin's words; she never asked him to go first. Scrambling to his feet when Sali hissed at him to stand up, Ashe wavered for a second, momentarily stunned into immobility. "Don't force it, just relax," Mrs. Rocklin encouraged. Ashe tried to relax. Really. He just couldn't. Everybody was watching.

Cheeks warm with embarrassment amid inescapable whispers, Ashe struggled with both the desire and the effort to turn. His mother always said his animal would speak to him when it was ready. Nothing spoke to Ashe. After ten minutes of exertion with no results, Mrs. Rocklin asked him to sit, moving on to other classmates who mostly met with success. Dori botched her turning, as did two others; the entire class was distracted over the beginning of spring break.

"Dude, you don't know how to relax," Sali said over lunch. Ashe pushed his tray over so Sali could spear his uneaten carrots. Sali didn't care what the food was; he was hungry.

"And I suppose you're going to tell me?" Ashe snapped, his voice harsher than intended toward his best friend.

"Nope. I don't do yogurt."

"That's *Yoga*, furball," Cori settled beside Ashe. "Besides, your animal is a given with two werewolves as parents. I heard Mr. Harris got a letter from Randy Smith."

Ashe might have been less surprised if a grenade had been tossed inside the cafeteria. He and Sali jerked their heads toward Cori at her statement. "But," Sali said.

"Yeah. That's what I said. I don't know that he would do something like that, especially after he was expelled and we had to move away. His mom and dad went to live in Santa Fe." Cori opened her milk carton and stuck a straw in it.

Ashe watched as Cori went through the routine of lunch, but her hands shook as she placed a paper napkin in her lap and lifted her fork. The news about Randy Smith's letter upset Cori more than she was letting on.

Ashe didn't know Randy Smith personally; he'd been five years old when Randy, the son of a human-werewolf marriage, was forced to leave their community at age thirteen and ordered to attend a human school. Children born to human and werewolf parents would never be werewolf. Barely six months later, Randy let something slip in the presence of humans regarding the hidden paranormal community and everybody had to pack their things and leave their homes in New Mexico.

Randy's parents had also been forced to seek a home elsewhere. Now, the exiled boy would be old enough to attend college and the community was comfortably settled in Cloud Chief. Randy's name was still whispered angrily among the adults, however. None of them had forgotten their betrayal at the hands of a thirteen-year-old half-human.

Only Randy's age had prevented the death penalty from being levied against him at the time. Revealing information on the Pack carried an automatic death sentence for any adult. Ashe's parents didn't think he knew anything about Randy Smith, but everybody did. The gossip at school was enough to give nightmares to the younger students.

"What did Mr. Harris do? When he got the letter?" Sali chewed carrots he'd taken from Ashe's tray. Cori frowned at him for talking with food in his mouth.

"I don't know. I just overheard the stuff about the letter when I went past Principal Billings' office. I'll bet the information is in Billings' computer, though." Cori smiled hesitantly at Ashe.

"Don't look at me. I had scary dreams for weeks after the last time." Ashe stared at his tray—Sali had emptied it. "I dreamed Billings turned into a bull and chased me through Cloud Chief."

"He never knew," Cori scoffed. "And all you did was get in to check grades. You didn't change anything." The year before, Ashe had hacked into the Principal's computer after Cori begged him to do so. Terrified that she wasn't passing algebra, Cori was sure her parents would ground her for a failing grade. Ashe discovered she had a low C after breaking into the Principal's computer, and Cori was satisfied with that. "I'll bet the password is still the same," Cori added, toying with her meatloaf.

Ashe snorted a laugh at Cori's statement. He figured Billings' password was still the same, too, unimaginative as it was. *BigWolf* had gotten him right in the first time. Benjamin Billings was an old werewolf, born long before the peace treaty between the vampires and the werewolves. The two races now cooperated and had for the past forty-seven years. Ashe knew his father was old, too, but Aedan never talked about the times before. Neither Ashe nor his mother knew how old his father was. When he'd asked once, Aedan had carefully steered him away from the subject.

"Come on, Billings always goes home early on Fridays. And it's the start of spring break. Everybody will be out of here in no time. We can slip into Billings' office and find out before we go home today," Cori wheedled, slipping a lock of long blonde hair behind an ear, her green eyes begging.

"What if he locks his office?" Ashe wanted to wriggle out of sneaking into the Principal's office, although Sali was now staring at him with mischievous interest.

"Lock's broken. Marco did that," Cori smiled maliciously at Sali. Sali's older brother had broken the lock; he and James Johnson had been sent to Principal Billings' office for disrupting class. They'd shoved each other while standing near the door, waiting for the Principal to call them in. Marco slammed into the door, breaking the lock and causing the door to swing wide. He'd gotten detention for a week over it.

"It's still broken 'cause Billings doesn't know how to fix it," Sali muttered. "And he won't ask Dad to come fix it for him." Cori snickered at Sali's explanation. Marcus DeLuca, the werewolf Packmaster, was also a locksmith with a small office in Cordell.

"Look, dude, everybody else is gonna be crazy to get away from here. And Old Harold won't come by to clean until eight." Sali was just as curious as Cori was. Ashe frowned at his friend; Sali wouldn't be the one in real trouble if they got caught.

"Come on, it won't take five minutes," Cori coaxed. "How are we going to learn what really happened if you don't?"

Shrugging his thin shoulders, Ashe gave in. "All right. If nobody is around and you agree to keep watch."

"Great!" Cori giggled and clapped her hands.

"This isn't going to work," Ashe muttered to himself as he and Sali hung back while their classmates raced away from the classroom. Spring break was officially started.

"Getting cold feet?" Sali slapped Ashe on the back. As a werewolf, even a young one, Sali was stronger than he looked, nearly knocking Ashe out of his chair.

"I had cold feet when Cori mentioned it the first time," Ashe replied, watching as Miss Campbell, their Social Studies teacher, left the room.

"Let's go find Cori. Maybe we won't have to dawdle after that," Sali gathered his backpack and slung it over a shoulder. They'd waited ten minutes before rising to leave the classroom behind.

"I think the others are gone." Cori found Ashe and Sali instead, right outside their classroom. Ashe blinked at Cori in near-darkness—

the hall lights had already been turned off as the last teacher left the school, leaving only weak afternoon sunlight shining through the school's front doors to illuminate the hallway. Ashe knew Cori and Sali, being what they were, could see much better than he could in the dimly lit corridor.

"I just walked past the Principal's office," Cori whispered, bringing Ashe's attention back to their intended espionage. "It's empty."

"Come on," Sali bent over, cautiously looked both ways and darted silently to the next classroom doorway, preparing to repeat the action.

"Dude, what are you doing?" Ashe stood in the middle of the hall, staring at Sali. Cori, standing beside Ashe, covered a smile.

"Spy stuff," Sali said, bending over again.

"Sali, the school is empty—I can't hear anything except us," Ashe pointed out.

"Oh." Sali straightened. "Well, let's go, then." His athletic shoes squeaking on tile, Sali trotted off toward the Principal's office. Ashe shook his head at Cori before following Sali down the hall; the young werewolf was humming the theme from *Mission: Impossible*.

"We'll be right outside," Sali shoved Ashe inside Principal Billings' office moments later and shut the door.

Ashe stood still, staring at the closed door for precious seconds, wondering how he'd gotten involved in the mess to start with. Shaking himself mentally, he surveyed the utilitarian cube of an office before turning toward Principal Billings' desk. Built of Mahogany, the solid wood behemoth was positioned toward the back of the small space.

Sliding onto the Principal's leather chair, Ashe tapped the keyboard to dismiss the screensaver and entered the password. All of Principal Billings' files popped right up. Thankful for the high-speed internet service the community paid for, Ashe went searching through files. He found one for Randall Smith, the ousted student, but right beside Randy's name, Ashe found his own. Gulping nervously and quaking a little, Ashe opened Randall Smith's file first.

Randall Smith is charged by the community with exposure of the community, punishment for which is expulsion with compulsion not to mention the community to humans for the rest of his life. Compulsion performed on Seventeen February, by Aedan Evans. Should perpetrator Smith commit a similar crime in future, according to Pack Law he will be condemned to death. Randall Smith may not approach or contact the community from this point forward or the death penalty will be levied.

The official-looking document was signed by Packmaster DeLuca and witnessed by three other werewolves. Principal Billings was one of those three. Ashe drew in a breath as he paged to the second document.

Letter received from Randall Smith on March 25. Paul Harris, a former instructor, neither requested nor condoned the forbidden communication. All information has been presented to Packmaster DeLuca for authentication. Authentication verified March 26. Pack Law is clear; Randall Smith should be sentenced to death—Benjamin Billings, Pack Secretary.

Principal Billings had inserted a personal note at the end. *I will volunteer to perform the execution,* he'd written. Ashe's breaths were ragged gasps. He knew Pack Law was different from the laws humans followed, but this—surely they couldn't do *this.* And how had Randall Smith found Mr. Harris to send a letter? That shouldn't have been. It made no sense at all to Ashe. He could see Randy contacting some of his former friends, but why a teacher?

Hurriedly Ashe closed that file, wondering what he should tell Cori and Sali. While he pondered that dilemma, he opened the file labeled with his name, coming face to face with the note Principal Billings sent to his parents.

"What did you find?" Cori pushed for information as they walked out of Cloud Chief Combined together a few minutes later.

"Just a note from Principal Billings, saying that the letter was neither requested nor condoned," Ashe replied. He wasn't lying; he just wasn't giving complete information. Randall Smith could be condemned to death during the next full moon, which fell on March thirtieth. The werewolves would take care of Pack business first, before making the change.

Nobody living in the community ever forgot when the full moons came—the wolves were forced to change and hunt. The shapeshifters also changed, but theirs was a less frenetic transformation. Ashe's mother, a peregrine falcon, went out flying by moonlight, his dad going out with her and watching over her; waiting on the ground below with a robe when she tired and came back to him.

Ashe hunched his shoulders, refusing to mention his file or the note that Principal Billings sent to his parents. If he couldn't find his ability (Principal Billings was convinced he didn't have one) then he would be enrolled in Cordell Junior High come August.

He'd never had human friends. He knew how to act around them for the most part, but never being able to talk freely about his life again? To be constantly on guard against anyone learning what he and his parents were? It frightened him. He could never bring human friends home; it was forbidden. Would they become suspicious? Ashe worried about that, too.

Shoving hands in his pockets, he walked silently beside Sali and Cori as they made their way home. The day was fine and warmer than the one before, even if the ground was still soggy after the brief snowfall. Ashe might have stood in silent wonder as a rabbit leapt from a clump of dead grass and raced away, but his mind was clouded with personal misery.

A hint of green lay across the prairie, with the beginnings of new grass and wildflowers peeking between the taller, pale-brown stalks left over from the previous year. Slender stems waved cheerfully in an Oklahoma breeze as Ashe walked quietly homeward. Cori broke away first—her home was less than a quarter mile from the school. Sali and Ashe split shortly after, Sali going north, Ashe following the gravel road that ran next to his house.

The Evans home had an elaborate alarm system; Ashe punched the code on the keypad located outside the garage, letting himself in. Another keypad waited beside the kitchen door, with a separate code to get through it. Ashe keyed in the second code to get into the house.

It was only four-thirty; his mother wouldn't be home for another two hours and his dad wouldn't be awake until an hour after that. The thing Ashe liked most about the winter months was that his dad was up earlier in the evenings. During spring and summer, the daylight hours stretched endlessly.

A note lay on the kitchen table when Ashe went to the sink to get a glass of water. *Your dad will take us to Oklahoma City to buy books tomorrow evening*, his mother had written. Normally, that would have made Ashe punch the air in delight. They'd leave right after sunset, eat at a nice restaurant and then visit one of the bookstores that stayed open late.

After reading the two files in Principal Billings' computer, Ashe was so depressed he didn't feel like doing anything. He'd never met Randy Smith, but he didn't think that writing a letter should result in someone's death. The contents of the letter hadn't been in the file; Ashe wondered what Mr. DeLuca had done with it. Briefly, he pictured himself as Randy Smith, with Principal Billings offering to execute him if he let anything slip at a human school. The thought made him shiver.

Ashe was working at his computer later when Adele looked in on him. "Honey, I'm about to start dinner, will you bring your laundry out? We'll work on it tonight." His mother gave him a warm smile.

"All right." Ashe shut off the computer and went to gather dirty clothes. While Ashe loaded the washer and added detergent, he wondered why his parents hadn't given him the full contents of the note. Perhaps they didn't want him to be upset over spring break. He certainly was upset after learning he was destined to attend a human school. Now he was forced to act as if he didn't know.

"Socks and underwear in the washer," Ashe washed his hands and dried them on the towel his mother always folded around a drawer handle in the kitchen. Painted a sunny yellow, the Evans kitchen had windows facing north and east. A hall on the southwestern side led into Adele's solarium, where plants and cooking herbs were grown. The door leading into the garage was also on the western wall, and it was kept closed and locked at all times, to protect Aedan while he slept.

"We're having smothered steak, honey," Adele said. Ashe loved smothered steak. Principal Billings' note meant his parents were more worried than usual about him. It was also the reason his mother was making his favorite meal. Wondering when they planned to tell him about the human school, Ashe went to the cabinet to get plates for the table.

"Son, how was school?" Aedan walked into the kitchen while Ashe and his mother were eating. Ashe watched as his dad leaned down to kiss his mother on the forehead. Vampires looked and acted human most of the time, as did werewolves and shapeshifters. They kept their other nature hidden, to protect the races. Ashe sighed at the thought. Humans, if they were aware those races existed, would be terrified of them and try to kill them. At least some of them would. If he couldn't change, Ashe would be forced to attend school with hundreds of humans. His silence would protect his parents; the humans could never learn what they were. It could become the most serious secret he'd ever kept.

"Have your list of books written out?" Aedan settled into an extra chair at the table and smiled at his son.

"I went looking on the computer. I have a few things," Ashe smiled back.

"You can ask Sali to come if you want." Adele picked up her plate and took it to the dishwasher.

"Are you sure you want to buy two dinners for him?" Ashe teased.

"That child can certainly eat," Aedan agreed.

"Call him in the morning," Ashe's mother nodded toward the peas still on his plate. Ashe turned to his food.

"Mom, can I go to Oklahoma City with Ashe tonight?" Sali shouted at his mother the following morning.

"Honey, I can hear you just fine." Denise DeLuca walked into the living room where Sali was talking with Ashe on the phone. Ashe had called first thing to invite Sali along.

"Sorry, Mom," Sali apologized, hoping ill manners wouldn't influence his mother's decision; he hadn't realized she was so close. Being werewolf, her hearing was just as sharp as Sali's.

"Going to the bookstores?" Denise gave Sali a smile instead.

"Yeah. And out to eat." Some things were simply more important to Sali than others.

"All right, but you have to clean your room and do a good job."

"I can go," Sali crowed into the phone.

"Sali's coming," Ashe replaced the cordless in the cradle. Adele was wiping down the kitchen counters after breakfast.

"I heard. And you should clean your room too, young man." Adele scooted Ashe out of the kitchen. Adele went to work, leaving Ashe at home to do his chores. After cleaning his bedroom, Ashe spent the day going through bookshelves his father had built for him, checking carefully to make sure he hadn't missed any upcoming sequels or favorite authors that might have new books out. The shelves lined one wall of Ashe's bedroom, floor to ceiling, and all were full.

His father was good with his hands. He, Old Harold and Cori's father, Nathan, had built a barn in four nights the previous year. The O'Neill's barn was knocked down by a tornado and they'd lost precious ewes and lambs in the spring storm. The three vampires had rebuilt the barn and others donated to help replace animals.

Ashe had seen the devastation the tornado caused early the following day. Tiny lambs lay nearly a quarter mile from the destroyed barn—all dead. They'd looked like bits of cotton fluff scattered in the fields until he'd gotten close enough to see what they were. Marco joked that you couldn't count them or you'd fall asleep. Ashe had never wanted to hit Marco so badly in his life.

"Time to clean up. Your dad will wake in half an hour." Adele interrupted Ashe's thoughts. She'd found him sitting in the floor, an open copy of the latest in his favorite series on his lap. Time had gotten away from him.

"On my way." Ashe grinned as he jumped up and raced toward his closet.

~

"Where are we gonna eat?" Sali asked excitedly as he slid onto the back seat of Aedan's SUV. The vehicle was newer and nicer than the old blue Ford Adele drove. Aedan had offered to replace Adele's battered truck with a new version many times, but Adele argued that she often carried plants or bags of feed in the back and didn't need something else; it would just get scratched up anyway. Aedan had stopped trying to convince his wife after a while.

"Feel like The Italian Grill?" Adele smiled over the back seat at Sali.

"Yeah." Sali loved The Italian Grill.

"Are you buying books?" Adele was still smiling at Sali.

"Yeah. Mom said I had to get at least three. And *read* them." Sali didn't enjoy reading nearly as much as Ashe did.

"Come on, dude. You liked the last ones I told you to buy." Ashe poked at Sali.

"I read those in self-defense, 'cause you wouldn't shut up about 'em." Sali grinned at Ashe.

"Whatever it takes dude." Ashe settled back in his seat as Aedan pulled away from the house. Oklahoma City was nearly a hundred miles away. They'd eat first, then visit the bookstores. Ashe was thankful the big bookstores stayed open late.

"Come on, you'll like this one," Ashe shoved a book into Sali's hands. He'd already dumped two others onto Sali's stack. "Besides," Ashe added, "that DVD you like so much—about the crazy inventor? That book was written by this author."

"Then why don't I read that instead?" Sali whined.

"You can read it first." Ashe dropped a paperback copy onto the growing pile, which shifted dangerously and nearly fell from Sali's hands.

"Ashe, please stop. Mom will expect me to read all this." Sali hefted his books dramatically, begging his friend not to add any more.

"Fine. I'll stop there." Ashe went to collect the stack of ten titles he'd placed in the floor nearby. His parents had approved ten books; Ashe had gathered them quickly.

Aedan and Adele were sitting in the coffee shop, waiting on both boys to finish shopping. "That's quite the stack there," Aedan remarked when Ashe and Sali showed up at their table.

"Dad, I'll have these read by the end of spring break." Ashe replied with a grin.

"Can you pace yourself a little? I was hoping to get some help at the store," Adele said. "And we'll pay for Sali's books if he'll help."

"I'd help for cookies," Sali agreed, his brown eyes pleading hopefully with Ashe's mother.

"I was throwing cookies into the deal, too," Adele laughed.

"All right," Sali breathed happily. "Cookies *and* free books."

"Come on, you two," Aedan rose and ruffled Ashe's hair.

On the drive home, Sali slept in his corner of the back seat and Ashe was nearly asleep on the opposite side when Aedan's cell rang. He passed it to Adele to answer. Aedan never talked on his cell while driving and normally wouldn't ask Adele to answer either. Something on the caller ID convinced him to hand the phone to his wife. Ashe woke completely as Adele said, "Nathan? What's wrong?" Usually, Ashe appreciated his gift of acute hearing. He heard Nathan's voice clearly as he explained that James Johnson's savaged body had been found in a field behind the Evans' home.

Ashe huddled into his corner of the back seat, utterly stunned. He wanted to wake Sali, and then thought better of it. James Johnson was Marco's best friend. He and Marco were often engaged in horseplay and frequently ended up in Principal Billings' office. That's how the lock on the Principal's door had been broken, Ashe recalled. And James was a werewolf—old enough to go hunting at the full moon with Marco and the other adults. It would take someone or something extremely strong to kill a werewolf.

Ashe listened while his mother informed Nathan Anderson that they were nearly home and terminated the call. Aedan, who'd listened in just as Ashe had, spared a glance for his wife and sped up.

When they arrived home, Ashe saw cars and trucks parked everywhere surrounding his house while people milled about in the front yard. Sali finally woke when the SUV's engine shut off inside the garage. Adele was out of her seat and opening Sali's door as Nathan and Lavonna Anderson walked into the garage, Marcus DeLuca right behind them.

"Have you told him?" Marcus DeLuca asked, gripping Sali's shoulders as he slid out of the vehicle, rubbing sleep from his eyes.

"No, we let him sleep," Adele replied.

"What's wrong, Dad?" Sali stared groggily at the Cloud Chief Packmaster.

"James Johnson was killed in the field behind this house, son," Marcus held Sali away from him as he explained. "Your brother Marco went crazy when he was told. Turned and broke through a window getting out of the house."

"But how?" Sali, still half asleep, wasn't sure he understood. Ashe, standing nearby, wasn't sure he understood either. Shivering in the early spring night, Ashe watched as Marcus knelt and pulled Sali against him. "Son, we don't know. James was strong. It would have taken somebody really tough to take him down. Micah is there, checking the ground and doing some sniffing with Ben, but we don't have anything yet."

"How did they find him?" Adele asked.

"Cori," Marcus turned to Adele with a sigh. "She and James have been dating on the sly, I suppose. Neither of their parents knew of it. When James didn't show up at the usual spot half a mile from here, Cori tracked his normal path, roughly six hundred yards behind your house. Her panther tracks are there, but we can't get a good scent off the ground around the body—it's still wet from the snow we had two days ago."

"How's Cori doing?" Ashe was worried for his friend. Even he hadn't known that Cori liked James.

"Understandably upset," Marcus raked fingers through his hair.

"Greta and three other wolves are searching for Marco. I hope they find him soon."

"Aedan, may I see you in the house for a moment?" Nathan hadn't said anything until now. Tall, with dark-blond hair and green eyes, Nathan, Cori and Dori looked very much alike. Cori and Dori were his daughters, after all, and Ashe wondered where both girls were since Nathan and Lavonna were inside his garage.

"Sure," Aedan answered, nodding to Nathan. He punched the code into the keypad at the back door and he and Nathan walked into the kitchen, shutting the door behind them. Adele rubbed Sali's shoulders as Marcus spoke softly to his son. Attempting to remain unnoticed, Ashe edged away until he was standing next to the back door. He could hear if his father were speaking to Nathan in the kitchen. He was.

"Aedan, we may have trouble," Nathan said. Ashe strained to hear the rest. "You're not going to like this," Nathan went on. "We've got at least three werewolves who think this murder is a vampire's work."

CHAPTER 3

"*B*oth of us have solid alibis," Nathan said as Ashe continued to listen to the private conversation. "But Old Harold was at the school, stripping the floors by himself. I called him —he wasn't lying when he said he hadn't gone anywhere else after sundown, but we must be on guard against any rumors. We don't need to go back fifty years because a werewolf decides to point the finger at a convenient vampire."

Ashe silently agreed. James, a senior and nearly eighteen, was still considered a child by the community and that made the crime worse. James and Marco had been born nearly a month apart and had grown up together. Ashe could understand Marco's grief and anger; he'd feel the same if anything happened to Sali.

"Have you been to the site? Did you scent anything?" Aedan asked.

"Yes, and it baffles me. I couldn't get any scents except those of Cori, Ben and Marcus. They were on the scene before I was called. Cori ran to Marcus' house since nobody was home here."

"Then someone was very careful," Aedan growled. Ashe knew what that growl meant; his father was becoming angry.

"Aedan, we may be reading this wrong and the perpetrator may be caught or come forward tomorrow, but it certainly doesn't look good.

Did anyone else besides Sali's parents know you were going to the city?"

"No." Ashe drew in a breath at his father's answer. Was someone trying to frame his father for this? At least Ashe knew his parents couldn't have been involved and were above suspicion. Not only did Marcus and Denise DeLuca know about the trip to Oklahoma City, but Sali had gone with them. Ashe wanted to talk the whole thing over with Sali, but Sali was walking out of the garage with his father, likely headed home to wait for news about Marco.

"Where did they take the boy?" Aedan asked.

"They took him to the O'Neill's barn. Obviously the Johnsons are distraught."

"Did you see the body?"

"No. The wounds were only described to me by Marcus. By the time I was called, they'd already moved James."

"You think Cori can tell you anything?"

"I had to place compulsion for her to sleep, Aedan. She was screaming and crying until I did."

"Do you think they'll let us examine the body? If they're going to accuse a vampire, we should have the right to defend ourselves. Old Harold didn't do this; I'd bet my life on it."

"As would I, but nobody was there to verify his whereabouts."

"And there's no motive," Aedan sighed. "Harold has very little contact with any of the children. He cleans the school long after they're gone for the day. Ours know him because he's vampire." Ashe recognized the truth in his father's words; Old Harold came by the house often to speak with Aedan. Nearly everyone called the vampire Old Harold, although he appeared as young as his father did. Old Harold acted old, if that was something you could gauge. He always smiled at Ashe, though, and asked about lessons during his visits.

"Aedan, I think we should contact the Council." Nathan's words interrupted Ashe's thoughts, frightening him. The Council. *The Vampire Council.* Ashe knew little about the Council, except to fear it. His father seldom mentioned it, but Ashe knew the Council was in charge of vampire Enforcers and Assassins; those elite among the vampire race that tracked down rogues or investigated other crimes.

"The werewolves may contact the Grand Master as well."

"Better that than allowing things to get out of hand. We're an experiment, Aedan. Don't forget that. There are only twenty communities like ours in the country, and both the Council and the Grand Master are watching." Ashe blinked. *An experiment?* He'd never heard that before. He wanted to ask questions. Itched to ask questions. But his father would know he'd been eavesdropping if he did. Who would have the answers that he could ask, anyway?

Ashe heard Aedan walk toward the back door. Quickly, Ashe slipped away to stand beside the SUV. Adele was still talking to a few others inside the garage and Micah Rocklin and Principal Billings had come in after examining the crime scene. In nearly thirteen years, Ashe had never seen anything like this. Ashe, at age six, had known that a werewolf died after an unsuccessful challenge against Marcus DeLuca, but that was werewolf tradition. None of the Pack had spoken that werewolf's name afterward, although his family had grieved privately for him. Ashe hunched his shoulders.

"Son, we'll get to the bottom of this." Ashe didn't know whether his father realized he'd been listening or if Aedan felt Ashe needed comfort as he slipped an arm around Ashe's shoulders.

"Mom, can we take Sali's books to him?" Ashe tapped the bag of books that lay forgotten on the kitchen table. Sali had left them in the back seat of the SUV the night before. Now, Sunday morning had arrived, accompanied by an aura of aching sadness. Ashe found his mother in the kitchen, putting a casserole together to take to the Johnson family. It was the way things were done in Oklahoma; if somebody died, you brought food to the family. Adele knew many of her human customers and did the same for them.

"If you'll hang on until I get this out of the oven, I'll put a batch of cookies together for Sali and his family."

"Yeah. Oatmeal raisin," Ashe nodded, naming Sali's favorite cookies.

Later, when they dropped by the DeLuca home after delivering the casserole to the Johnsons, Ashe learned from Sali's mother that Marco had shown up just before dawn, naked, filthy and exhausted. Denise expressed relief that he'd come home on his own and explained that Marco was now in bed, sleeping. Sali gripped Ashe's elbow, pulling him down the hall and into his bedroom while Adele talked with Denise.

"Dude, what's going on?" Ashe whispered the moment Sali's door was closed. Sali's room looked normal for Sali—the bed made but rumpled, with a few items of clothing flung carelessly across the furniture. Schoolbooks were piled in a stack on the floor, mostly forgotten. Sali was a sports fan and posters of athletes littered his walls.

"Dad called the Grand Master last night," Sali whispered his answer to Ashe's question, flopping onto his not-so-neatly made bed. Ashe sighed at Sali's words. To him, the Grand Master was the Werewolf King.

"Is somebody coming to investigate?"

"Yeah. Dad thinks it's for the best."

"Yeah." Ashe wondered if Sali's mom was telling his mother the same thing. "Sali, what do you think happened to James?"

"Don't know. Dad and Micah couldn't get any other scents around the body except Cori's, and she's the one who found him. They'll question her, too."

"Cori wouldn't kill James."

"I know that. You know that. Do the adults know that?" Sali flipped over on his back. "This is so messed up."

"Did Marco say anything? When he came home?" Ashe realized he was still holding tightly to Sali's bag of books. He half-rose to pile them on the bedside table.

"Mom and Dad pulled him into the den and shut the door. I didn't hear anything."

"Dang."

"Yeah. And now he's asleep," Sali added glumly.

"Why would somebody want to kill James?" Ashe was back to the question that was circling his brain so often it threatened to develop racecar sound effects any moment.

"No idea. Did you sleep last night?"

"Not much."

"Me either. Not after we got to your house, anyway."

"Yeah."

"Want to get a cookie?" Sali blinked hopefully at Ashe.

"Yeah. Let's get a cookie." Ashe wasn't hungry, but he wanted to humor Sali.

"Sali, only two, lunch is just half an hour away," Denise DeLuca warned as Sali carefully lifted aluminum foil off the plate of oatmeal raisin cookies. The pile of cookies was meticulously inspected as Sali searched for the two largest. Ashe waited patiently for his friend to make a choice.

"We were gonna go to Six Flags," Sali munched on a cookie. "On Thursday. Mom said I could invite you. That's not gonna happen now."

"We'll go another time." Ashe spared a glance at Sali—no doubt, his mother already knew and had kept it a surprise. Ashe thought he'd be working at Cordell Feed and Seed the entire week of spring break. And it wasn't often that Marcus offered to take Ashe along on a family outing. Ashe also wondered how this would affect the whole Randy Smith thing. Full moon was Tuesday, during spring break.

"I'll come over early tomorrow and go to Cordell with you and your mom," Sali stuffed half a cookie into his mouth.

"You still want to?" Ashe was surprised.

"Yeah. Bein' around the house gives me the shivers."

"As long as it's okay with your parents." Ashe remembered the conversation his dad had with Nathan the night before.

"Mom says it's okay."

"Good. Maybe we can go to the Burger Hut for lunch."

"Yeah. That would be great." Sali pulled Ashe toward him. "Dude, I want to talk to you," he said so quietly that Ashe barely heard.

"Tomorrow morning? Mom leaves early," Ashe covered Sali's whisper as his mother walked into the kitchen.

"Sali, are you sure you want to come?" Adele brushed Sali's thick black hair away from his forehead. Sali blinked nearly black eyes at her before smiling slightly.

"Yeah, Mrs. Evans. I want to come."

"He'll just mope around the house if he doesn't get to spend the day with Ashe," Denise observed.

"Then be at the house at seven-thirty," Adele said. "I'm expecting azaleas, onions and more petunias. Plus a load of feed."

"I get to water the plants," Sali put his bid in right away.

"Mom, what do you think happened to James?" Ashe asked as his mother drove home.

"I don't know," Adele reached out to pat Ashe's arm. Ashe nodded. He didn't either, and it bothered him. He had so little information, outside the conversation his father had with Nathan Anderson the night before. Now, the Grand Master of the werewolves was sending someone and the Vampire Council could send someone, too. Ashe itched to ask his mother about Nathan's comment the night before—the one regarding Cloud Chief being an experiment. He couldn't. He'd be in trouble for listening to a private conversation and getting information he wasn't supposed to have.

"Dad," Ashe sat next to his father on the sofa after helping his mother clear away dinner dishes. Aedan had wakened only a few minutes earlier.

"What, son?" Aedan settled an arm over the back of the sofa.

"Dad, Sali told me that the Grand Master is sending someone to investigate."

"Your mother told me."

"What will they do? This sounds scary."

"Son, it's already scary. A boy died who shouldn't have. Now we have to solve this, somehow. You'll find out soon enough, so I'm telling you now that the Vampire Council is sending an Enforcer."

"An Enforcer?" Ashe stopped breathing for a moment.

"They know it's only an investigation," Aedan replied. Ashe realized his father clearly heard when his breath caught. "I hope the Grand Master's man and the Council's Enforcer can work together on this. It will make it easier on everybody," Aedan added.

"When will they get here?" Ashe asked.

"The Grand Master's investigator will arrive on Thursday. That's what Mrs. DeLuca told your mother. The Enforcer will get here on Friday or Saturday, according to my source."

"Where did they put James?"

"That's a morbid question, but if you must know, he's in the O'Neill's barn, locked inside their walk-in refrigerator. Marcus has the keys so nobody else can get in and disturb the body."

Ashe knew the investigator and the Enforcer would examine James's body to see if they could determine how he'd died. Both would have good scenting ability, so they'd look into that as well. Ashe hadn't done it in a long time, but he leaned his head against Aedan's shoulder.

"Son, it'll be all right," Aedan said softly. "Why don't you go read one of your new books?"

"Okay." Ashe slid off the sofa and walked toward the stairs. His bedroom, like the others, was below ground. Once the door was shut at the top of the stairway that led downward, Ashe leaned against the door and listened.

"They're sending someone named Radomir," Ashe heard his father say. "The Council has to find someone older than Harold, and Radomir couldn't get here before Friday at the earliest."

"So the Grand Master's investigator will have a full day ahead of the Enforcer," his mother replied.

"Adele, don't read more into this than necessary." Ashe didn't hear anything else, so he slipped down the steps as softly as he could.

"Sali, I don't know why they needed to send a vampire older than Old Harold," Ashe said for the third time. Adele had driven them to the Burger Hut for lunch Monday, warning them not to mention anything about James. It was understood—you didn't talk about James's murder unless you wanted human authorities involved and Cloud Chief didn't. Adele hadn't stayed; she normally didn't close the store during lunch so she went back, promising to pick up both boys around one-fifteen.

"Well, there has to be a reason, don't you think?" Sali was still curious about the vampire.

"Yeah, but I don't know what it is." Ashe was beginning to feel grumpy. There were too many questions and he didn't have any answers. He hated that. Ashe wanted problems that he could solve. He wasn't sure he could solve any of this, beginning with James's death. "What did you want to talk to me about?" Ashe asked to steer Sali away from incessant questions.

"Dude, I really wanted to listen in on the Pack meeting tomorrow night," Sali said, biting into his double meat, double cheese with bacon burger. A pile of fries occupied the remaining space on his plate. Ashe knew Sali would eat every bite. "And I would listen in, but Mom has a sitter coming," Sali continued.

"A sitter?" Ashe didn't understand. Cloud Chief would empty on the night of the full moon. Any adult would go through the shift or the turn and hunt or run or fly. Who would be babysitting Sali?

"Nathan, Cori and Dori are coming to stay with me," Sali muttered. "And Staci, Brad and Timothy are coming over, too." Sali named three werewolf children younger than he was. Six other young werewolves were old enough to hunt with the Pack, although they hadn't finished school yet. Fifteen was considered old enough and Marco was one of six remaining teens that met the requirements. James Johnson had been the seventh.

"Wait, did you say you would listen in if you didn't have a sitter?"

Ashe's eyes narrowed at his best friend. He'd never heard this before from Sali.

"I've done it twice before. Almost got caught, too, but I didn't." Sali grinned, preening over his apparent prowess. Somehow, he'd spied on the Pack when he should have been at home.

"Sali, how did you do that? And why haven't I heard this before?"

"You think I want to be grounded for the rest of my life? Dad will shout the house down if he ever finds out. I know where to go and that's where you'll be tomorrow night while your dad is out with your mom on the full moon." Sali's smugness washed over Ashe. Sali had not only fooled the Pack twice but had kept the secret from Ashe for who knew how long. Ashe blinked at Sali in surprise, listening while Sali explained how and where.

"That's where they meet? In that clearing?" Ashe recognized the spot Sali meant as he described it. A small stand of trees stood a quarter mile behind the DeLuca home. There weren't many patches of trees in that portion of Oklahoma; most of it was farmland or prairie. Marcus had chosen the property with trees and the Pack hunted on his land during the full moon.

"Yeah. But you have to get in that old oak tree on the eastern edge. You won't be able to see much but you'll be able to hear. Probably better than I can. I want to know what they're saying, Ashe. About James and Randy Smith."

"Dude, if you get caught doing something like that, you'll get grounded. There's no telling what they'd do to me if I got nabbed." Just the idea of being caught by angry werewolves frightened Ashe.

"Dude, it's the only way we'll know," Sali shot back. "I think Cori still wants to know, too."

"And what if I say no?"

"Then we may never know what's going on."

"Dang."

"Yeah."

"What time do I need to be there? I'll have to wait until Mom and Dad are out of the house," Ashe pointed out.

"The wolves won't be there until nearly ten. You should have plenty of time to sneak away and get back."

"This sounds like imminent disaster," Ashe grumped, gathering paper wrappers and napkins to dump on his way out of the restaurant.

~

Ashe and Sali spent the afternoon cleaning up the back room of the store before unloading onion sets and the rest of the plant deliveries, and then unloading a shipment of seeds, gardening supplies and bags of chicken feed. Ashe was tired and ready to go when six o'clock rolled around.

"Sali, do you want to be dropped off first?" Adele smiled at him as he climbed into the old Ford.

"Yeah. I think I can grow plants from the dirt on my jeans."

"And you smell like onions, dude." Ashe grinned and poked Sali in the ribs.

"And I smell like onions," Sali admitted. "But I'll be at your house again tomorrow morning."

"Glutton for punishment, Sali?" Adele laughed.

"I guess." Sali ducked his head to hide the grin.

"We'll clean the store and put those new seed packet displays together tomorrow," Adele started the truck and put it in gear. Ashe sat quietly next to Sali on the way home. The work had taken his mind off James's death, and James's death had taken his mind off his own problems. Those problems now seemed insignificant next to the other things.

~

Sali studied the diagram for the cardboard display the following morning while Ashe helped a customer at the register. Adele had gone to the back to inspect another shipment of plants and gardening tools before signing off on it. "These good gloves?" the old man placed a pair of leather gloves on the counter. Ashe knew he was one of his mother's regular customers. Stooped slightly, the man had thinning gray hair, plenty of wrinkles and twinkling blue eyes.

"Yeah. Mom wears this brand all the time," Ashe said.

"I'll take 'em, then." The man drew his wallet out of a back pocket slowly and deliberately. Ashe wondered if the older ones pondered things before expending the effort. At the moment, it made sense to him, somehow. And then James came to mind. James, whose life was over after seventeen years. Most werewolves lived two hundred years or more. That life might be cut short if you were a Packmaster and didn't survive a challenge.

Ashe stole a glance at Sali, whose face was set in concentration as he folded the cardboard seed packet display and slipped tabs into slots. Shapeshifters lived the same number of years a werewolf might, but vampires lived forever unless they were killed somehow, or walked into the sun. Ashe took the old man's twenty, rang up the sale and gave change back, then handed him the bag containing the gloves.

"Thank you," Ashe said. The old man grinned and nodded before shuffling toward the door.

"Hey, I actually got it together." Sali set the assembled display in the floor.

"There's hope for you yet, you've mastered cardboard," Ashe smacked Sali on the arm.

"Yep. Cardboard today, string theory tomorrow," Sali laughed.

"Dude, you're into string theory?" Ashe teased, grabbing the box of seed packets that came with the display and stuffing the small envelopes into empty slots.

"Yeah. I think Dori plays with a ball of yarn when she turns to ocelot," Sali grinned.

"That looks great," Adele said, admiring their work on the display when she returned. "I can fix lunch here or take you by the Burger Hut or Taco Palace," she offered.

"Taco Palace," Sali said immediately.

"All right. Come on, then." Adele flipped the closed sign in the window, setting the little clock on it so customers would know she'd be back in fifteen minutes.

"What's going on?" Sali and Ashe stared at three highway patrol cars sitting in the Taco Palace parking lot as the old Ford bounced through the entrance.

"They probably wanted to have lunch together," Adele said. "Here's money. Try to bring some of it back." She handed Ashe a twenty.

"I'll try to keep the taco vacuum turned on low," Ashe elbowed Sali and slid out of the truck behind his friend.

"I'll be back in an hour," his mother promised before driving away, the truck creaking a little as it pulled out of the parking lot.

Ashe blinked when he walked up to the counter—the county sheriff was also there with one of his deputies, their wide backs blocking the counter from Ashe and Sali's view. The sheriff and his deputy carried their trays of food to a table shoved against the same one the highway patrol officers were using. "What's going on?" Ashe asked the woman behind the counter as he and Sali came forward to place their orders. They recognized her; her family owned Taco Palace.

"They found a body south of town," the woman replied. She looked to be in her late forties, but her red hair was still red, no gray, and she had a nice smile.

"Wow. Anyone from Cordell?" Sali asked.

"No. Not that I know of," she said. "It'll probably be on the news tonight." Both boys turned in their order, grabbed a table and Sali offered to pick up the tray when their names were called.

"Mom, the police found a body south of town; that's why they were at the Taco Palace." Ashe and Sali climbed into Adele's old truck when she came to pick them up.

"I know, honey," Adele said softly.

"How did you find out?" Ashe watched his mother's face; it appeared pale and drawn.

"Greta Rocklin called. She said it was Terry Smith, Randy Smith's father."

CHAPTER 4

"What was he doing here?" Ashe and Sali both knew Terry Smith was human. Randy Smith's mother, Dawn, was werewolf.

"No idea. Greta said he was shot and left in a ditch south of town. It was on the noon news."

"Do they know who did it?" Ashe's eyes were wide with shock and worry.

"Not yet. They're waiting for the Oklahoma State Bureau of Investigation to make a statement. Since the Smiths lived in New Mexico, they've called state authorities in on this."

"This is terrible," Ashe muttered softly. Sali dug an elbow into Ashe's ribs.

"You two shouldn't even know who Terry Smith is," Adele pulled away from the Taco Palace.

"Mom, the older kids gossip sometimes—about Randy Smith," Ashe's voice was nearly a whisper. "They're all afraid of getting into trouble if they let something slip."

"Honey, don't worry about that, all right?" Adele patted Ashe's knee. Ashe knew what his mother was thinking; he'd thought it often enough recently. But his mother didn't know that he'd hacked the Principal's computer and read the full contents of the note.

Watering the plants later, Sali glanced at Ashe a time or two. And when Adele was far enough away, Sali whispered at Ashe. "You're still going tonight. Right?"

"Yeah." Ashe stared at his shoes. The water from the hose Sali held made a tiny river that parted around Ashe's old sneakers and ran toward the drain in the greenhouse.

"You'll be all right, just get in that tree and don't make a sound," Sali hissed.

"That's easy for you to say," Ashe mumbled. The more he thought about it, the more worried he became. His desire not to get caught warred with his craving to know what the Pack would do about Randy Smith and what the latest on James and Terry Smith's murders might be. The chance to hear that information firsthand made Ashe itch with longing.

"Dude, I'd go myself if I were able." Sali's words forced Ashe away from his thoughts.

"Sali, will you do something for me?" Ashe gazed at Sali. Sali's black eyes stared back across a slatted table filled with plants.

"What?" Sali lifted the hose again to water plants on the table.

"Tell Cori I'm sorry about James."

"Son, keep the doors locked," Aedan instructed as he prepared to take Ashe's mother out for her full moon flights.

"Okay, Dad." Ashe nodded at his father.

"Don't let anyone in," Aedan continued. "I don't care who it is, don't open the door. Your mother and I can let ourselves in. Is that understood?"

"All right, Dad." Ashe was worried, now. What was making his father afraid? He'd watched the six o'clock news with his mother and there wasn't much information to be had regarding Terry Smith's death. The only evidence given was that he'd been shot, his body left in a gully south of Cordell. A reporter had interviewed the Washita county sheriff, but all he said was the investigation was ongoing. Ashe wondered what they'd say if they knew about James's death.

Both parents walked through the back door into the garage while Ashe watched. Aedan had one of the automatic door openers in his pocket and closed the garage door behind him. It was only a few minutes after nine, so Ashe gave his parents fifteen minutes to get away before sneaking out of the house and shutting the garage door again, using the keypad outside the garage. Slipping into his denim jacket, Ashe began to run.

"Dang." Ashe was halfway up the tree when he looked down. If he fell, he could break something—at least fifteen feet stretched between him and the ground below. "Don't think about it," Ashe grumbled to himself, grasping the trunk firmly and climbing farther up. His watch showed nine forty-five as he settled into a fork where the trunk split and branched out.

Each of the forked branches was as thick as Ashe's waist and quite solid. Ashe wriggled on his perch to get comfortable, braced his shoes against the tree trunk and prepared to wait for the werewolf Pack to arrive. It didn't take long, as it turned out. Marcus and Denise DeLuca came to the clearing with Micah and Greta Rocklin; Packmaster and Second, with their mates. Ashe heard them clearly and blinked several times when he heard Marcus say a word that he'd ground Sali for using. They were discussing Terry Smith and why he'd come to Cordell, followed by discussion and speculation on why he'd been murdered.

"And right after James," Greta Rocklin, Ashe's Transformational Arts teacher said. Ashe could tell from her voice that she was troubled over the event.

"No way the two are connected. This is just a strange coincidence," Marcus said. "Has to be."

"You think Terry found out that Randy sent the letter?"

"It's possible. He may have come to plead Randy's case. He has a right to petition the Pack before we make a decision."

"As a human mate. That doesn't carry much weight," Micah observed. "It would have been better if Dawn came."

"Maybe not. She was really mad and accused us of framing Randy," Denise DeLuca pointed out.

"That's ridiculous. Ben heard Randy talk about werewolves with that human child. Nathan placed compulsion on the human so he'd forget. All those records are in the Grand Master's files, now."

Ashe knew who Ben was. Benjamin Billings. Principal. PhD. Werewolf. The one who would volunteer to execute nineteen-year-old Randy Smith. Ashe shuddered, gripping the tree trunk even tighter. He couldn't help but wonder where Randy was right then and if he knew his father was dead.

"The Hoffs think Old Harold killed James." There it was; part of the information Ashe waited for. Sali wasn't aware of this and Ashe hadn't mentioned eavesdropping on his father's conversation with Nathan Anderson.

"Old Harold wouldn't do that." Greta Rocklin snapped at Marcus, her voice clear in the moonlit night.

"I don't think so either, but the Hoffs and Pat Roberts do," Marcus' voice sounded placating, as if he were attempting to calm Mrs. Rocklin down. "They're the reason I called the Grand Master instead of the Packmaster from Oklahoma City."

"If it wasn't a vampire, then who might have done it? And no scent around the body except Cori's? That's really strange." Ashe could see Sali's mother through the oak's branches; she'd wandered away from the others, staring at the full moon overhead, her arms hugged tightly against her body. Ashe knew her well enough to realize how upset she was.

"Cori couldn't have done it," Micah Rocklin said. "James would have gotten away from her. He was a fully-grown werewolf and she's still not a mature panther." Micah was defending Cori, making Ashe appreciate Marcus' Second more than usual.

"We're back to the scents, then. Even Old Harold couldn't erase his scent. I don't think it's possible." Marcus paced in agitation.

"Well, James didn't just drop from the sky," Greta pointed out. "We don't have any bird shifters large enough to carry the body." The four werewolves went quiet as others approached. Ashe heard them too—Marco shuffled dejectedly behind Mr. Dodd, the history teacher. More werewolves came, including the Hoffs and Pat Roberts.

Pat was an aging male werewolf, with wrinkles lining his face and gray in his hair. Ashe figured Pat had to be two hundred years old or more—werewolves didn't turn gray until they were quite old. None of the gathering werewolves carried lights; their night vision was nearly as sharp as his vampire father's. Ashe could see well enough in the moonlight; colors weren't visible to him, but he knew the barest tips of green grass were showing through the dead foliage on the ground and tiny, new leaves were out on the oak in which he sat.

Ashe was as still and quiet as he could be once all the werewolves were assembled. Marcus raised the question of what action the Pack should take regarding Randy Smith. Only a small amount of discussion was devoted to Terry Smith's death, and by a nearly unanimous vote, it was determined that Randy Smith should be executed for breaking Pack Law.

Marcus would submit the decision to the Grand Master, and the Grand Master's trackers would be dispatched to take Randy into custody and bring him before the Cloud Chief Pack during the next full moon. Ashe swallowed nervously at the verdict. Randy Smith had a month to live, and true to the note in his computer, Principal Billings offered to take the execution when Marcus asked for a volunteer.

"Now, you all know the Grand Master is sending an investigator on Thursday," Marcus went on. "So we won't officially discuss James's death tonight. We can hold a special meeting after the investigator gets here and sniffs around. I don't want anyone speculating and spreading rumors while we gather information. Is that clear?" Marcus paused and Ashe imagined that Sali's father was staring the Pack down. "The Vampire Council is also sending an Enforcer, so we'll have two working the case."

"Like any vampire will tell the truth if it involves one of theirs," Pat Roberts spat. Ashe recognized the old werewolf's voice easily.

"Pat, did you hear what I said?" Marcus growled. Ashe looked up—the Moon was riding high overhead and he knew what that meant. The werewolves were restless and about to turn. Tempers were flaring and becoming volatile.

"I heard. Don't have to agree," Pat growled back.

"Keep your mouth shut. That's an order," Marcus growled louder. Engrossed in the conversation and ignoring his growing discomfort, Ashe's foot slipped against the tree trunk where he'd braced it, sending a cascade of bark tumbling down. Ashe froze.

"What was that?" Micah hissed.

"Came from this direction," Marcus walked swiftly toward Ashe's tree. Right then, Ashe wanted to be invisible. Desperately. Fervently. He was going to get caught, his parents would be notified and he'd be punished at the very least. It was an unspoken rule in Cloud Chief; you didn't interfere with Pack business. And if the werewolves gathering below were angry enough and moon-touched enough, Ashe might not make it home at all.

"It came from right around here. Smell anything?" Principal Billings asked. Several male werewolves milled about the oak where Ashe sat. Ashe had never been so terrified in his life.

"I don't smell anything except the usual," Frank Dodd replied. "Kids have been running through here again."

"No, it came from this tree." Principal Billings was staring up at Ashe's tree. Staring *right at him.*

"There's nothing up there." Marcus pulled out a flashlight and shone it right at Ashe. "See?" Ashe stared down at Marcus and the others, who were all peering up at his branch. How could they miss him? Ashe was thin, but he wasn't small.

"Could have been an owl," Micah said, turning away. Ashe would have been puzzled if he weren't so frightened. They'd all stared right at him. The other werewolves were following Micah as he walked away from the tree. Ashe was ready to breathe a sigh of relief when he realized he wasn't breathing. Looking downward, Ashe couldn't see his feet. As werewolves began turning for the hunt, a terrified Ashe floated away.

~

Ashe had no idea how he'd managed to float home but he'd done it. Astonishingly, once he'd focused on where he wanted to go, he'd sped off in that direction. But what to do now? Ashe was still floating as he hovered before the keypad on the garage door. *Need to be solid. Need to be solid*, Ashe chanted silently. Miraculously, Ashe became corporeal, dropping onto the gravel drive with a thump.

"Still here? Shoes, clothes?" Ashe whispered to himself as he patted his chest with hands that shook. How had this happened? He'd wished to be invisible and that's exactly what he'd been. Thirty-seven adult werewolves had stared straight at him and none of them had seen a thing. And then, to make it more wondrous, Ashe had floated home, much swifter than he'd made the trip on foot, even running. Trembling slightly, it took several seconds for Ashe to recall the code that would get him inside the garage. Closing the heavy steel door afterward, Ashe punched the second code to get through the door into the kitchen, nearly falling as he lurched through the entryway once the code released the lock.

"Now what?" Ashe wanted to tug his hair out by the roots. He wanted to tell Sali. And then not tell Sali. If everybody found out he could become invisible, then it wouldn't take much to add two and two and come up with his spying on Pack business. Telling everybody would have to wait, Ashe decided, still quivering from his accidental discovery. Just to be sure, Ashe raced downstairs to the bathroom and concentrated on becoming invisible again. In less than a second, Ashe stared at nothing in the large mirror. How was he doing this? He'd never heard of anything like this before. Concentrating again, Ashe watched as his body reappeared in a blink.

"Wow," Ashe whispered to his image, watching as his lips formed the word.

~

"Ashe, honey, are you asleep?" Ashe's mother slipped inside his bedroom later.

"Mom?" Ashe had been asleep but was glad his mother came in to check on him.

"It's just us, hon. We're back." Adele Evans sat down on the edge of Ashe's bed and brushed hair away from his forehead. "Go back to sleep." She patted his shoulder and got up to leave.

"G'night, Mom."

"Goodnight, honey."

~

"Sali, they're gonna execute Randy Smith." Ashe waited until they were in a corner booth at the Burger Hut on Wednesday to whisper the news.

"They'll do it at the next full moon then." Sali dipped a French fry in a puddle of ketchup and stuffed it into his mouth.

"Sali, that's almost an entire family wiped out in the space of a month." Ashe stared at the young werewolf. How could he eat while discussing someone's death so casually?

"Pack Law," Sali mumbled around a mouthful of food.

"Sounds a little callous, don't you think?"

Sali chewed thoughtfully and swallowed before answering. "Dude, look at it this way. We have to stay hidden. People will kill you and your mom and dad if they find out what you are. Oh, some humans will think it's cool, but there are others who'd hate us and they'll get all of us. They think we're evil or something."

"Anybody has the capacity for that," Ashe shoved half his burger in Sali's direction. "Not every human is good. Not every vampire or shifter is good either."

"You're not gonna turn into a philosophizer, are ya?" Sali grinned and bit into Ashe's burger.

"Sali, I may have to alter my impression of you," Ashe said. "You just used a five-syllable word."

"I'll try not to let it happen again," Sali laughed.

Picking dead leaves off caladium plants was their job for the afternoon. Brown or yellowing leaves were dumped in an old cardboard box as Ashe and Sali made their way through potted plants lined up in neat rows at the back of the greenhouse. While they worked, several customers came in to select plants. Ashe dutifully hauled out cut-off boxes filled with seedlings and loaded purchases into waiting cars or trucks. The weather was definitely warming up and people wanted to plant.

Ashe and Sali walked to the Dumpster behind the store to empty the box of dead leaves before Adele closed up for the evening. "Dude, do you smell anything?" Sali asked after pounding the bottom of the box to get the last of the plant detritus out of it. The box would be reused—Adele didn't like throwing anything away if it could be recycled or repurposed.

"Smell what?" Ashe's nose wasn't as sharp as Sali's, even when Sali was in human form.

"Weird. Like ozone or something." Sali was still sniffing and following after whatever he'd smelled.

"What?" Ashe trailed behind Sali, mystified.

"You know, sort of like after a spring rain or something?"

"Dude, I can't smell anything," Ashe grumbled, but didn't doubt Sali's ability to detect the scent. It hadn't been raining, either, although a spring storm was predicted for the following day.

"Boys?" Adele's worried voice reached them from the back door of the greenhouse. They'd wandered behind the Dumpster, walking toward the wooden stockade fence at the edge of the property.

"Here, Mom." Ashe grabbed Sali's arm, halting his best friend's search for a source of the mysterious scent.

"Thank goodness." Ashe's mother muttered the words so softly that most people wouldn't have heard. Ashe heard.

"Come on," Ashe hauled Sali toward the greenhouse and his mother. "Sali thought he smelled ozone," Ashe poked Sali in the ribs.

"Ozone?" Adele lifted an eyebrow in Sali's direction.

"Yeah." Sali ducked his head, suddenly unsure of his own abilities.

"If you say you smelled ozone, then there was probably ozone. Come on, I'll make dinner and we'll have cookies for dessert. Sali's mother had to run an errand and asked if Sali could come over until she got back."

"Sweet," Sali grinned.

⁓

"Hey, Mr. Evans," Sali said when Aedan joined them at the dinner table nearly two hours later.

"Salidar," Aedan smiled at Sali. "How's your brother Marco?"

"Marco's okay, but Mom says he's depressed." Sali picked at his green beans while Ashe watched his friend. Ashe knew not to talk about Marco. Sali felt overshadowed by his older brother much of the time so Ashe hadn't brought Marco up the past few days. He figured if Sali wanted to talk, he would.

"I'm sorry to hear that. What about you, Sali? Everything all right?"

"Yeah. I'm good." Sali speared two whole green beans and stuffed them in his mouth.

"You can take your cookies to Ashe's room if you're careful with the crumbs," Adele handed a plate of cookies and a small glass of milk to Sali after the dinner dishes were done.

"I wanted to do some surfing anyway," Ashe received his plate of cookies next. He led the way toward the middle door separating the upper and lower floors. Aedan closed it behind them as they clumped down the steps. Ashe heard, even though Sali didn't. His mother was explaining to his father about the scent of ozone Sali picked up behind the shop in Cordell.

⁓

"Dad, has any shifter or paranormal ever been able to disappear?" Ashe stood beside his father as they watched Denise DeLuca drive away. Sali waved from the passenger seat of the DeLuca's Honda sedan. Ashe waved back as he waited for his father to answer the question.

"Son, that's impossible, I think. Maybe some of the witches or warlocks can put up a shield so people can't see them, but they're not truly invisible. There are two very rare types of vampires, though, and one of those can turn to mist. The other can mindspeak."

"Really? Some vampires can turn to mist and read minds?"

"They can't read minds, but they can send messages to someone else with the talent," Aedan smiled down at Ashe. "And that may be more useful at times."

"What about the ones who can turn to mist? How do they do that?" Ashe blinked curiously at his father.

"Ashe, only two or three of those exist at the moment," Aedan herded Ashe inside the garage and shut the door. "The rest of us don't know much at all about them. All that information is kept secret and I imagine all of them work for the Council in some way or another."

"But what happens after they turn to mist? Are they still shaped like their bodies?"

"I've heard tales through the years that misters can slip through the smallest cracks or keyholes, even. And I heard an old vampire say once that their clothing and such turned to mist as well. I didn't believe that. After all, your mother and all the others must disrobe before they turn or their clothing can hamper them in their other shapes."

"Yeah. I've gathered up clothes for Sali and the others in class," Ashe agreed gloomily.

"It'll come," Aedan misinterpreted Ashe's comment. "Just relax. It will come." Aedan placed an arm around Ashe's shoulders as they walked into the kitchen together.

~

"You missed your chance to grab the boy!" Wolf's hands clenched as his eyes angrily grazed his two accomplices. They'd missed a perfect opportunity. Ashe Evans wasn't like the others and didn't belong in Cloud Chief. Let the shapeshifter mother and the vampire father worry over the boy's kidnapping and subsequent death. If human authorities found the body, there was nothing to indicate the boy wasn't just as human as they were. Wolf growled—they'd botched a perfect opportunity. At least nobody could connect him to the crime when the boy was captured and destroyed; he'd refused to give these accomplices his real name, ordering them to call him Wolf instead.

"There was much danger that we might be seen. The boy's mother was nearby and he was not alone; you said yourself that no more werewolf children were to be harmed." Only one of the two accomplices could speak; the other was misshapen—a genetically enhanced warrior whose specialty was killing.

"You could have distracted the other boy," Wolf hissed. This was turning out badly, all the way around. James's death was a mistake and threatened to tip their hand. Now, others would die before both targets could be acquired and disposed of. And all to cover up the first death and point accusing fingers in other directions. "You know what you have to do," Wolf snapped. "Do it!" Shockingly, both accomplices disappeared before his eyes, leaving the scent of ozone behind.

Ashe awoke Thursday morning with a terrible taste in his mouth, only to discover it was still dark. Turning on his side with difficulty, he searched for the bedside clock, finding only more darkness. *What the heck? Dang.* He was buried beneath the blanket. Flopping and struggling with the fabric that felt extremely heavy for some reason, Ashe worked his way toward the edge of the bed—and then dropped out of it. Well, plopped out of it might have been a better term. The word aptly described the sound he'd made after falling out of bed.

Ashe looked around, blinking in astonishment. Everything was huge. Really, *really* huge. And he could see popcorn and cookie crumbs on the carpet beneath his nightstand. *What was going on?* Ashe crawled toward the nightstand in question. The space between the wooden legs, normally a spare two inches off the floor, now looked like a massive cave entrance. Ashe crawled and fumbled his way toward that entrance. What was the matter with him? Was he dreaming? This might be the strangest nightmare he'd ever had, except he could feel the carpet fibers beneath his—*wait. Those weren't hands.*

CHAPTER 5

orcing himself to remain as calm as possible, Ashe flopped and tumbled toward his dresser. A mirror was there and he'd get to the bottom of this as quickly as he could. Provided he could climb up the dresser that now resembled a forbidding vertical mountain of polished wood, that is. Hooking a tiny claw into a crack between the side of the lower drawer and the dresser, Ashe heaved himself up. Then, hooking the opposite claw into a higher position in the same crack, he heaved again. Ashe figured it took the better part of half an hour (with much slipping and scrabbling) to make his way to the top of the dresser.

Panting as he reached the top, Ashe navigated around the brush, comb, deodorant and pile of unread books that now dwarfed him until he could hook a claw into the bottom frame of the mirror. Cautiously he lifted himself up, frightened and unsure of what the mirror might tell him.

Dude, you're screwed, Ashe thought as he examined his image in the reflective glass. He knew exactly what stared at him from the mirror; he'd studied it in science class. A tiny, not yet fully-grown bumblebee bat frowned back.

I can't tell anybody about this. This is too embarrassing. Backing up against the bottom of the mirror frame, Ashe wrapped tiny wings around his body as he shivered, envisioning all his classmates laughing as he turned into one of the smallest mammals on the planet. His minuscule, fur-covered torso was reddish-brown, tipped with golden-hued fuzz about his head. Ears that seemed too large for such a small body picked up every sound inside the house. A tiny, pig-shaped snout wiggled a bit as he sniffed the air around him. He still couldn't scent things as well as Sali, but then bats relied on echolocation to find their prey. *While they flew.*

Unfurling wings that trembled with uncertainty, Ashe dragged himself to the edge of the dresser. Gulping in a breath, he launched himself off it, hovering briefly in mid-air before dropping to the floor with a squishy plop. Thankful that he had thick carpet on the floor, even if he did see that it needed vacuuming from such close range, Ashe flapped his wings and lifted partially away from the fuzz-filled rug. And then dropped immediately to the floor. Determined now, Ashe pulled himself up and tried again.

It took at least ten tries with partial successes before he was flapping and hovering around his room. The hovering was great—Ashe flapped for several seconds before the mirror, watching as his wings kept him aloft and bobbing about in the early-morning air.

"Ashe, time to get up!" His mother's shout and subsequent knock on the bedroom door brought him back to reality with a bang. Ashe lost his concentration and dropped onto the dresser, bumping his tiny head on the corner of a book. He discovered he could read while a bumblebee bat; *The Last of the Mohicans'* title looked to be as wide as Ashe's wingspan.

Need to be human, need to be human, Ashe chanted mentally and promptly dropped off the dresser in human form, completely naked and knocking a shower of books, toiletries and other bric-a-brac down on top of him.

"Ashe, are you all right?" His mother was still standing outside his door.

"Yeah, I just knocked some stuff off the dresser. Books and stuff," Ashe called back. "I'll be out in a minute."

"Clean up the mess," his mother said as she walked away. "Breakfast is nearly ready."

Ashe was still trying to get a heel stuffed into his right sneaker as he pounded up the steps to the kitchen. Somehow, all the changing had made him ravenous.

"Hon, slow down," Adele cautioned as Ashe pulled two more pancakes onto his plate and added syrup. Ashe was getting a taste (literally) of what Sali went through every day. "Sali's mother called, Sali won't come with us today. Marcus wanted him to ride along to the city to pick up the investigator."

Ashe nodded, his mouth full. His mother didn't like it if he attempted to talk around his food. "When?" he asked after swallowing. His mother answered while Ashe busily cut another triangle of pancakes to shovel into his mouth.

"The plane arrives at one this afternoon, so I figure they'll be back around three or four. They'll probably take the investigator out to eat before leaving the city."

"Are they gonna be out in the pasture behind the house?" Ashe and the others had been warned to stay away, but he now had the means to investigate with no fear of being caught. He could turn to mist or to bumblebee bat and fly around the area without ever putting a foot to the ground.

"Yes. Tonight or tomorrow, after the Enforcer looks at the body, I think."

"Mom, we're calling James a body. That has to be wrong, somehow."

"I know, honey. But we have to believe that James is somewhere else. That what he left behind is just a shell."

"Yeah." Ashe's appetite had suddenly deserted him.

"Go brush your teeth and let's get to work."

~

"The witch is coming to renew the concealment spells," Adele said during the drive into Cordell.

"I forgot about that," Ashe huffed out a breath.

"Not a surprise, with everything else that's happened," his mother agreed. "I almost forgot about it until Marcus mentioned it when he called your dad last night."

Ashe nodded. Every spring a hired witch came to renew the spell that hid all the aboveground structures from the outside world. Anyone driving by would only see empty fields. Non-residents would have to breach the spelled area and come within a few feet of the structures in order to see them. It kept Cloud Chief safe from the outside world. Aedan explained it to Ashe when he was eight.

"Son," he'd said, "With the weapons and technology available now, we wouldn't stand a chance if somebody truly wanted us dead. They have machines that can even detect things underground. They have radar, sonar and any other number of things to locate us, and any number of deadly weapons to kill us after they find us. That's why we remain hidden. We can't afford to expose ourselves."

Ashe understood that better as time passed. It terrified him to think that a hunting rifle could shoot his mother out of the sky during one of her flights. Shifters and werewolves healed notoriously fast, but a shot to the head or heart and they'd be just as dead. He shook himself to eliminate such morbid thoughts. "When will the witch do the new spells?" he asked.

"Next week, I think. She'll have to do the prep work, walking the perimeter and such." Ashe nodded at his mother's words. He had no idea if a witch might be able to detect him while he was mist or bat, and that concerned him for some reason. Leaning his head against the worn upholstery of his mother's truck, he stared out the window the rest of the drive into Cordell.

Fifteen tomato plants and six pepper plants went into a box later as Ashe rushed around helping customers. Everybody wanted to plant over the weekend, so they were buying plants that Thursday in preparation. Ashe figured Friday and Saturday would be even busier.

It was a good thing he and Sali had gotten all the seed packets out and stocked; those were flying off the shelves, along with gloves, trowels, hoes and hand plows. A few customers bought more expensive gas or electric tillers. His mother liked making those sales; they were a good return on investment, as she called it.

Adele was on the phone to her supplier right after lunch, ordering replacement supplies. Most of that would come in early the following week. Ashe realized he'd be back in school by then and he'd have to make a decision. Turn in class or not. A tough choice. Somehow, he didn't want to let anyone know he could become mist. That was a secret he wanted to keep.

"Tired honey?" Adele locked the door to the shop behind her.

"Yeah."

"Me, too. Let's go to Betsy's and order takeout."

"Okay. Sounds good." It did. Betsy's Diner made chicken and dumplings as a regular menu item. Ashe intended to get that if they hadn't run out of it. Five minutes later Ashe and his mother sat at a table in Betsy's, looking the menu over.

"I'll have the roast beef-dinner with mashed potatoes, spinach and a dinner salad," Adele handed the menu back to their waitress.

"I want the chicken and dumplings, with two pieces of cornbread and a side of fried okra," Ashe gave up his menu.

"Are you growing again?" Ashe's mother teased as they waited for their order to come. Adele asked for it to go, first thing.

"Maybe," Ashe shrugged and sipped the complimentary glass of water the waitress brought when they arrived.

"We'll have to shop for more jeans," Adele said absently.

"Can I get cargo pants?" Ashe asked hopefully.

"Maybe a couple pairs."

"When?"

"We can go to the city sometime next month I think." Adele turned her attention back to Ashe.

"What's wrong, Mom?" Ashe knew his mother was worried about something.

"The Council's Enforcer? Your dad said his name was Radomir," Adele said.

"What about him?" Ashe asked.

"He'll be staying with us while he's here," she sighed.

Later, Ashe carried the last box of Christmas decorations up the steps leading to the second bunker beneath the basement. His mother was already vacuuming the carpet in the nine-by-nine room, preparing to dust the dresser and bedside table. His father's bunker was a twelve-by-twelve square beneath the master bedroom. This second bunker had never been intended for anything other than storage and the occasional visiting vampire. In all his twelve years, Ashe had never seen a visiting vampire. He guessed his father's foresight was a good thing, since that's exactly what they were getting. Radomir wasn't just any vampire; he was an Enforcer for the Vampire Council.

"Bring clean sheets when you come back," Adele called up the steps. Ashe was headed toward the attic in the garage with the box of ornaments. His mother didn't like to keep things up there; Oklahoma summers could be sweltering in their intensity.

"Okay," Ashe called behind him and kept going.

"Will these do?" he brought the best queen-sized sheets he could find, with matching pillowcases.

"These are good," Adele nodded, unfolding the fitted sheet onto the bed. "Get the comforter out of the closet." Ashe pulled the comforter out of the protective plastic sleeve and unfolded it, grateful that his father had installed plenty of lighting. Otherwise, the bunker would be dark as a tomb. That might not matter to a vampire, but Ashe needed light to see while he was human. Ashe went still for a moment. *While he was human.* He'd never had that thought before. It comforted him in an odd way.

He helped his mother get the top sheet and the comforter on the bed, then set about slipping pillows into pillowcases and two additional pillows into shams that matched the comforter. "There." Blowing a stray strand of honey-blonde hair away from her face, Adele Evans smiled at her son. "And just in time for your dad to wake, too. Come on." Ashe followed his mother up the steps and watched while she let the trapdoor down. If someone went inside the bunker, the door could be locked from there and nobody would be able to get in unless a grenade or something stronger was tossed inside the bedroom overhead.

"Son, you've got dust in your hair." Aedan found them closing the trap door leading to the second bunker. He ruffled Ashe's hair affectionately for a moment.

"He's been hauling Christmas decorations into the attic," Adele said.

"I could have taken those up."

"It wasn't a big deal, Dad. Everything is up there and the bunker's clean and ready to go."

"So, your mother told you." Aedan searched Ashe's face.

"It's kinda hard to miss, Dad."

"He'll be here sometime before dawn tomorrow morning." Aedan leaned over to kiss Adele. "Go clean up, son. You look like you've walked through a haunted house."

Ashe awoke the moment the door opened to the stairwell, and then listened while his father showed their guest where the trapdoor was located leading to the smaller bunker. Shivering in the cool morning air, Ashe checked the time on the clock—six-thirty was displayed in big, red, digital numbers. They wouldn't have time to search the field behind the house—sunrise came at seven-fifteen. Unless the Enforcer arrived earlier and he and Aedan had gone out to look first. Ashe resolved to examine the site as quickly as he could.

"It'll be busy today and tomorrow," Adele set a plate of ham and eggs in front of Ashe.

"Is Sali coming?"

"Not today. Denise called and said she's keeping Sali at home. The investigator is staying there with them, so Denise needs Sali's help at the house."

"Is Marco doing any better?" Ashe cut into his ham.

"Not really. No."

"Did you meet him?"

"The investigator?"

"The Enforcer." Ashe bit into a chunk of ham.

"He seems nice enough. Taller than your father by a couple of inches. Dark hair, dark eyes. Looks strong."

Ashe was chewing so he nodded at his mother. He figured the *nice* comment was to keep him from thinking that an Enforcer was scarier than anything he'd ever met before. "What about the investigator?"

"Denise says it's somebody from Dallas named William Winkler. I think she knows more than she's telling, but that's Pack business."

"Mom, the Pack has a Grand Master and the vampires have a Council. What do the shifters have?" Ashe stopped eating for a moment to ask the question. He'd never really thought about it before.

"We don't have anything," Adele sighed regretfully. "We're too scattered and disorganized. The vampires are all vampires, the werewolves all werewolves. Shifters can be almost anything. We're all different, so there's never been any movement to band together. Can you see all the lions getting together, or all the horses or caribou?"

"There are shapeshifting caribou?"

"In the north. They're quite common there. We're so scattered it would be extremely difficult to organize. These paranormal communities have been the best we could do so far."

"How many communities like this are there, Mom?"

"Not a lot, and they're all here inside the U.S. Europe still hasn't tried it; I think they're waiting to see how we do."

"Sounds like an experiment." Ashe was turning Nathan's words around, making them sound like idle curiosity. He was rewarded with an answer.

"We sort of are," Adele lifted her fork. "That's why it's so important to find out who killed James and why. The answer might determine whether Cloud Chief stays together or disbands."

"That's possible?" now Ashe was worried. He and Sali would be separated, he just knew it.

"Ashe, don't worry, all right? Things will work out. Finish your breakfast."

The day was busy at Cordell Feed and Seed, just as Ashe expected it to be. He rang up customers. Talked about the advantages of this piece of equipment over that. Listened sagely as an old woman spoke about the different kinds of tomatoes and then sold her two dozen plants, as well as squash, zucchini and watermelon seeds. His mother worked tirelessly with the more difficult tools and plants, between helping with bags of feed and fertilizer. Both of them missed lunch and Ashe was starving by the time the workday was done.

"Come on, we'll run by the grocery store and I'll broil steaks," Adele hugged Ashe as they walked toward his mother's old truck. Dinner was finished and Ashe had eaten every scrap of his T-bone, salad and mashed potatoes when Aedan walked through the door into the kitchen, a tall, dark-haired vampire right behind him.

"How was your day?" Aedan sat down at the table just as he always did. "This is Radomir, Enforcer for the Council," Aedan invited the other vampire to sit down with his family.

"The store was extremely busy. We had a good day and missed lunch, so I fixed steaks." Ashe noticed his mother was chatting nervously, something she seldom did.

"What time do you normally rise, Mrs. Evans?" Radomir asked, leveling a dark gaze on Adele. Ashe watched as his mother lowered her eyes. She was worried and too frightened to look Radomir in the eye.

"Around five-thirty. Aedan usually wakes me," she replied, staring at her hands.

"Aedan and I may be busy, so please set an alarm clock for tomorrow morning."

"Of course," Adele whispered. Ashe didn't like that his mother felt so uncomfortable, but he felt helpless. His father couldn't say anything, because Radomir worked for the Vampire Council. He wondered if Sali were feeling the same about the investigator the Grand Master sent. Ashe itched to phone Sali, but that was impossible as long as Radomir remained inside the house. He could easily listen to any conversation, and Ashe wasn't allowed a cell phone to make a call from outside the house. His father said he could have a cell phone on his fifteenth birthday. Until then, his parents felt that Ashe was just too young to have one.

"I'll clear away the dishes," Ashe lifted his plate off the table and walked toward the sink. He could try to instant message Sali on the computer, but Sali didn't have his own computer, as Ashe did. The conversation might not be private.

"Here, honey." Adele stood and took her plate to Ashe. Together they loaded the dishwasher and wiped down the stove and countertops. Radomir and Aedan were still sitting at the kitchen table when they finished.

"Is there anything I can get for you?" Adele asked Radomir.

"I am fine, Mrs. Evans."

"Then Ashe and I will go downstairs and watch television." Radomir inclined his head slightly in acknowledgement, so Ashe went down the stairs ahead of his mother, who closed the middle door behind her. Neither spoke until they were inside the living room downstairs. Ashe's mother closed that door as well.

"Mom, is Dad gonna be okay?" Ashe had to work to keep himself from trembling.

"I hope so," Adele replied. Ashe didn't miss the tiny crease of worry between his mother's brows.

Ashe watched one program with his mother before asking if he could go to his room to read. Adele gave permission so he walked down the hall toward his bedroom. He'd heard the kitchen door open and close ten minutes after he and his mother walked downstairs, so Ashe knew Radomir had gone out with his father. Standing in front of his dresser, Ashe quickly turned to mist, hoping mightily that his mother wouldn't come to check on him and find him gone while he was out.

Discovering that his father's information was correct, Ashe slipped through the barest of cracks around doors to leave the house. Once outside, he lifted high into the air to look around. Spotting his father and Radomir in the pasture behind the house, Ashe zoomed his mist in that direction.

"No other scents were found?" Ashe hovered over their heads as Radomir asked questions.

"No. I wasn't here initially, but when Nathan and I went out after the others left, we only found evidence of the boy, the little female panther, Micah Rocklin, Marcus DeLuca and Benjamin Billings," Aedan explained. He stood amid knee-high prairie grass, arms crossed over his chest as he examined the spot where James' body had been found.

"Who was first at the scene?"

"After Cori, I believe Marcus and Benjamin were. Micah came after they arrived."

"Hmm." Radomir walked around the area, sniffing for scents and searching for clues with sharp, vampire sight. "Too much time has passed," he said after a while. "The scents are confused now and any clues are obliterated."

"I feel the same." Aedan sounded defeated and Ashe wasn't used to that. His father was always strong and confident. This worried Ashe more than he wanted to admit.

"Are they prepared to show us the body tonight?"

"Yes, I only have to call Marcus and they'll meet us there."

"Then we will go now."

Without a word, Aedan lifted his cell phone from a pocket and hit a number on speed dial. Ashe heard it ringing just as well as he might if he still had corporeal ears. He heard Marcus' answer, too. "We're ready to see the body, if you're free," Aedan said.

"We'll meet you there in twenty minutes," Marcus's voice was soft, but Ashe heard. Ashe followed his father as he strode purposely toward the house, Radomir beside him. Tossing good sense and caution away, Ashe misted inside his father's SUV as Aedan and Radomir loaded into it. Ashe was going to do what none of the others his age could—he was going to see James's body first-hand.

Marcus and a werewolf Ashe didn't recognize stood outside the O'Neill's barn when Aedan drove up. Ashe figured it was the Grand

Master's investigator, William Winkler. Black-haired, black-eyed and taller than Marcus but not quite as tall as Aedan or Radomir, William Winkler moved with an easy grace that spoke of power and confidence. Misting away from the SUV as soon as his father opened the driver's side door, Ashe followed closely behind Aedan as the two vampires approached the werewolves.

"Aedan, this is William Winkler," Marcus introduced the investigator. Aedan offered his hand and the tall werewolf clasped it firmly.

"Mr. Winkler and I already know one another," Radomir said, shocking Marcus, Aedan and Ashe.

CHAPTER 6

"We met several years ago," William Winkler explained. "And call me Winkler, everybody does." Ashe found he liked the werewolf investigator. He put everyone at ease, whereas Radomir seemed more stiff and formal.

"Come on in; I have the key." Marcus held up the key in question. Ashe followed invisibly as Winkler slid the barn door back and walked inside. The others followed the werewolf investigator's lead. The O'Neill's walk-in refrigerator had a bright light that blinked on when the door opened. Grateful for the light and for the discovery that he didn't feel the cold when he followed his father inside the refrigerator, Ashe might have gasped his surprise if he'd been corporeal; James had died as werewolf. Somehow, he expected James to be, well, *James*.

"So, he went down fighting, you think?" Radomir was speaking directly to Winkler, as if he valued the werewolf's opinion. Ashe realized that this was both unusual and true. Radomir and Winkler not only knew one another, they respected each other as well.

"Couldn't be otherwise," Winkler agreed. Radomir leaned in to examine the deep claw marks running across the young werewolf's torso.

"These are impressive wounds, but surely they wouldn't have killed him," Radomir observed. Ashe was sickened by what he saw. Globs of dried blood covered strips of fur and skin that had been cruelly torn from James's body. Eyes that still shone golden in the artificial light were nearly closed but not completely. The tongue was blackened and hanging from the mouth. Ashe stared at James's lengthy canines. Sali's weren't that long, but Sali wasn't fully grown as a werewolf, either.

"They didn't kill him," Winkler agreed. "But the boy died somehow. Now, all we have to do is figure out how and why. One of our werewolf physicians is coming in from Chicago next week. He'll perform an autopsy. Perhaps he can tell us what really happened here."

"I would like to be present when the autopsy is performed," Radomir said. Ashe might have gulped if he'd been solid. No way he'd want to see that. No way he could stand there and watch without tossing his lunch.

"I intend to be here as well," Winkler agreed.

"Both of you are confident this isn't the work of a vampire?" Marcus asked.

"Yes. A vampire would have shredded the boy. These claw marks aren't deep enough." Radomir pointed out the deepest of the gouges. Ashe estimated they couldn't be more than one or two inches deep. "What about the girl? The panther shapeshifter?" Radomir asked.

"We sniffed her for blood and only found it drying on her clothing when she knelt down beside the body. No blood under her nails. I've questioned her and believe she's telling the truth, but I was waiting for you to place compulsion for the whole truth." Winkler nodded at Radomir.

"I will do this Monday evening. Arrange it for me, please." Radomir spoke to Marcus.

"I'll call Nathan," Marcus said. "And I and the boy's father will be present when the physician examines the body."

"As you wish it," Radomir agreed. Ashe got the idea that it might be extremely difficult to surprise or gross out Radomir the Enforcer. He couldn't decide whether that was truly frightening or really cool.

Then, anxious not to be locked inside, Ashe zipped out of the refrigerator ahead of the others and waited next to the SUV until his father opened the driver's side door.

His father and Radomir were silent as they drove toward Cordell. Ashe was shocked—he imagined they'd go back to the house. They didn't. Ashe was becoming frightened; where were they going? He didn't find out until Aedan stopped to get gas for the SUV at a truck stop off I-40. Radomir and his father were driving to Santa Fe.

Longing to be in two places at once, Ashe watched his father's SUV pull away from the gas pump, driving toward the exit that would take him toward New Mexico. Turning his mist southward with a mental sigh, Ashe reluctantly headed toward Cloud Chief.

Wishing later that he could have timed his trip from the interstate back to his home, Ashe became himself again inside his bedroom, noting that the clock said eleven-thirty. He'd made good time, no matter how you looked at it.

"Ashe, are you in bed?" his mother tapped on the door ten minutes later.

"Getting into pajamas now," Ashe called out.

At the breakfast table the next morning, Ashe itched to tell Sali what he'd seen and heard the night before, but that would get him into trouble. Ashe felt he might burst with all the secrets he was keeping lately, but there wasn't anything else he could do without getting into serious trouble. Why were his father and Radomir driving to Santa Fe? That made no sense.

Ashe had found his mother reading the note his father left for her the night before when he'd come upstairs for breakfast. Aedan didn't tell her where they'd gone, just that they'd be back on Sunday if possible. If Aedan hadn't said something while pumping gas about how long it was likely to take to get to Santa Fe, Ashe wouldn't have known either. His mother was terribly worried and Ashe couldn't tell her where his father had gone. This had to be about Terry and Randy Smith, Ashe decided. They'd lived in Santa Fe. But what did that have to do with James's death?

"Ashe, will you settle for a bowl of cereal for breakfast?" his mother sounded defeated, just as Aedan had the night before.

"I'll make instant oatmeal for both of us." Ashe went to get the packets out of the pantry and put the water on to boil in the kettle.

"You were supposed to be coming back from Six Flags today," Adele said absently as she drove toward Cordell. "It's funny how things got so messed up, isn't it?"

"Yeah." Ashe muttered. So many lives had changed in the past week. He wondered how many more might be affected before it was over.

The store was busy, just as predicted. Ashe watched the store while his mother had a sandwich inside the tiny kitchen in the back. He knew she was making phone calls while she ate, but he couldn't hear with all the noise from customers and outside traffic. When Adele came out to take over, she sounded more depressed than before. Ashe thought she might have left a message on his dad's cell since he'd be asleep somewhere. At least Ashe hoped his dad was sleeping somewhere. He'd never really worried about his father until now.

"Mom, it'll be all right," Ashe took his mother's hand as they walked toward the truck after closing for the evening.

"Honey," Adele Evans stopped at the edge of the sidewalk where the old Ford was parked, "I wish I could say that for sure. There are so many things you don't know." She pulled him to her and hugged him hard.

"Will I ever know those things?" Ashe, nearly as tall as his mother, searched her eyes with his.

"You seem so grown up most of the time." Adele rested her forehead against his. "Maybe when you're older, you'll know those things." Pulling the truck keys out of her sweater pocket, she unlocked the door. "Get in, Ashe. We'll find something to cook at home."

Dinner was tomato soup and grilled cheese sandwiches. Ashe didn't complain; he just had an extra sandwich. He washed up afterward, too, so his mother could lie down—she had a headache. Ashe listened while Adele walked into her bedroom and shut the door.

"Ashe, meet me at the place behind your house where they found James." Sali's voice was soft over the phone. Ashe had gotten the call and as soon as his mother knew it was Sali, she hung up the extension.

"Why?" Ashe was puzzled.

"They're done with it, so we can go poke around."

"Sali, do you think you'll find anything that the others haven't? We're not supposed to go out there." Ashe wasn't sure about this. He'd gone the night before as mist and his father and Radomir hadn't found anything. What could Sali hope to do?

"Just meet me there, okay?" Sali hung up.

"Sali, you're gonna get me killed," Ashe muttered, hitting the off button on the cordless. Nevertheless, Ashe was at the proper spot, waiting for Sali to arrive ten minutes later. He'd misted through the cracks, just as he'd done the night before. Twilight was falling and the light was fading when Sali came trotting up, completely naked.

"Sorry. Ran most of the way as wolf," Sali panted an apology.

"Here." Ashe slipped out of his jacket and handed it to Sali, watching while his friend tied the windbreaker around his waist. According to Sali, all werewolves lost their modesty when they began the change. "What are we looking for?" he'd stayed away from the exact spot, electing to lean against a fencepost not far from the actual site while waiting for Sali to appear.

"Anything, dude. Cori is terrified that she'll be accused when she didn't have a thing to do with it," Sali said, walking toward the site. "I can smell it, Ashe. Death. It was here. At least for a while, even though it's fading."

"Sali, I am in awe of your amazing nose," Ashe said truthfully.

"All werewolves have it," Sali said distractedly. He was busily sniffing around.

"I can only use my eyes," Ashe said, and started looking right behind Sali.

"Dude, I can't find anything." Sali kicked at a clump of dirt half an hour later. The sun was now completely down and all Ashe had was fading twilight in which to see anything. That meant he almost didn't catch the tiny glint as the dirt that Sali kicked rolled away.

"What's that?" Ashe jumped toward the rolling ball of dirt, grabbing it before it was lost in six-inch weeds and dead grass.

"Just dirt," Sali said.

"No, I saw something." Ashe turned the lump of dirt over in his hands. "See?" he wiggled the shiny bit of metal that had caught his eye. It broke away from the dried dirt, but Ashe had to rub it between his fingers to discover it was a button.

"Looks like a button from somebody's jacket," Sali carefully examined the small gold disc. Werewolves had good night vision, so he could see it better than Ashe. "Not from anything I've seen Cori or James wear," Sali added.

"It's not big enough for a coat button," Ashe added what he could.

"Let's take it to your house and wash it off," Sali offered.

"Dude, Mom's in bed with a headache and I didn't tell her I was coming. I'll take it home and clean it off. You can come over tomorrow and we'll look at it."

"All right. I think Mom will let me come. Mr. Winkler isn't hard to take care of."

"You gonna see Cori before school starts on Monday?" Ashe asked.

"Doubt it," Sali was kicking dirt again.

"Then I'll talk to her on Monday," Ashe sighed. "Come on, it's dark, dude. Let's go home." The boys split up after a few minutes, and Ashe waited until Sali turned back to wolf pup before retrieving his jacket. Silently he watched as his friend loped away before turning to mist and racing toward the house.

Aedan wasn't home when Ashe woke on Sunday morning, and he'd been hoping that his father might come in while he was sleeping. Adele seemed listless as she prepared bacon and eggs for breakfast. Ashe didn't like seeing his mother like this. And he wondered if she'd gotten any replies from the numerous messages left on his father's cell. Ashe cleaned up the kitchen while his mother went back to bed.

Sali rang the doorbell outside the garage two hours later. Ashe shouted to his mother that it was Sali; she told him not to make a lot of racket and left him alone. "Mom's not feeling good," Ashe muttered as he led Sali down the steps to the lower level of the house.

"Marco either, and I figure Cori isn't doing all that well." Sali shut the door to Ashe's bedroom behind him.

"Here's the button, but I've been thinking about this. People walk through the field back there all the time. It could belong to anybody." Ashe handed the button to Sali.

"But I've never seen anybody wear anything with gold buttons like this." Sali turned the gold-colored button in his fingers. It had a raised design on it.

"That's a Celtic knot; I looked it up," Ashe said.

"Who'd be wearing that?" Sali frowned at the button in his hand.

"Could be what the designer chose."

"Yeah, but I've never seen a button like this before." Sali handed it back to Ashe.

"Me either, but I don't think I've seen everything that everybody wears in Cloud Chief. Want to take it to your dad?" Ashe asked.

"No, dude. He didn't know I was out last night, and you're right, somebody just dropped this. Keep it." Sali handed it back to Ashe, who slipped it into the top drawer of his bedside table. Neither of them wanted to admit to their parents that they'd disobeyed and gone out to the pasture to look around.

"Wanna play Frisbee?" Sali asked, changing the subject. Ashe knew what that meant; Sali wanted to turn to wolf and go chasing after the neon green Frisbee he had stuffed inside his closet. It bore teeth marks from Sali doing the same thing for the past two years.

"Yeah. I'll tell Mom."

Ashe laughed as Sali leapt high in the air to catch the Frisbee, snapping the edge between his teeth and landing with a semi-graceful roll on the ground. It was a warm, early spring day, the old grass blowing in a slight breeze while new green sprouted beneath it. Ashe hoped a roadrunner or some other potential prey wouldn't pop up— Sali enjoyed the chase, although he usually lost interest if it were a roadrunner. Ashe had no desire to go running after Sali, reminding him that his mother had said to stay in the yard.

"Ashe?" Ashe turned quickly to find Cori standing ten yards behind him.

"Cori? Are you all right?" Ashe walked toward her, leaving Sali behind, the Frisbee still dangling from his mouth.

"Ashe, I have to talk to you." Cori's green eyes were worried, the ever-present Oklahoma wind blowing blonde hair into her face. Her hair was past her shoulders long and pretty when she left it down. It was down now.

"Sali, let's go to the house so you can change," Ashe turned to his werewolf friend, who'd trotted up. Ashe took the Frisbee from Sali's mouth.

"Ashe, I'd like to talk to you alone," Cori said softly as Sali raced toward the house, tongue flying from his mouth in joyful abandonment as he ran.

"I'll think of something," Ashe promised, opening the kitchen door to allow Sali to slide inside. Sali's paws and toenails always slipped and slid on Adele Evans' tiled kitchen floor and he nearly collided with a cabinet before righting himself.

"Sali, your mother called. She wants you to come home," Adele was there, the phone in her hand, staring down at Sali's half-grown wolf who flipped a paw over his nose in embarrassment. He gave a whine at Adele's words but rose and trotted obediently down the steps to get to the basement and Ashe's bedroom.

"We'll give you a few minutes to change," Ashe yelled at his retreating friend.

"Cori, honey, is there something I can get for you?" Adele sounded tired.

"No, Mrs. Evans. I just came to talk to Ashe for a little while. If that's all right with you."

"Of course it is," Adele offered Cori a weak smile.

"Mom, do you need some ibuprofen or something?" Ashe asked. He was ready to run down the steps to the bathroom and get the bottle of pain reliever for his mother.

"No, honey. I need to get up and get around. I feel sluggish for some reason."

"Sit down. I'll make coffee for you."

"That sounds good."

Ashe busied himself at the coffee pot. Once he had that going, he offered a soda to Cori, who took an orange. Sali clambered up the steps and looked expectantly at Ashe, who sent him on his way with an orange soda as well. "See you tomorrow," Ashe called as Sali went out the back door. Sali waved and disappeared, hitting the button to close the garage door behind him. As soon as Ashe poured out a cup of coffee for his mother, he and Cori went downstairs.

"What is it, Cori?" Ashe shut the bedroom door.

"Ashe, you're the only one I can trust with this, I think." Cori at sixteen was five feet, two inches tall—two inches shorter than Ashe and not likely to grow any taller. Her mother, Lavonna, was around that height as well.

"Trust with what?" Ashe sat on his bed, gazing expectantly at Cori Anderson. Choosing a corner of Ashe's bed to sit, Cori scooted next to the wall that bumped against it.

"Randy Smith didn't write that letter to Mr. Harris." Cori hugged herself tightly, her eyes cast downward.

"Cori, how do you know that?" Ashe put his back against the solid wood headboard, kicked off his shoes and drew his knees up as he stared at Cori.

"He wouldn't. He knew better." Cori met Ashe's puzzled gaze.

"How can we know that for sure? Nobody has been in contact with him or his family for seven years." Ashe shook his head.

Cori heaved a ragged sigh. "I know for sure," she said. "You didn't know Randy because you hadn't started school yet. But I did. And James did, too."

"But it's been seven years," Ashe was still trying to make his point.

"Ashe, Randy doesn't write letters. He makes phone calls. Or did. To James. And James made calls to him. They were best friends, before. James never stopped calling Randy, Ashe. They just had to find a way to do it. Why do you think I asked you to hack Billings' computer? James wanted to know what was going on and if he and Randy were in trouble. When I told James what you said, he called Randy and told him. Randy worried that somebody would come for him and he'd be killed by the Cloud Chief Pack. But that's not all, Ashe. Randy never said anything to anybody about any of us. Not intentionally, anyway. James knew but he wouldn't talk about it. All he'd say was that Randy was framed, somehow. I think this is tied up with Pack business and we could get into the worst kind of trouble if we tried to get in the middle of it."

"Cori, what do you think I can do about any of this?" Ashe chewed his lower lip and wished he were older. Perhaps he could deal with it better, that way. Now it all seemed a muddled mess and he was helpless against it.

"I'm telling you this in case something happens to me. What evidence do they have that the letter came from Randy? Do you know? Where was it mailed? Was it in his handwriting or typed on a computer? Were his fingerprints on it? Or his scent? Somebody has the answers to these questions and if they're sharing, it's only with the Pack. I don't like it when they set themselves up as judge, jury and executioner and the rest of us have no say whatsoever." Cori angrily brushed a tear away. "What are we going to do?"

"I don't know." Ashe was afraid to tell Cori what he knew; that Randy Smith was scheduled for execution during the next full moon. And what if Cori was right? What if Randy was framed? The wolves would execute an innocent. Who would do this? Who? "Cori, why would somebody do something like that to Randy? He was thirteen at the time."

"I don't know. James refused to tell me anything, and now he's dead."

"This is so messed up," Ashe muttered.

"Yeah." Cori wiped another tear away.

"Who has the letter now?" Ashe thought to ask. "The one Randy Smith supposedly sent to Mr. Harris?"

"James asked Marco. He said his dad didn't have it now, but

Packmaster DeLuca saw it after it came in. Mr. Harris turned it over to Principal Billings, and Billings called Mr. DeLuca."

"You think Billings has it?" that hadn't been on the Principal's computer—it only said it was authenticated by Marcus DeLuca, not what happened to it afterward.

"He might, but I don't think he'd keep it at the school."

"Why not?"

"I wasn't thinking when I asked you to go into Principal Billings' office, both times. He can scent you, you know."

Fear washed over Ashe and he muttered a word his mother would ground him for saying. "Cori, I believed you when you said he wouldn't know," Ashe's hiss threatened to become a full-blown shout.

"Ashe, I'm sorry. I said I wasn't thinking."

"No wonder he was smiling when he handed me the note to give to my parents." Ashe was so frightened and angry he thought he might explode.

"What note?" Cori's confusion showed on her face.

"He can't wait to ship me off to Cordell Junior High because I can't turn," Ashe snapped. "He had a file on me, just like the one on Randy Smith. Mom and Dad haven't told me everything in the note because they don't want me to feel bad. But the whole thing was right there on Billings' computer. He's known since the first time that I hacked his system. Now, he's going to punish me in the worst way he knows." Ashe shifted angrily on the bed. He wanted to punch something. Wanted to shout as many obscenities as he knew, and with Sali's help over the years, he knew quite a few.

"I didn't know. I wasn't thinking. James knew you did it the first time—I told him. James convinced me to get you to do it a second time."

"Did you intend to get me killed too? Did you?" Ashe slipped off the bed and tugged wildly at his hair.

"I never meant to hurt you. Ever. I was stupid. James and I both were stupid."

"And now James is dead." Ashe didn't mean for his words to be accusing. Cori began to sob.

"Don't cry," Ashe pleaded. "I don't know what to do about it."

"I know. And I deserve every bit of the blame in this," she wept. "I asked James to meet me in the grove behind the DeLucas' house. Only he never came."

"Cori, somebody else killed James. You didn't. Stop blaming yourself for that."

"Then find somebody to blame for it. Find the guilty one, Ashe. You're smart."

"I don't know if the best detective ever can solve this mess. I mean, your dad and the others went out and checked the area where James was found. They didn't find anything. What do you think I might do?"

"I was hoping you'd have some ideas about all this. I didn't mean to upset you by dumping it in your lap. Besides, you're the objective one. You even call Sali out when he's wrong or teases Dori too much. I don't know," Cori tossed a hand up in a helpless gesture. "Somebody needs to save us, Ashe." Cori slid off the bed. "I'll go home, now. Mom will be frantic, and I sure don't want to be out after dark. Ever again."

"I'll walk you up," Ashe sighed. "I want to check on Mom anyway. She's not doing too good since Dad's been gone."

"When is he coming home? My dad said he went to run an errand."

"Don't know," Ashe shrugged.

"Cori, I told your mother I'd drive you home," Adele said when Ashe and Cori walked into the kitchen. "She called and said she was worried."

"I'm sorry, Mrs. Evans. Thank you for offering." Ashe and Cori loaded into the old Ford for the drive to the Andersons' home. Cori didn't say a word on the way, giving a half wave after she closed the passenger-side door and turned to walk toward the house. Adele waited until Cori was safely inside.

"She's afraid something will happen to her, now," Ashe confided softly to his mother.

"I know," was all Adele said.

CHAPTER 7

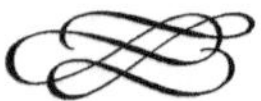

Two things happened before dawn on Monday, April fifth. Aedan came home with Radomir and Ashe decided not to reveal the tiny bat in class. Perhaps he'd play that card later, but for now, he'd pretend it didn't exist. His father slipped into Ashe's room a few minutes past five that morning, waking Ashe. Ashe's arms were wrapped around his father immediately, hugging him as tightly as possible.

"I need to get back to your mother," Aedan pulled Ashe's hands away. "She's not doing very well right now."

"I know," Ashe mumbled.

"Go back to sleep if you can; I just wanted to see you before daybreak."

"Goodnight, Dad."

"Goodnight, son." Aedan left Ashe's bedroom, closing the door noiselessly behind him.

The April morning was frosty and chill bumps stood out on his arms as Ashe walked toward Cloud Chief Combined. It was the first day of class following spring break and his mother offered to drive him to school. Ashe preferred to walk and think, so he'd turned down her offer. Adele looked as if she wanted to say something, but didn't. She'd have gone to the store late just to drive him and Ashe didn't want to be the reason the store didn't open on time.

Silence greeted Ashe as he shuffled into the Transformational Arts classroom and took his seat. His classmates stared at him, too—several with open mouths. Ashe reasoned it out quickly. Cori had told Dori, Dori had told Wynn and now everybody knew Principal Billings wanted him out. And James was still dead. Ashe wondered how many of his classmates were truly upset over that. James and Marco often teased the younger ones mercilessly. Was that what some of those around him would do when they grew older? Ashe sighed at the thought.

"Class, we won't be transforming today," Mrs. Rocklin walked in and sat at her desk. "Instead, we'll talk about loss."

Ashe felt Principal Billings' gaze on his back as he followed Sali to the lunchroom at noon. The Principal's arms were crossed over his chest and he'd smiled a contented smile as Ashe walked past. Ashe hoped his scent had faded since his visit to Billings' office nearly a week and a half earlier, but figured that the first visit to check Cori's grades was still fresh in Billings' mind. And Cori? She couldn't wait to tell her sister what Ashe had told her, yet there he was, keeping Cori and James's secrets.

"Know why everybody was staring at me in Transformational Arts this morning?" Ashe asked sullenly as Cori set her lunch tray on Ashe and Sali's table. Sali was busy vacuuming up the last of his spaghetti and meatballs, slurping noisily on an extra-long spaghetti noodle and ignoring Ashe's conversation with Cori.

"I'm sorry." Cori turned her head away.

"Me, too," Ashe said, lifting his tray and walking toward the drop-off. He hadn't eaten half his food and he'd been hungry when Cori sat down. Ashe didn't know what to do. He'd trusted Cori and he should have known better. He wondered if she knew that Radomir would be questioning her after darkness fell. Shrugging off that worry, Ashe walked toward the History classroom to sit and mope.

"Here." Sali sat down at the desk next to Ashe's, passing over a folded note. "And I didn't even read it."

"You can read?" Ashe grumped, taking the note.

"Sporadically," Sali grinned.

"Wow. Another five-syllable word. I think you need a brain scan, dude. They may find something yet." Ashe began to open the many-times folded note.

Ashe, the note began, *Mom asked me what we talked about. I made it sound like you were the one who needed help. I had to tell her so she wouldn't ask questions.* Ashe read the note twice before stuffing it in his book bag.

"Getting lurve notes?" Sali teased.

"Sali, Cori liked James. She just wanted to talk about that with somebody who might be objective over the whole thing."

"So, Cordell Junior High, huh?" Sali said what he wanted to say.

"Sali, the year's not over yet. I have until the start of the fall semester."

"Dude, we'll work on it this summer. You can't fraternize with humans."

"Sali, my dad was human once. He just didn't stay that way."

"Didn't mean to bite your paws, man."

"Is that werewolf humor?"

"You know it."

Ashe and Sali were loaded down with homework at the end of class. In the fall, they'd start geography and algebra. Ashe was looking forward to it. Just for a moment, he wanted to tell Sali not to worry; Ashe had no plans to attend Cordell Junior High. Sali was fretting over the whole thing, Ashe could tell.

"Dude, tell me we're gonna use stem-and-leaf plots in real life," Sali hefted his backpack over a shoulder for the walk home after school.

"I like the geometry lessons better," Ashe admitted.

"You would." Sali walked in silence for a while before speaking again. "Dude, if Marco wasn't in such a funk, he'd drive us to your Mom's store."

"Sali, Mom's not doing that well either, right now. Probably not a good idea."

"Some doctor is supposed to fly in today; Mom had to drive to Oklahoma City to pick him up," Sali grumbled. "So it'll be me and Marco until Mom and Dad get home."

"Where's Mr. Winkler?"

"He said he had errands to run and he'd be back tonight, too. He lives in Dallas—he could have gone home for all I know."

"Yeah, I guess that's true," Ashe agreed. He wondered if the doctor would wait until the following evening to start the autopsy on James's body, since Radomir was supposed to question Cori that evening. Cori's betrayal still stung. She'd done it to protect herself, leaving Ashe vulnerable to the entire school. Now they all thought him a failure, destined to spend his life among humans. Not that humans were bad, but the others were essentially tossing him aside, as if he had no business living in Cloud Chief among them. Ashe knew exactly how Randy Smith must have felt.

"Do you ever wonder what Randy Smith said to get him kicked out?" Ashe asked.

"Nobody will tell me," Sali said. "All I know is that Dad growls every time somebody mentions Randy's name."

"What would your dad do if Randy didn't say those things? What would happen if he really didn't write that letter to Mr. Harris?"

"But Mr. Harris got a letter from Randy," Sali stopped and stared at Ashe.

"What if Randy didn't send it?"

"Then who did? Ashe, that's BS and you know it. Randy broke the law and now he's dead meat."

"Like I'd be dead meat if I contacted you? Sali, listen to yourself."

"Dude, you're smarter than that." Sali started walking again. "Have you decided what you're going to write about for the end of school essay?" Sali asked when Ashe caught up with him. "I can't think of anything, and I really could use that money. Mom said that if I won the contest, I could get a cell phone."

Sali referred to the essay contest the community sponsored every year. The first-place winner received five hundred dollars. Second place was awarded three hundred and third place would get one hundred. Usually someone from the higher grades won. The subject had to be about some aspect of life in their paranormal community. The teachers got together and voted on the winners, who were announced at the end of the school year. The essays were always handwritten, so penmanship was under scrutiny as well.

"I hadn't thought about it yet," Ashe grumped. "Too many other things going on."

"Come on; Mr. Harris said last year that yours was noteworthy," Sali nudged Ashe with an elbow.

"But it didn't win anything."

"But seventh-graders hardly ever get any of the prizes," Sali pointed out. "You can check the list outside Billings' office. All the winners are posted there."

"I know." Ashe had walked past the list for seven years. Students' names were painstakingly engraved on shiny metal strips affixed to a polished wooden plaque, along with the year in which they won. Ashe had never paid much attention to it before. He decided to do that the following day.

"See ya, dude," Sali waved and took off toward his home. Ashe still had a ways to go.

"Mom, they won't hurt Cori, will they?" Ashe still worried about her, even if she had betrayed him. His father and Radomir left the house shortly after rising to question Cori under compulsion.

"She might be afraid at first, but they only want the truth. Besides, Marcus, Mr. Winkler and the werewolf physician are all going to be there, with Lavonna and Nathan. Nathan won't let anyone harm his girls." Adele placed leftovers inside the fridge before turning her gaze on Ashe.

"What are they going to ask her?"

"They won't pry into her private life. They only want to know the facts surrounding James's death. They'll ask her if she killed him. We know the answer to that already, but it has to be placed in the records that she said it under compulsion. And then they'll probably ask her how she found James. Where he was, what she saw, things like that."

Ashe nodded. If it were he, he'd be scared to death. It didn't matter how many times somebody said that no harm would come to him, compulsion or not. "I think I ought to go do my history homework." Ashe slid off the kitchen chair and walked toward the door leading downstairs. "I'm glad you're feeling better, Mom."

"I felt better the moment your father came home," Adele sighed. "Go do your homework. I know you're worried about Cori, so if I hear anything, I'll let you know."

"Thanks, Mom." Ashe opened the door and clomped down the steps. He found out about Cori sooner than he imagined he might; her father, Nathan, brought her over after the questioning was done.

"She wanted to see you," Nathan said as Ashe stood inside the kitchen, staring openmouthed at Cori.

"I'm sorry I blabbed," Cori hugged Ashe tightly, crying on his shoulder.

"Blabbed?" Adele asked. Of course, Nathan was still listening, causing Ashe to flush to the roots of his hair.

"I told Mom and Dori that Ashe will be sent to Cordell Junior High in the fall because he can't turn," Cori wept, clinging to Ashe. Ashe stood, his arms limply at his side, unsure what to do with the moist affection.

"Ashe, young man, how did you find that out?" Adele now stared at her son, who was peering at his mother over Cori's shoulder. Cori still had a death grip on Ashe's slender body.

"Mom," Ashe disentangled Cori's arms and stepped away from her as she wiped her eyes and offered him a pitiful expression. "It wasn't hard to figure out, was it?" Ashe lifted his shoulders in a shrug. "I mean, everybody was in an uproar over Randy Smith's letter, right after I got the note from Principal Billings. It didn't take a genius, Mom. I can add two and two, just like anybody else." Ashe's voice was grim as he grabbed a still-sniffling Cori's hand and led her to a chair at the kitchen table. After getting Cori seated, he sat in the chair next to hers.

"We're in the clear, everything was just as Cori described it," Nathan sighed, taking a seat across the table.

"Cori, can I get you a soda or something?" Ashe's mother asked.

"A soda would be nice. Do you have more orange?" Cori wiped the last of her tears with the heel of a hand.

"I do." Adele pulled two bottles from the fridge and handed one to Cori and the other to Ashe. "Ashe, you don't need to let this worry you. I think everything will be fine and you won't be sent off to that school." Ashe noticed his mother said *that school* with distaste.

"Mom, humans are okay. They're like us. Most good. A few not." Ashe twisted the cap off his bottle of orange soda and drank.

"That's an insightful opinion from a twelve-year-old," Nathan observed.

"He's twelve, going on forty," Adele laughed.

"I read books all the time—humans write them," Ashe pointed out. "They write about werewolves and vampires and witches and wizards. While most of their stuff isn't based in actual fact, there's one theme running through all of them." Cori was now staring at Ashe as he spoke.

"What's that?" she asked. Cori didn't like to read, much like Sali.

"That even though you're different, you don't have to mistreat other people because they have differences, too. The bad ones need to be removed from society, but that's true for every race and culture."

"He is forty," Nathan laughed. Ashe smiled. A laugh from a vampire was a rare occurrence, indeed.

~

Ashe knew something was wrong the moment he walked into the

school building Tuesday morning. Teachers were lined up outside Principal Billings' office and whispering. They became quiet whenever a student walked past, but Ashe could hear them perfectly before and after he walked by. The whispers concerned Old Harold. He hadn't come to clean the school the night before.

Ashe knew nobody could check on the school janitor until after nightfall, unless his home had been broken into. Right then, Ashe was wishing for the cell phone his parents said he was too young to have. He wanted to call his mother and tell her. He desperately wanted to tell his dad so he wouldn't have to worry about the old vampire caretaker alone, but his father was asleep. Ashe began to notice the trashcans that needed emptying and shoe streaks on the tiled floor that hadn't been cleaned away. Old Harold never got sick and never shunned his duties. Ashe's worry ramped higher the more he thought about it.

"I already know," Ashe held up a hand to keep Sali from bursting with the news. Ashe dropped his book bag beside his desk and gave Sali a helpless look. "What if he's dead?" Ashe had to concentrate to keep his emotions under control. Old Harold had come to the house many times to talk with his dad. He'd always treated Ashe kindly. Ashe had also listened while three werewolves admitted that they thought Old Harold killed James. Had someone gone after him when they knew Radomir, Nathan Anderson and Aedan Evans would be elsewhere? Ashe didn't like where his thoughts were going.

"Oh, my gosh," Ashe stood up and then sat down again.

"What? What is it?" Sali was concerned, now.

"Old Harold. If he's dead, he could have died anytime during spring break, after he cleaned the school the Friday before. Oh, my gosh." Ashe rubbed his forehead. He felt a headache coming on.

"Wait, didn't your dad and Radomir talk to him sometime last week?"

"They may have, but I didn't hear about it," Ashe muttered. There wasn't any way to question any of them until nightfall. Once again, Ashe felt out of his depth, with too many questions and too few answers.

"The autopsy is happening tonight, too," Sali said. "And that ties up the Enforcer and the investigator."

"Yeah. So if anybody goes to check on Old Harold, it'll be Dad and Nathan."

"Dude, won't he just be ash or something, if he is dead? I mean, there won't be a body to look over so we can figure out what happened, will there?" Sali was right, Ashe knew. When a vampire died, their bodies turned to a dusty ash. His father always said it was nature's protective measure, so the humans wouldn't have a vampire to dissect and prove they actually did exist.

"Pat Roberts has disappeared—Marcus can't find him anywhere," Ashe heard Mrs. Rocklin's voice from outside the classroom as clearly as if he'd been standing next to her. He didn't know to whom she spoke, but Ashe was now doubly worried. Pat Roberts certainly thought a vampire killed James. Did he kill Old Harold in retaliation and then run away?

"Dang," Ashe whispered.

"What is it?" Sali hissed.

"Shhh, Mrs. Rocklin's coming," Ashe warned. Most of the class heard and turned away from gossiping with their neighbors.

Class resumed once Mrs. Rocklin took her seat, but Ashe thought she looked pale and wasn't as attentive as usual during the transformations. She didn't call on Ashe, and he was fine with that. He just picked up clothing after the others.

"What are we going to do?" Cori was almost in tears at lunchtime. She'd sat next to Ashe, who noticed that her hands shook as she held her fork. The entire school had done nothing but gossip and speculate all morning about Old Harold.

"Cori, it'll be all right, just don't go out alone, okay?" Ashe was becoming very worried. Cori held secrets that would certainly result in punishment if they were discovered, and Ashe knew that was eating away at her. Radomir hadn't asked her anything about Randy Smith, and the werewolves would be furious if they found out what Cori knew.

"I don't think that's a problem, dude." Sali jerked his head toward the cafeteria door, where Denise DeLuca stood, keys in hand. Spotting Sali, she walked right over.

"I'll be taking you three home this afternoon, with Wynn and Dori," Mrs. DeLuca said.

"Mom, do they know anything yet?" Sali was about to burst from curiosity.

"Not yet. Your father went to Old Harold's house, but the place is still locked up so we won't know anything until sundown. He's tried to call Pat Roberts over and over again, and gets no answer. Micah and Mr. Winkler have gone to Pat's house, but they haven't found anything yet. Your dad is thinking about pulling Marco out of school to go sniff around with some of the others. Ashe, I've talked to your mother, and she says under no circumstances are you to go outside unless an adult is with you, and to call her the minute you get home."

"Okay." Ashe couldn't help it; he gripped Cori's hand under the table. Cori gave his fingers a grateful squeeze.

"I'll be waiting outside in the van when school lets out." Denise DeLuca rose from the bench beside Sali.

"Thank you, Mrs. DeLuca," Cori remembered her manners.

"Sweetie, it's no trouble." Mrs. DeLuca walked out of the cafeteria.

"Where are you going?" Sali asked when Ashe didn't walk directly to history class after finishing lunch. Cori separated from them, heading toward tenth-grade English with Mr. Harris.

"To check something," Ashe replied, heading directly for Mr. Billings' office. Principal Billings was standing outside his doorway, brown eyes watching intently as the students went this way and that, most focused on getting to their classrooms to talk for a while before the bell rang. Ashe ignored the deep frown Principal Billings cast in his direction as he looked over the list of essay contest winners. First, second and third place was listed on each strip of engraved metal, along with the year the students won.

Ashe found the one he wanted. There it was—it hadn't been altered. Seven years earlier, the winner had been Randy Smith, a seventh grader at the time. Barely three months later, Randy had been sent to a human school and shortly after that, he'd been banished for spilling secrets. Ashe wanted more than anything to read that essay—he just didn't know what happened to any of them after they were submitted. He knew he'd never gotten any of his back. Maybe they went into the recycle bin after the judging; he'd never thought to ask.

"What were you looking for?" Sali whispered on the way to history class.

"Just what I found," Ashe replied, making Sali snort.

After school let out, Denise DeLuca waited in the school parking lot as promised, but Ashe was shocked to see the number of other vehicles parked on the wide strip of gravel beside the school. Even Mr. Thompson, in buffalo form, was standing in a field nearby, keeping watch over the students. Every child had a ride, however. Ashe thought it safer, if he were honest, climbing into the third row of seats inside the van. *DeLuca's Locksmith Services* was painted in red on the outside of the white van and that meant Marcus DeLuca must be driving the Honda so Denise could drive the kids. Sali was already inside and scooting over to give Ashe room.

"Everybody in? Anybody forget anything?" Mrs. DeLuca asked. "Good," she said at the shaking heads. "Let's go. We'll drop Dori and Cori off first." She navigated around two other cars that were pulling closer to the school before going down the dusty dirt and gravel road that ran between fields in Cloud Chief.

"Anything new, Mrs. DeLuca?" Cori asked.

"No, sweetheart. And your mother said she'd be in from the fields early. She drove the tractor out to check on fences but she'll be back before dark," Denise kept her eyes on the gravel road as she answered Cori's question.

"Dad is supposed to do the plowing for the community vegetable garden tonight," Cori sighed.

"I'm sure someone will go out with him," Denise DeLuca reached over to pat Cori's hand. Cori sat in the front passenger seat; Dori had the middle section to herself since Sali didn't want to sit beside his nemesis, and Ashe had elected to sit beside his friend.

"Cori, call me if there's any problem," Ashe said as Cori and Dori climbed out of the van in front of their house. Like Ashe's home, most of it was below ground to benefit Nathan. Ashe had vague memories of when both homes were built; Aedan and Nathan had built them with help from Old Harold.

Like Aedan's private bunker, Nathan Anderson's was below the master bedroom floor. The rest of the house was quite different from the Evans' home. The Anderson's kitchen was below ground and only the garden room and a sitting area were above. Ashe liked having the kitchen upstairs. He could watch sunsets while helping with dinner or the dishes.

"Why don't you boys move up here?" Denise suggested before putting the van in gear. Ashe and Sali moved forward. Sali got the front passenger seat; Ashe sat directly behind him. "Ashe, will you tell your father that Mr. DeLuca wants to talk with him and Mr. Radomir as soon as they rise?" Denise said as she drove toward Ashe's home.

"Sure, Mrs. DeLuca. I'll tell him."

"Good. This has all of us spooked, I'm afraid to say. I hope there's a good explanation for all of it, but right now we're in the dark."

Denise DeLuca waited until Ashe opened the garage door and closed it again before driving away. Ashe fumbled with the door code to get into the kitchen, finally getting it on the third try. He shut and locked the door behind him, breathing a relieved sigh.

"Mom, I'm home now, Sali's mom gave me a ride," Ashe said when his mother answered the phone with her usual "Cordell Feed and Seed."

"Honey, is the house locked up? Is the alarm on?"

Ashe knew his mother was frightened. "Yeah. Mom, I'm okay for now."

"I'll be there as soon as I can, but everybody wants everything today. I think I've filled up three trucks with chicken feed."

"Good sales day," Ashe observed.

"It is, but I've got other things on my mind. Be safe, baby." Adele hung up the phone.

His mother must have made record time getting home; she was closing the door behind her at six-twenty. His father wouldn't be up until nearly eight. The days were getting longer and that meant less time to spend with his dad. "Mom, Mrs. DeLuca said that Mr. DeLuca wanted to talk to Dad and Radomir as soon as they were up," Ashe pulled the pizza pan out of the cabinet; they were having homemade pizza.

"I'll make sure they call," Adele sighed. Normally, Ashe enjoyed making pizza. His mother made up the dough and then spread it on the pan after letting it rise; and then they dropped the toppings they wanted on their half. Ashe dumped mozzarella over the tomato sauce before spreading pepperoni slices and black olives on his side. Neither he nor his mother talked much as they ate. Ashe felt hungry and nauseous at the same time. They'd know soon enough if Old Harold was home or not. He wondered, too, whether anyone had heard from Pat Roberts.

"They'll be up soon." Adele glanced at the kitchen clock. It was seven forty-five, the dishes were done and the kitchen cleaned. Neither Ashe nor his mother thought to do anything other than sit and wait at the kitchen table. Five minutes past eight Ashe heard his father's steps on the stairs, followed by Radomir's lighter footfall. They were in the kitchen quickly.

"I see something's wrong," Aedan said right away.

CHAPTER 8

"Aedan, Old Harold didn't clean the school last night. And Pat Roberts has disappeared." Adele gave the news straight away. "Marcus wants to speak with you, too. As soon as you were up, he said."

"I'll go outside and make the call," Ashe's father walked through the kitchen door, Radomir right behind him.

"I'll go do my homework," Ashe sighed and went toward the basement door.

"All right, honey." Adele was staring at the door to the outside and not at Ashe as he walked down the steps toward the lower level of the house.

It didn't take three seconds to turn to mist once his bedroom door was closed, and Ashe was zooming upward and under doors—twice—to get outside. His father was still on the phone with Marcus DeLuca.

"We'll pick Nathan up on the way to Harold's and call if we find anything," Aedan said and snapped his cell closed. Ashe fully intended to ride along invisibly with his father.

"We're going to get Nathan, and then we'll go to Harold's," Aedan poked his head through the kitchen door to let Adele know. "Make sure the doors are secure," he added before climbing into the SUV.

Radomir settled on the passenger seat and Ashe misted inside before Radomir shut his door. The garage door closed behind them as Ashe watched, only wondering then how it was that he could see and hear while he was mist. Giving up the conundrum after only a moment or two, he gave a mental shrug, grateful that he could do those things.

Hovering behind Nathan's head later after Nathan slipped into the back seat, Ashe watched as his father drove down the narrow dirt track leading to Old Harold's house. Harold had never bothered to put gravel down around his home. He didn't drive much, preferring to walk or run everywhere. Vampires could and did run—quite fast, actually, when they wanted.

"Do you have the code?" Radomir asked as he, Aedan and Nathan stood outside Old Harold's garage door later.

"We have the code to the garage," Aedan said. "We can knock down the inside doors if necessary." He rang the doorbell next to the keypad. And rang it again. When there was no answer on the third try, Aedan punched in a code. The garage door lifted readily on well-oiled tracks. Ashe would have drawn in a breath if possible while turned to mist; the inside door into Old Harold's upper floor was hanging loose on its hinges.

"Claws out," Radomir ordered. Ashe was shocked as perilously sharp, foot-long claws grew on all three vampires' hands. Ashe, feeling shaky even as invisible mist, followed along behind as all three vampires, alert for any sound or movement, crept through the house. There was no light to see and nothing there to warrant the claws, so all were retracted quickly. Somehow, Ashe's night vision had greatly improved. He could see much better in the dark, now. Perhaps it was the bat in him, tiny as it was.

They didn't have to go far, as it turned out. Radomir found what he was searching for in Harold's aboveground sitting area. A pile of ash lay there in the shape of a headless man. Disturbed, Ashe wanted to fly away and stare at the same time.

"Head over here," Aedan found a second, smaller dusting of ash. Nathan cursed while Radomir remained silent, examining everything around the body before sniffing through the room.

"I believe he knew the one that killed him. Harold likely allowed his visitor inside the home and led him into this room, where the murder took place. Afterward, the back door was knocked down when the perpetrator rushed to get away. Perhaps he wasn't strong enough to break down a steel garage door, so he opened it with the button and closed it the same way. The button is near enough to the door to get out if you hurry."

"Ashe does it all the time; he and Sali make a game of it," Aedan agreed. Ashe shifted his mist uncomfortably at the sound of his own name.

"I will do some sniffing in the garage, then." Radomir walked toward the broken door.

"Will you recognize this scent again?" Nathan asked Radomir later, after Radomir searched the garage.

"A werewolf was certainly here," Radomir observed, "but the scent is strange. As if it has been mixed with something else to nearly destroy the scent, somehow. I don't know that I could truly connect it with anyone."

"Pat Roberts' disappearance could certainly be connected," Nathan suggested.

"Of course, and we will demand to see his home," Radomir inclined his head in agreement. "But that will still not guarantee that I can distinguish the scents. I wonder how this was accomplished." The Enforcer was definitely puzzled over the scent.

"Let's go to Marcus and let him know. He may have a way to get into Pat's house," Aedan walked out of Old Harold's garage. Ashe waited outside the house as Nathan closed the door. Silently, sadly, Ashe said good-bye to Old Harold.

"So, he's dead, then?" Marcus asked later, standing in his brightly lit kitchen.

"Yes. There is some scent there, likely werewolf, but it is confused, somehow," Radomir stated flatly. Ashe, hovering over his father's head, desperately wanted to drop onto his father's shoulders and hug him. He would certainly be in trouble if he did that, so he held himself away and watched while Sali's father paced.

"We have nothing on Pat," Marcus growled. "Message after message left on his cell and no reply. We'll go over there now, but Micah and I went earlier. There's no sign of him."

"I only wish to get the scent," Radomir said.

"Then come. The autopsy can be performed afterward. Mr. Winkler and the doctor are at the O'Neill's now, but they know things might be put off for a little while." Once again, Ashe misted inside his father's SUV, but the vehicle was becoming crowded. Marcus climbed into the back seat and rode with Nathan. Ashe was hovering in the cargo area as his father drove to Pat Roberts' farm.

"It looks as if he hasn't been home for at least two days," Marcus observed, once they were all inside Pat's small farmhouse. It only held one bedroom, a kitchen, the small sitting room and a bath, with no lower level. Ashe had spent all his life in a home where most of the rooms were below ground. He felt exposed, somehow, in Pat Roberts' house.

"I can't tell," Radomir was sniffing around the house. "This makes things so much more difficult."

"How did Harold die?" Marcus thought to ask.

"Beheading," Aedan growled. Marcus didn't reply; he merely nodded. "Old Harold didn't kill that boy," Aedan said. "You don't know what he was—who he was—before. I promised not to tell while he was alive. But since he's dead, now," Aedan didn't finish.

"Then who was he?" Marcus demanded.

"How good are you with Roman history?" Aedan asked.

"Not good," Marcus admitted.

"Wealthy Roman families at times employed Greek tutors for their children. Harold was a Greek scholar teaching language and mathematics nearly a thousand years ago. He cared for the children he taught. You never knew that he might have taught the children of Cloud Chief Greek and Latin. Better than anyone else, more than likely. Yet he settled for being a janitor and cleaning the school at night, before helping Nathan and me guard the perimeter. Harold would never harm any child from this community. It wasn't in him." Aedan shook his head.

"And now he's dead. Just like that." Marcus flung up a hand. "If Pat did this, I promise I'll kill him myself." Ashe wanted to shiver at Marcus DeLuca's words. "Come on, the doctor's waiting." They trooped toward Aedan's SUV. Ashe had no desire to be anywhere near when they cut into James's body, so he misted home instead.

"Ashe, are you in there?" Adele was banging on Ashe's bedroom door when Ashe misted inside the house. Hurriedly he slipped under the door, materializing immediately and opening the door, feigning a yawn.

"Sorry, Mom, I fell asleep," he mumbled, rubbing his eyes. Ashe felt guilty for lying to his mother, but he'd had no desire to stay behind and miss the chance to learn what happened to Old Harold.

"Your father called a few minutes ago. Old Harold's dead."

"Mom, that's awful."

"I know, honey." Adele pulled Ashe into a tight hug.

"Who cleaned?" Sali began complaining the moment he set foot inside the school Wednesday morning. It smelled strongly of disinfectant and that offended every student's nose, but the werewolves most of all. Old Harold had somehow struck a balance that wasn't overpowering when he used cleaning agents.

"Don't know, but I don't like it much," Ashe agreed. The one thing he could say was at least the trash was emptied and the floor looked clean again. He still felt bad about Old Harold, especially after his father explained who the old vampire really was. Ashe heaved a weary sigh. He could have asked Harold so many questions, and now that opportunity was lost forever. News of Harold's death was all over school, giving students yet another topic for their daily gossip. Ashe itched to ask Sali if he knew what the autopsy revealed. His chance came when they sat down in Transformational Arts.

"Did you hear anything? From the doctor?" Ashe whispered, kicking his book bag beneath the desk.

"Yeah. I wasn't supposed to, but I sneaked halfway down the hall so

I could listen while they talked in the kitchen," Sali whispered back. "Dude, you cannot say anything. Promise."

"Promise," Ashe agreed.

"They said James's heart exploded. Like a bomb or something. Dude, that's just not natural."

"You're kidding. That's not possible. Are you sure you heard right?" Ashe couldn't believe what Sali was saying.

"I heard it, all right. Just don't tell, okay? Dad will be mad for sure."

"Mrs. Rocklin's coming," Ashe hissed and students rushed for seats as the class quieted.

"Honey, Denise says the witch will be here tomorrow to renew the concealment spells. Denise will be going out with her, so Sharon O'Neill, Wynn's mother, will pick you up after school."

"Okay," Ashe nodded and stared at his plate. He'd eaten two pork chops; he couldn't help himself. Maybe he was growing again, besides being able to turn. "Mom?" Ashe looked up at his mother.

"What, hon?" Adele asked.

"What happened to Old Harold? Did Dad say anything?" Ashe shivered, remembering the piles of ash in the floor from the previous evening. More and more he recalled that his dad might die the same way, leaving nothing behind except a scattering of grayish dust.

"It's not something I want to talk about right now," she said. "Finish your dinner; I'll wash up." She lifted her plate and walked to the kitchen sink. Ashe noticed she hadn't eaten much—perhaps she was thinking the same as Ashe.

"Mom, where did my name come from? Why did you choose it?"

"Your dad picked it out. Said it was from someone he knew."

"Oh."

"We're planning a service for James on Sunday. There'll be a smaller one afterward for Old Harold."

"Mom, we shouldn't be going to either one. Both of them should still be here."

"I know, honey. But we can't pull them back. We have to go on without them."

"Yeah. I'm done, Mom." Ashe took his plate to the sink.

"Any homework?"

"Only a little. And I wanted to start kicking around ideas for the essay contest."

"That's a good idea. The end of the school year is almost here. It's getting away from us, isn't it?"

"Mom?"

"Yes?"

"What happens to the essays after we turn them in? I've never gotten one back."

"Well, all the teachers vote on the winners. Ben Billings keeps them in a file somewhere, I think. Copies are sent back to the winners' parents. Jamie Waters' mother got a copy last year."

"But that's a copy and not the original?" Ashe persisted.

"I saw a copy, yes. Why are you so curious about this?"

"No reason. Sali wants to win this year, because his dad says he can buy a cell phone if he wins."

"Is that what this is about? You want us to promise a cell phone if you win?" Adele smiled at Ashe.

"Mom, a cell would be great."

"If you win, I'll mention it to your father."

"Sali, did your dad say anything about Old Harold?" Sali called later, while Ashe wrote and then crossed through potential essay subjects. His notebook was now littered with words obliterated forcefully with Ashe's favorite pen.

"No, dude. Even Marco asked, and Dad wouldn't tell him. He just clammed up and wouldn't talk."

"Dang." Ashe marked out *human interaction,* his pen nearly going through the paper when the notebook slipped on his knee. He'd braced it against his leg with one hand while holding the cordless in the other.

"But your dad and Cori's dad are supposed to plow the garden tomorrow night," Sali offered what little information he had.

"It was supposed to be done last night," Ashe pointed out.

"Yeah. I figure we'll be planting on Saturday, since James's funeral is Sunday."

"Old Harold's service is right after."

"Dude, I don't know if I want to go to that."

"Suit yourself, but you might learn some things you didn't know before."

"You going?"

"Yeah."

"I'll come, then."

"Okay. Did you finish your English homework?" Ashe knew Sali was probably stalling for time. He hated English.

"Not yet."

Ashe realized Sali's mother was listening when she told Sali to hang up the phone and do his homework. He figured Sali would ride him the following day about getting him in trouble. Ashe grinned and punched the off button on the cordless.

"Thanks for making Mom stand over me while I finished that book report on *Huckleberry Finn,* Sali poked Ashe in the ribs on their way to class the following morning.

"Come on, it was a good story," Ashe said.

"You already read it. It was easy for you," Sali grumped.

"I read it twice," Ashe grinned, knowing that would cause further retaliation. He wasn't wrong; Sali side-kicked him, nearly tripping afterward. "But the good news is," Ashe moved away from Sali, the kick *hurt,* "you can read *The Hobbit* for your last assignment."

"*The Hobbit?*" Sali made a face at Ashe.

"One of those books I loaned you last year. Haven't you opened that box yet? I carry all that stuff to your house, and it's probably still stuffed in your closet." Ashe poked a finger in Sali's ribs. Sali elbowed Ashe. Ashe stomped Sali's toe. Sali went after Ashe. They might have made it through the door of Transformational Arts if Principal Billings' wide body hadn't been blocking it.

"That's enough," he snarled. "Both of you, come with me." Sali's eyes were huge as he stared at Ashe. Ashe shrugged at his friend and fell in behind Principal Billings' sturdy body.

"Now, you will explain what this is about," Principal Billings demanded, once both boys were seated inside his office.

"Ashe poked me," Sali said right away.

"Because you haven't even looked at those books you borrowed from me last year," Ashe accused.

"I may have a bruise," Sali lift the hem of his shirt.

"Whiner," Ashe wrinkled his nose at Sali.

"Bookworm," Sali shot back.

"Principal Billings, I'm afraid there's something going on in eleventh-grade Math," Mr. Dodd, the history teacher poked his head inside the office.

"Stay here and try not to damage one another," Principal Billings snapped at Ashe and Sali before rushing out the door.

Sali grinned at Ashe. "It worked," he whispered. "Get to it, dude, you have five minutes, maybe." Ashe was up and hauling file drawers open as quickly as he could.

"Not here, these are old grade books." Ashe shoved the top drawer shut and opened the next one down. "Nope, not this one either," he said, finding folders of invoices for school expenditures. Shutting that one, Ashe moved down to the third drawer of the five-drawer cabinet. It failed to yield the desired paperwork. Ashe dug through both remaining drawers, then opened drawers in Principal Billings' desk. It wasn't there. "He must keep the file of essays at his house," Ashe muttered, shutting the last drawer with a thump and frowning at Sali. "He's coming!" Ashe shot around the Principal's desk and was sitting innocently in his seat when Principal Billings walked back inside.

"How many times do I have to tell them not to shift in class," Billings muttered as he sat in his leather chair. It creaked a little under his solid body. "Now, where were we?" Billings leveled a frown at Ashe and Sali.

"We promise not to do it again," Ashe said meekly, ducking his head.

"Besides, he won't be here next year," Sali said, jerking a thumb in Ashe's direction.

"True." Principal Billings suddenly seemed in a better mood. "Do this again and you'll have detention. Now get to class." Ashe and Sali scooted out before Billings could change his mind.

"Good job." Ashe grinned at Cori when she sat beside him at lunch.

"It wasn't hard. If I turn, then idiot Jeremy has to turn, too," Cori buttered her roll before taking a bite. She was right; Jeremy Booth was a shapeshifting wildcat and couldn't stand that Cori was a larger cat when she turned. Usually they hissed and yowled at one another after shifting. Ashe figured Jeremy was too much of a coward to take it farther than that.

"And I didn't even get into trouble," Cori grinned. "Principal Billings already had two culprits in his office."

"I didn't find the essays," Ashe said, disappointment thick in his voice. "So Billings must have them at his house. That sucks."

"Yeah. I didn't think to look at the winners," Cori said. "This might give us some information on Randy that we didn't have before."

Ashe had gotten Sali and Cori on board with his plan on their way to school. Wynn's mother drove and she busily chatted with Wynn and Dori in the front seat while Ashe, Cori and Sali hatched their plan in the back. It had worked perfectly. "We won't have the chance to see it now, if Billings has all of them locked up at his house," Sali groused. He'd been just as curious as Cori, once Ashe pointed out that they might get something out of Randy's essay. Of course, Cori and Ashe held more information than Sali and didn't intend to share.

"Yeah." Ashe made tracks in his mashed potatoes with the tines of his fork.

"Dude, you don't have enough there to reenact *Close Encounters,*" Sali observed, tilting his head slightly to make the assessment. "And I'll eat it if you don't want it."

"You can have the potatoes, but I want the chicken." Ashe shoved his tray toward Sali, who happily accepted the offered mashed potatoes.

"You think we can ask to see the essays?" Cori said.

"You have English coming up, why don't you ask Mr. Harris?" Ashe suggested.

"I will," Cori nodded.

"Tell me what he says after school," Ashe said.

"Will do."

"Mr. Harris said they won't consider it, because it might tempt us to use the same subjects or benefit from the essays themselves. It's to discourage copying," Cori heaved an irritated sigh later as she, Ashe and Sali squeezed into the back seat of Sharon O'Neill's small import. At least they weren't forced to share a seat, like Dori and Wynn.

"Dang," Ashe muttered.

"So, there's no way now," Sali leaned back and sighed. "Could Miss Patterson load us down any more with homework?"

"Come on, dude, it's just a reading assignment."

"Twenty pages."

"You make it sound like a lot."

"I'll fall asleep after three. Guaranteed."

"The text is a little dry," Ashe admitted. He'd wondered if there weren't a better science textbook available from somewhere.

"Dry? I dumped a glass of soda on it once and it soaked right in and disappeared," Sali joked.

"That's so funny," Dori turned in the front seat and glared at Sali.

"Hey, nobody asked you," Sali snapped back.

"Children," Mrs. O'Neill cautioned as she drove away from the school building.

"At least tomorrow is Friday," Cori wiggled her way between Sali and Ashe so she could lean back, too.

"Cori, are you coming to the service?" Ashe asked quietly.

"Yeah. I'll be there."

Cori and Dori were dropped off first, before Sharon O'Neill turned toward Sali's house. Denise DeLuca was waiting in the front yard when they drove up. Sharon rolled her window down as she pulled to a stop in the DeLuca's driveway.

"What is it Mom?" Sali asked, climbing from the car. His mother hugged herself as she leaned down to talk with Mrs. O'Neill.

"Mr. Thompson and I went out to check the boundary with the witch today," Denise quavered. We found Pat Roberts' body."

CHAPTER 9

"The doctor is doing an autopsy now," Ashe's mother said after hanging up the phone. Ashe hadn't gotten much information from Sali's mother; she'd told Sharon O'Neill that she'd call her later with details, leaving Ashe in the dark until his mother got home. Now he knew Pat Roberts' body had been buried outside the boundaries of Cloud Chief. The witch, having her senses open to any flaws or gaps in the previous year's shield, felt the presence of the body. Denise DeLuca and Amos Thompson had sniffed out the grave. Now Mr. Winkler, Marcus DeLuca and the werewolf physician had taken charge of Pat Roberts' remains.

"But how?" Ashe was at a loss to put exactly what he wanted to know into words. "I mean, if he killed Old Harold, then who?"

"I know, honey. Micah is out at the site, trying to find any scents left behind. Maybe he'll pick something up. I'm sure your father, Nathan and Radomir will all go out when they wake."

"The garden isn't going to get planted this year, is it?" Ashe's eyes were level with his mother's.

"You've gotten taller," Adele said, patting his shoulder. "You could end up being taller than your dad. And we will plant the garden. I'm bringing the tomato, onion and pepper plants home tomorrow. The seed packets are here already." She nodded toward the cardboard box sitting on the kitchen table. "Feel like sandwiches tonight?"

"Yeah. Do we have ham?" Ashe scooted toward the fridge.

~

"Adele, how would you feel about flying overhead?" Ashe's father asked her later when he and Radomir came upstairs. "Maybe you can see something we can't," he added. Ashe studied his father—Aedan's face looked grim at the news of Pat Roberts' death.

"I will, and I'll go out again early tomorrow if I can't see anything tonight," she offered. "Ashe, while we're gone, you need to make sure the alarms are on and you're downstairs, locked in," Adele cautioned. "I shouldn't be gone long."

"Sure, Mom," Ashe agreed. He fully intended to mist along behind his parents, but only he knew that.

Later, Ashe watched as his mother carried a robe with her out the door. She'd hang it on a peg outside the garage and slip into it when she flew back to the house. Ashe dutifully locked the door after his parents left with Radomir. When he heard the garage door sliding down, he closed the door to the lower section behind him, locked it and set the alarm before turning to mist and zipping right out of the house.

This time, Ashe followed his father's SUV as it drove away. Pat Roberts' body had been found on the eastern side of the boundary, so Ashe flew higher still; the dust and debris raised by the vehicle was flying through his mist and obscuring his vision. Ashe hovered as his father, mother and Radomir exited the SUV roughly ten minutes later, outside the barbed-wire fence marking the edge of the property. Micah Rocklin was still there, waiting.

"It's the damndest thing," Micah said. "Same as with James. No scents, other than Pat's, around the grave. Denise and Amos Thompson found the body after the witch said there was something here."

"How long do you think he was out here?" Aedan asked.

"Two, three days maybe," Micah replied. "Sounds like he may have died around the same time Harold did."

"This doesn't make any sense at all," Nathan grumbled, running fingers through his short, dark-blond hair.

"I'll change in the truck," Adele said and walked toward the SUV. Moments later Adele's peregrine falcon flapped away from the SUV, her wings catching the winds and flying gracefully into the night sky. Ashe watched as his mother flew widening circles around the area, looking for any clues from above. Her call, piercing when she gave it, put everyone on alert. What had she found? Ashe blazed through the night air in her direction.

Sure enough, his sharp ears caught the noise of something moving, but it was moving swiftly through the trees that ran along the eastern edge of the boundary and he couldn't pinpoint the source. Ashe increased his speed, desperate now to find whatever it was. Still he wasn't catching up. It was running away, that was certain, and Adele had been left behind long ago. Images of trees and fences blurred past as Ashe flew by them, still no closer to his quarry. Was there any way to tell what it was? How large it was? There might be. *Echolocation.* Ashe's clothing dropped away when he became the bumblebee bat in mid-air, his jeans, shirt and underwear falling onto a tall tree as he flapped tiny wings, still in determined pursuit of his prey. Ashe sent out a high-pitched call. Wondrously, it took a few seconds but it bounced right back to him. His mother always said instinct would take over. It did. Ashe knew his quarry was large. He could almost feel the shape of it. The bulk of it. Man-tall it was. Perhaps larger. But what man might move that fast, besides a vampire? Somehow, Ashe knew it wasn't that. A vampire could move more swiftly than this. It was traveling at top speed, whatever it was, and leaving Ashe's tiny bat behind. Ashe sent out one last call and waited interminable seconds for the echo to return. He'd lost this race, but he'd learned the size of the quarry.

Misting back to the tree, Ashe wondered how to pick up his clothing again. He couldn't materialize in the treetop; only thin branches sprouted there, with newly formed leaves budding from them. He couldn't lift anything as the tiny bat and he didn't want to leave his favorite shirt in the tree, waiting for someone to find it and point an accusing finger. Ashe moved closer until his mist touched the shirt. Incredibly, the T-shirt disappeared once he came in contact. Ashe drew back—the shirt reappeared. Lowering himself, he touched it once more. The shirt vanished.

Grateful that he'd been barefoot, Ashe quickly gathered his jeans and underwear the same way and flew homeward, arriving bare seconds ahead of his mother. Well, it worked with his clothing—Ashe flew right through the door, a feeling of elation hitting him as he passed through the heavy steel, ending up inside the kitchen. He performed the miracle twice more, through the middle door to the basement and then through his bedroom door.

"This is the best ever!" Ashe whispered as he danced and punched the air, his clothes hurtling across the room as he sent them flying.

"Ashe?" his mother called as she came down the steps.

"Just getting into pajamas, Mom," Ashe called out, calming himself. "Be there in a sec." Ashe pulled his PJs from a drawer, stepped into underwear and then slid into his favorite top and striped bottoms. "Did you find anything?" Ashe opened the bedroom door, finding his mother standing right outside.

"I thought we did, but it must have been a wild animal or something," she said. "Feel like a cup of cocoa?"

"Yeah." They had more than cocoa. They had a snack of cheese and crackers, too. Adele was always hungry after turning; Ashe discovered that he felt the same.

"An animal?" Ashe crunched his cracker, spread with soft cheese.

"We spooked it, I think," his mother said. "It ran away. It probably smelled the body and came to investigate."

"Oh. I never thought about that," Ashe said, sipping cocoa with tiny marshmallows floating in it. He felt his mother was attempting to protect him. He realized he was doing the same. Aedan, Nathan and Radomir walked in while Ashe and his mother were sitting at the table.

"Didn't find anything," Aedan said. "And Marcus called. Whatever killed James killed Pat. Same claw marks. Same problem with the heart." Ashe set his cup down. Was it aiming for all of them, whatever it was? Catching them alone so it could make their hearts explode? And who—or what—could do that?

"Aedan, will we have to move?" Adele stood, her face filled with worry. Ashe knew she was frightened.

"We can't. Not until we discover what it is. We could be moving it with us, you know," Aedan raked fingers through his hair in a gesture of frustration. Ashe knew his father was more than upset—he seldom showed this much emotion.

"I'll go downstairs." Ashe placed his cup in the sink and walked toward the door.

"Son, I'll stop by and talk to you later," Aedan said. "I have to drop Nathan off. Sharon and Jonas are going to plow the field tomorrow afternoon." Ashe nodded at his father before closing the door and walking heavily down the steps.

"Son, don't go outside alone," Aedan cautioned later as he sat on the edge of Ashe's bed. Ashe was sitting with his back to the headboard, an open book on his lap when his father knocked and came in.

Ashe nodded, wondering what his father might do if he knew what Ashe had done already and intended to do in the future. "Dad, what's happening?" Ashe placed a bookmark inside his book and closed it. Aedan took the book from his son's hands and set it down on the bedside table.

"We don't know, son. I've never seen anything like this before and I've seen plenty of strangeness in my lifetime. Scents either aren't there or confused somehow, and I don't know what can do that. Marcus plans to talk to the witch tomorrow and see if she knows anything. Micah thought she might be involved at first, but she was in Tucson the past three days and in Phoenix before that."

"Have you heard anything else on Terry Smith?"

"The human authorities have the body and there's no way we can get in to check on it. Besides, they've said already he was shot. That's not how any of ours died."

"Yeah." Ashe picked at his thumbnail. The edge was ragged and needed trimming.

"Here." Aedan didn't do it often, but he allowed a bit of a claw to slide out; barely an inch or so, and carefully shaved Ashe's fingernail.

"That's so cool, Dad." Ashe examined the neatly trimmed nail.

"It has its perks. And its downside. If I could only be available if needed during the day, I'd give up some of these perks." Aedan rose to go.

"Dad?" Aedan already had a hand on the doorknob.

"What, son?"

"Mom needs a hug."

"I know." Aedan walked out of Ashe's bedroom.

"So, James and Pat died the same way." Ashe didn't have to tell Cori, Sali did. He'd heard his father discussing it with Mr. Winkler and the doctor.

"You still think Pat killed Old Harold, and then whoever killed James killed Pat?" Sali asked Ashe, who'd remained silent on the ride to school and now on the trek to Transformational Arts.

"Sali, think about this for a minute. Old Harold's heart didn't work anymore, so it might not have done any good to make it explode. What if the same one killed him, and wanted to make it look like Pat did it? Only they didn't expect us to find Pat, maybe. He was buried, you know, and James wasn't."

"How did you know he was buried?" Sali demanded.

"Mom said so," Ashe defended himself.

"Then why wasn't James buried?" Sali asked.

"Dude, how should I know? Maybe the killer got spooked or something."

"Ashe, no more." Cori looked green.

"Time to shut up, dude," Ashe warned. Sali closed his mouth.

Ashe was called on for the first time all week. It would have been so easy to give in and make the turn as Ashe stood in front of the class, feigning an effort. He sat down with a sigh as soon as Mrs. Rocklin said he could.

~

"You're all coming home with me today, since Sharon and Jonas are plowing and Adele won't be home until later," Denise DeLuca announced when everyone piled into her van. Wynn shrugged at Dori before both girls turned and glared maliciously at Sali. "I didn't do anything." Sali raised his hands in surrender.

Ashe thought Sali would have a continuous fight on his hands the entire time Wynn and Dori were inside his house, but the moment both girls saw Mr. Winkler leaning against the kitchen counter with his shirt off while drinking a cup of coffee, all they could do was stare. He grinned at their openmouthed adoration and found a Yahtzee game somewhere. Soon, Ashe, Sali and Cori were playing and laughing at the kitchen table with Winkler, Dori and Wynn.

"I have twins," Winkler informed Wynn when she asked if he had children. "A boy and a girl. They're nearly grown and will graduate high school next month. They're both pre-enrolled at the University of Texas."

"So, not married?" Wynn worked up the courage to ask.

"Not anymore. There was someone else, but she died," Winkler's gaze lost focus for a moment. Shaking himself, he smiled at Wynn and Dori. "That was years ago. Now, whose turn is it?"

~

"We played Yahtzee with Mr. Winkler," Ashe said as he climbed into his mother's old truck when Adele came to get him.

"He's the Dallas Packmaster," Ashe's mother said, causing Ashe to blink. "Your father says he owns a security company. The Grand Master must have exerted quite a bit of pressure to get him here."

"He seems nice," Ashe said. "He said he has twins who are about to graduate from high school."

"And he may be nice outside the Pack, Ashe. Just never forget that every Packmaster has killed to get where he is."

Ashe had to digest that. He'd never thought much about it before. Sali's father was Packmaster. "Who did Sali's dad kill?"

"I don't know. Marcus was Packmaster already when Aedan and I joined the community. You know that Hollis Daniels died in a challenge against Marcus not long after that. Now, Georgia Daniels and her son lower their heads around Marcus."

"Mom, whose idea was it to put these communities together?"

"Don't worry about that right now, all right? I shouldn't have said anything. Sali's your friend. Don't forget that."

"How hard would it be for us to live among humans?" Ashe asked.

"Well, think about that for a moment. Your dad can never come out in daylight. How long before the humans start to notice? How long past that before they begin to ask questions? Your father can't place compulsion on all of them. And when the full moon comes, I have to change. There's no way I can avoid that. Here, everybody knows what I am and accepts that. I don't have to hide from any of them. I did before, though. Before I met your father. My parents waited a long time before I was born. They both died before you came along."

"What made you marry Dad? Since you're so different?"

"When I saw your dad the first time, that was it," she said. "He says it was the same for him. I was having a sandwich at a pub in London —I'd saved enough money to spend two weeks there. I always wanted to see England, Ireland and Scotland. So I scrimped and put the money together. The third night I was there, I was having dinner in the pub near my hotel. Your father came to sit beside me and that was that."

"Why haven't I heard this story before?" Ashe asked, curious.

"Someday, we'll tell you. Your father and I. In the meantime, just remember that we love you and wanted you. Nothing else matters. Now, Denise will pick you up tomorrow morning around nine. You'll help the others plant the garden."

"I want to plant the tomatoes," Ashe said.

"Sharon will be handing out the assignments, so talk to her."

Ashe did get to plant tomatoes in the early Saturday morning sunlight. Much of the rest of the community was there, too, all dropping seeds into neatly tilled rows, or covering them up or carrying water. The land was right next to the O'Neill's barn and Ashe never forgot that James's body lay inside their walk-in refrigerator within that barn. Heaving a sigh, Ashe placed another tomato plant and pushed dirt around the slender stem.

He and his mother would come later and place wire cages around the plants to keep them from drooping and breaking when the tomatoes came and weighed down the plants. "That's what we all need right now," Ashe said to himself as he worked. "Something to prop us up and keep us from drooping."

"Dude, did you say something?" Sali carried the hose past the end of the tomato rows. Ashe smiled. Sali liked to water; he didn't like to plant.

"Just talking to myself," Ashe replied and placed another tomato plant.

Ashe was tired and covered in dirt and mud by the time the planting was over Saturday afternoon. Sali was worse off, since the wind had blown water back at him as he sprayed newly planted seeds and plants. Someone brought sandwiches and sodas for lunch and now Ashe was looking forward to dinner after a long, hot shower. His muscles ached from exertion in the cool, spring air. A brisk, freshening breeze had blown all day, although sunlight had shone in abundance while they worked.

"Take your shoes off and put them inside these bags," Denise DeLuca handed garbage bags to Ashe and Sali. Marco had come but hadn't contributed much, Ashe noticed. He'd also driven himself and left before the others. Ashe wondered if Marco would come out of his depression at all. Muddied shoes went inside the bag and Ashe tied it before sliding into the back seat of Denise's Honda as carefully as he could, grateful for the leather seats. They'd still need cleaning after he and Sali sat on them.

"Be sure and lock the doors and set the alarms," Denise called after him as Ashe walked in his socks through the garage door. Ashe waved at Sali while the garage door closed. He immediately turned to mist and zoomed downstairs, going straight into the bathroom. Shucking his clothes once he rematerialized, he turned on the taps and went to pull the cordless out of its cradle.

"I'm home, Mom; the garden's planted," Ashe told his mother while waiting for the water to warm up. "I'm getting in the shower—I got covered in dirt."

"I'll be home in a while, hon," Adele hung up. After dumping the phone on top of his towel, Ashe climbed into the shower.

Ashe had never been to a funeral before, and since it was held in the afternoon, the vampires weren't able to attend. Ashe got a good look at the werewolf physician, though. Sali said he was scheduled to fly back to Chicago on Monday. He had reddish-brown hair curling thickly around his ears, golden-brown eyes and wore a dress shirt with gold cufflinks. Ashe decided he was wealthy.

Mr. Winkler, who accompanied the physician, wore a black polo, black jeans and black boots. If Mr. Winkler challenged Sali's dad, Ashe had no doubt as to who might win that fight. Mr. Winkler appeared easygoing, but Ashe felt there was power there, and he certainly wouldn't want to aggravate it. Radomir, the Enforcer? Ashe shivered just thinking what Radomir might be capable of if angered.

Micah Rocklin, Marcus DeLuca's Second, delivered the eulogy at James's funeral. "We have to believe there is love," he said, "Although love is lost. That there is hope, although hope is lost. And that there is faith, although faith is lost. We have to believe that what we lose, we will find again." A carved wooden box lay at the front of the meeting hall inside the school. Ashe knew that James, as werewolf, lay inside it while Micah spoke quietly and eloquently over his remains.

"That's what Mr. Winkler left to get," Sali nodded toward the wood box later. It looked to be made of oak and was polished, with delicately carved trees across the top. "He brought it back in a van."

"And now they'll stick it in the ground," Ashe sighed. Is this what there was for all of them in the end? He'd never had those thoughts before. Now, three deaths had come to Cloud Chief and Ashe worried that more might come.

James was buried beneath the tree that Ashe had sat in to spy on the Pack. Sali cast a covert glance at Ashe while the box was lowered into the ground. Someone had already dug the grave before the body was carried out of the school and transported to the site in Mr. Winkler's van. James's parents were visibly upset and Ashe felt sorry for them. Most of the adults were attempting to comfort, but Ashe decided that grief was a personal thing; something you had to come to terms with and find a way to get through somehow.

"Dude, there's food at Mom and Dad's; that's where everybody's going afterward," Sali said. Ashe nodded and followed his friend. He and Sali rode with Ashe's mother; Mr. and Mrs. Johnson went with Marcus and Denise DeLuca. Marco hung at the perimeter, never said anything and disappeared before anyone could stop him. Cori, wiping away tears and trembling, leaned on her mother the whole time. Ashe worried for her, too.

"Ashe." Cori only said his name as she sat beside him later. Ashe hadn't wanted any food, grabbing a bottle of soda instead and heading toward Sali's bedroom to avoid the gathered crowd. Cori found him sitting in the floor, his back to the wall and staring at Sali's posters of the Oklahoma City basketball team.

"Cori," Ashe picked at the plastic ring that remained around the top of his soda bottle. "I'm really sorry."

"Me, too."

"I think I've drank more soda in the past two weeks than I did all last year," Ashe said.

"Me, too." Ashe and Cori sat silently for a few moments, shoulder to shoulder and lost in thought.

"When are they holding Old Harold's service?" Cori finally asked.

"Around nine tonight."

"Dad says they'll bury Pat Roberts tomorrow morning. I think only the werewolves are going."

"I can't recall anyone saying much about him," Ashe observed.

"He was a bigot." Ashe stared at Cori, thinking for a moment that he hadn't realized Cori knew what the word meant. "James told me some of the things he'd say in the Pack meetings," Cori added. Ashe just nodded his head. He'd heard Pat Roberts say some of those things himself.

"He was old." William Winkler walked in silently; sitting on the edge of Sali's bed and making it creak a little beneath his weight. "The older the werewolf, the better they remember the race war," Winkler added. The Dallas Packmaster held a cup of coffee in his hand and sipped it thoughtfully for a moment. "But like every major shift in history, there will be those who find it difficult to deal with the changes," Winkler observed. "It's like a rising tide. The water comes in and then recedes. Floods in again and recedes. But each time, it rises a little higher. We have to keep our eyes on the place that marks our highest goal and refuse to let the receding waves drag us away from it." Winkler brushed Cori's blonde hair away from her face and smiled kindly at her before standing and walking out of Sali's bedroom.

The werewolf students were noticeably absent from school the following morning. Ashe knew why. He and Cori huddled together at lunch—they'd had substitute teachers in many of their classes because the regular instructors were werewolf, too. Ashe had never put that into perspective before, only now coming to realize that Cloud Chief was very much involved with the werewolf race. He also wondered how Lawrence and Clarice Hoff had taken the news of Pat Roberts' death. It was certain Old Harold hadn't killed him. Surely, too, they couldn't point the finger at his father, Cori's father Nathan or Radomir.

Old Harold's service the night before looked to be a poorly attended affair, too, until the multitude of expensive automobiles had driven into the schoolyard. Ashe, Cori and Sali had gaped at the well-dressed vampires whose limousine doors were opened by vampire drivers. Radomir had walked up to one of them, dipped his head respectfully and called the vampire he spoke with "Honored One." Ashe didn't know what that meant until after Old Harold's service was over and he and the others watched the vehicles drive away.

"Son, that was the Head of the Vampire Council," Aedan had pulled

Ashe against his side. "His name is Wlodek, and he knew Old Harold longer than any of us."

"He was a friend?" Ashe had searched his father's face, watching as Aedan grimaced. Ashe realized his father had been surprised by Wlodek's visit. Radomir may have known and kept the information to himself.

"A good friend to Harold. He was much upset over this. Come, we will take Salidar home." Sali's parents hadn't stayed for Old Harold's service, and Aedan had promised to see Sali home safely. Ashe thought it a shame that the Cloud Chief Packmaster hadn't stayed; Marcus might have been surprised to see the Head of the Vampire Council.

Now, Sali wasn't at school to talk about the night before. Cori, too, had been shocked that so many important vampires had come. Another visitor had been a member of the Council. He, Radomir and the Head of the Council had talked at length before the visitors drove away.

"What do you think this means for the peace agreement?" Cori pushed peas around her tray with a fork.

"What?" Ashe was pulled away from his thoughts by Cori's question.

"That somebody—maybe a werewolf—killed a friend of the Vampire Council's chief."

"I don't know, Cori." Ashe sighed and pushed his tray away. The food suddenly tasted like dust. "But I'm worried that they'll break up the supernatural communities, and that means we won't get to see our friends."

"Yeah. Something like that would definitely break up a lot of friendships. Ashe, I miss James."

"I know."

"It was nice of Mr. Winkler to come talk to us last night."

"Yeah. Cori, there's a bunch of people coming down the hallway outside." Ashe heard more footsteps than usual. Principal Billings strode down the hall, leading a group of werewolf parents and their children, smallest to tallest, as they walked inside the school cafeteria.

"Has anyone seen Marco?" Marcus DeLuca stepped around Principal Billings and looked about Cloud Chief Combined's cafeteria. Ashe saw Sali, partly hidden behind his father. Sali looked frightened and Sali didn't frighten easily. Heads were shaking all over the cafeteria now; none of the students had seen Sali's older brother.

"Oh, no," Cori's hand went to her mouth and it was shaking.

"Cori, don't jump to conclusions," Ashe grabbed her fingers and held them.

"Ashe," Cori wiped tears away with her other hand.

"Dad! I'm here, Dad!" Ashe heard Marco's voice from the front doors of the school. Marcus heard it too, a bare second after Ashe did. Marco was running.

"Son, what happened?" Marcus now gripped a panting Marco's shoulders in strong hands.

"Dad, somebody killed her. Somebody shot Megan." Marco sobbed in Marcus' arms. Cori's arms were around Ashe quickly, and she was crying as well. Ashe blinked as he awkwardly patted Cori's back. Megan was the girl Marco went to see at the Burger Hut. She was human and she'd been killed, just as Terry Smith had. Whatever this maelstrom was, it was pulling humans into it, too.

"Early this morning," Adele explained the circumstances surrounding Megan's death as Ashe picked at his dinner that evening. School was let out in Cloud Chief after Marcus and Principal Billings had come to the cafeteria. Rides were found for all the children, even if two trips had to be made. Nobody was allowed to walk home. They all waited, holding their breath to see whether Megan Lindley, the seventeen-year-old human girl, had been shot with the same gun that killed Terry Smith.

"Where?" Ashe asked as he watched his mother. Her head was down, her eyes staring at her plate as she grimly dipped into the enchilada casserole she'd made for dinner.

"On her way to school. She was walking through a neighborhood when the shot rang out. Nobody saw anything. The sniper had to be on foot; there wasn't a car driving through."

Ashe had watched the six o'clock news before his mother came home, and all they'd said was the girl had been gunned down by an unknown assailant. The journalists were waiting for a statement from the authorities, who couldn't make a comment at the time. Ashe had seen Megan many times at the Burger Hut; she worked there after school. Had even seen Marco talking to her often during the previous summer, when school was out and he'd been helping his mother at Cordell Feed and Seed. Ashe worried about his mother, working in Cordell as she did, six days a week.

Aedan found them still sitting at the kitchen table when he walked through the middle door later. Neither Ashe nor his mother had cleared the table. "Adele?" the question was heavy in his father's voice.

"That girl that Marco liked in Cordell? She was shot and killed this morning." Ashe heard his father curse, and Aedan's eyes were red. Ashe dropped his head into his arms at the kitchen table. Radomir came up the steps and stared at the family sitting at the table. Aedan growled as he explained what happened to the vampire Enforcer.

"I am glad that the Honored One and the others kept their visit a secret," Radomir said, causing Ashe's head to jerk up in surprise. Radomir suspected that those vampires might be targets if the community had known they were coming? This bore thinking about. Ashe rose and started clearing away the dishes. Adele rose to help.

"I'll do this, Mom, if you and Dad want to talk."

"We'll go outside for a bit, son. Do you have homework?" Aedan asked.

"No, Dad. They let us out today at noon, when we found out about the murder." Aedan nodded at Ashe's statement.

"Just get the dishes into the washer, I'll get it started when I come back inside," Adele caressed Ashe's head, her fingers bringing a little order to Ashe's slightly curly hair.

"All right." Ashe nodded and emptied uneaten food down the disposal.

"Sali, Mom has to go there to work every day. What if they come into the store?" Ashe poured his fears into the phone later as he talked with his best friend.

"Can't we hire bodyguards?" Sali asked.

"Who would you hire? Sali, the one you hire could be the bad one." Ashe wanted to talk to Sali about what he'd chased the last time he'd gone out as mist; he just couldn't. If he revealed those secrets, he'd be in trouble for sure.

"Mom has to take the doctor back to Oklahoma City tomorrow, so Marco is supposed to drop us off at your mother's store," Sali said.

"How's Marco doing?"

"He won't talk to anybody, dude. He barely nodded when Mom told him to take us to Cordell tomorrow after school."

"At least he's taking us. What about Cori and Dori?"

"Wynn's mom is taking them home."

"All right." Ashe rolled over on his bed. "I wish I knew who was doing this," he said.

"Dad just growls every time somebody mentions it," Sali said. "I don't think they'd last long if Dad got his hands on 'em."

"Yeah."

"Everyone should be thinking about the essay contest," Mr. Harris said during English class the following morning. Shorter and thinner than most werewolves, Mr. Harris had light-brown, nearly blond hair—another anomaly. Devoted to his subject, Mr. Harris always made sure the rules were followed as written in his English classes.

"Think about it, choose a topic and start writing," Mr. Harris went on, pacing before his seventh-grade class. "Remember, anything between one and five pages, handwritten, is acceptable. The shorter ones must be exceptional, if you recall. And your writing must be legible," Mr. Harris lifted an eyebrow in Sali's direction, causing Sali to sink uncomfortably in his seat. Ashe knew how much Sali coveted the prize money; he desperately wanted a cell phone. Ashe figured it was because Marco had one; Sali constantly struggled to compete with his older brother.

"I love lasagna days," Sali blissfully cut into his rectangular wedge of lasagna later in the cafeteria. Three shapeshifter women cooked for the school and all were good cooks. There weren't many complaints over what was served in the lunchroom.

"Look, it's the *empty*." Chad Daniels pointed at Ashe, who had his fork halfway to his mouth. The bite of lasagna dropped off and landed in the tray as Ashe froze. *Empty.* It meant completely human. Not having any nature other than that. Ashe hadn't heard it since James was murdered. Jeremy Booth, Chad's friend, snickered as Ashe went red at the insult.

"Chad, get out of here or I'll go straight to Mrs. Rocklin," Cori hissed, setting her tray beside Ashe's. Mrs. Rocklin was on cafeteria duty but she was far enough away and the noise level was such that she hadn't heard.

"Look, it's the one who got her boyfriend killed," Jeremy couldn't pass up the opportunity to dig at Cori.

"That's enough," Ashe stood and snarled at Jeremy, although his face still bore the flush of embarrassment.

"Mrs. Rocklin's coming," Sali snapped, beginning to rise as well. Jeremy and Chad walked away quickly, carrying their trays to the far side of the cafeteria.

"What's going on?" Greta Rocklin stopped at Ashe's table.

"Nothing," Ashe lowered his head.

"We don't need a division in the ranks," Mrs. Rocklin muttered as she walked away. Ashe knew what she meant. This was the time for everyone to stand together; he just didn't think Chad and Jeremy knew that. Sali growled low when he saw Chad and Jeremy sitting at the end of Marco's table. Marco ignored the newcomers as he toyed with the food on his tray. Ashe couldn't understand why Chad and Jeremy had chosen now as the time to dig at him.

"It's my fault. I should have kept my mouth shut," Cori hung her head.

"Cori, it would have come eventually—they all knew I couldn't change," Ashe heaved a distressed sigh. He kept telling himself that Chad and Jeremy didn't know that things were different now. A part of him knew that it shouldn't make any difference, but it did.

Marco was silent while driving Ashe and Sali to Cordell Feed and Seed after school. "Dad told him he couldn't go to Megan's funeral last night," Sali said as Marco did a U-turn in the street and screeched away.

"That's gotta suck," Ashe said. "Come on, dude. Let's go inside before Mom comes looking for us." Ashe grabbed Sali's arm and turned him toward the glass door leading into the shop.

"Ashe, Sali, can both of you help customers?" Adele looked frazzled and there were several people inside the store, gathering supplies. Ashe and Sali hauled out plants, fertilizer and gardening tools. Both put in more than two hours of work and were looking forward to six o'clock when Adele would close up and lock the doors. At ten minutes before six, a woman walked in. Sali elbowed Ashe—hard.

"Adele?" the woman walked toward Ashe's mother, who was busy filling a display with gardening gloves.

"Dawn?" Adele straightened and blinked at Randy Smith's mother.

"What is she doing here?" Sali hissed as he and Ashe moved the newest shipment of plants onto slatted tables inside the greenhouse. Adele had told them earlier that this job could wait until the following day. Now, she and Dawn Smith were locked inside Adele's office while both boys set out the small plastic containers of seedlings. Ashe couldn't hear from this distance and he chose not to tell Sali what he'd seen when Dawn Smith walked inside the shop. She was wearing a green blazer with gold buttons at the cuffs—buttons that matched the one he had at home. One of Dawn's buttons was missing.

"Dude, her husband got killed south of town. Why wouldn't she be here somewhere?" Ashe mumbled, carrying another flat of petunias to the table.

"Yeah. I guess you're right."

"I'm sure they're still investigating, and since Megan got killed, they'll probably compare the two deaths," Ashe said. Sali hadn't noticed the buttons; he'd just noticed the scent. Sali's nose had told him the woman was werewolf; he just hadn't known who she was until Adele called her Dawn.

"Your mom knew her before?" Sali blinked curiously at Ashe.

"Everybody did. Think about it, Sali. Everybody in Cloud Chief knows everybody else."

"Yeah. You gonna tell your mom and dad about Chad and Jeremy?"

"Would you?" Ashe stared across the table at Sali. Sali hefted a tray of periwinkles onto the table before answering.

"I guess not," Sali went to get another tray.

"What good would it do?" Ashe said, following Sali. "It'll just get worse if somebody says anything." Ashe's burden of plants plunked down beside Sali's.

"Yeah."

"Boys, come on," Adele stood in the doorway, keys in hand.

"Mom?" Ashe looked at his mother as he walked toward her.

"Ashe, no questions," Adele lifted a hand to hold him off. "I have to talk to your father and Radomir tonight. I'd appreciate it if you wouldn't say anything. Sali, will you ask your father to call Aedan tonight after sundown?" Adele's voice was weary and troubled.

"Sure, Mrs. Evans," Sali nodded.

"Good. Come on. Let's lock up and get out of here."

Ashe itched to know what Randy Smith's mother had said. If he'd been there alone, he'd have misted inside his mother's office and listened. Now, he might never know what prompted the visit. And the missing button bothered him. He still had it in the drawer of his bedside table. Wondering whether he should take it to his father, Ashe remained silent on the drive home.

"Sali, thank you for your help today," Adele said as Sali climbed out of the truck in front of his house. "I'll buy your lunch Saturday if you want to come in with Ashe and me."

"Sure. Can we go to Betsy's?" Sali loved Betsy's fried chicken.

"I'll buy at Betsy's," Adele promised. Sali waved at Ashe and went to the front door, letting himself in. Adele sighed as she watched Sali disappear. Ashe examined his mother's face; her expression was shuttered. He remained silent.

"Honey, will you go downstairs and read or do your homework?" Ashe's mother asked when his father and Radomir appeared in the kitchen. The sun had disappeared below the horizon a few minutes earlier and Ashe heard his father's footsteps on the stairs.

"Sure, Mom." Ashe stopped cleaning countertops and went downstairs, closing the middle door behind him. Knowing his father could hear his footsteps and the bedroom door closing, Ashe went through the motions, turning to mist immediately and flying through both doors to get back upstairs.

"She walked into the shop?" Ashe arrived in the kitchen as invisible mist while his father asked the question.

"Yes. She's been in Oklahoma City, hoping the investigation into Terry's death will yield results. So far there hasn't been anything; the Chief Medical Examiner's office hasn't released their final report and now that Megan Lindley is dead, she wanted to come and sniff around for herself," Adele shook her head in confusion.

"Have the authorities come to any conclusions?" Radomir asked.

"Nothing yet. They're still examining the girl's body."

"Of course."

"What did she want?" Aedan turned back to Dawn Smith's visit.

"She wanted to know where the letter was and if the Pack has made a decision on Randy. I told her I didn't know anything about it. She knows the Pack doesn't hand out that information." Adele was clearly upset.

"Did she say anything else about the letter?"

"No. She said she didn't know anything about it until someone from Cloud Chief contacted her. When I asked who it was that called her, she wouldn't tell me."

"Did she say what Terry was doing here?" Aedan asked.

"He came to plead Randy's case with Marcus. He just never made it."

"Did anyone know he was coming?"

"I didn't ask her that." Adele heaved a sigh. "I'm sorry, Aedan, I was just so shocked that she walked into the shop, I couldn't think straight."

"Mrs. Evans, do not concern yourself over that, we will get to the bottom of this," Radomir assured her. "Your husband used to be a fine Enforcer for the Council. Wlodek still holds hope that he will return soon."

If Ashe could gasp as mist, he might have at Radomir's statement. His dad, an *Enforcer*?

"Aedan has promised he won't as long as I live," Adele said stiffly, rising from her seat at the kitchen table. Ashe realized that Radomir knew that, somehow. Radomir was looking to the time when Adele would die, as all shifters did. If nothing happened, his father would live past that.

"I did not intend to upset you, Mrs. Evans," Radomir apologized.

"Oh, don't worry," Adele tossed up a hand. "Do you think I haven't thought of that, over and over again? That Aedan will live on when I'm dead?" Adele flung open the door to the stairs and walked through it, slamming it behind her. Ashe scooted through it, rushing toward his bedroom and materializing there, listening as his mother made her angry way downward.

Ashe was fingering the gold button later when his father knocked on his bedroom door. Hastily Ashe shoved the button into the drawer of his nightstand and shut it before sliding off the bed to answer the knock. "Dad?" he asked, looking up at his father's shuttered features.

"Son, I want you to keep quiet about Mrs. Smith's visit earlier," Aedan said, taking Ashe's arm and leading him into the small bedroom. It always seemed smaller when his dad was inside it.

"I will, Dad." Ashe sat on his bed and scooted forward until his back rested against the headboard.

"Radomir and I spoke to Marcus. He says there's no need to worry the others with this. He knows Dawn was here, attempting to get information on her husband's death."

"Yeah." Ashe nodded, ducking his head. He knew he ought to pull the button out of the drawer and give it to his father. He ought to. He just didn't. He wanted to ask his father about being an Enforcer for the Council, too, but couldn't. His parents held so many secrets. Now, Ashe had secrets of his own.

Sali must have gotten a similar talk from Marcus, because he didn't mention Dawn Smith's visit either. Ashe figured Sali might be about to burst over it, but held the information inside. Ashe blew out a sigh in Transformational Arts, picked up clothing as usual and went on to the next class. What Ashe knew that Sali didn't, though, was that someone from Cloud Chief had contacted Randy Smith's mother.

When Terry Smith had come to Cordell, someone had killed him. Ashe wondered if it hadn't been a carefully laid trap. What he couldn't fathom, however, was why Terry Smith had been shot when James and Pat's hearts had somehow exploded. If the killer was capable of that sort of thing, why hadn't they done it to Terry Smith?

"Come on, you're always slow to get to lunch," Sali dragged Ashe along the tiled hallway of Cloud Chief Combined, nearly running over a second-grader, who scooted out of the way at the last second.

Ashe's mother turned on the small television sitting on a corner of the kitchen counter. Ashe listened as she switched the channel to one of the news stations out of Oklahoma City. "Police fear they are dealing with a mass murderer in St. Louis," the newscaster announced. "Four children are reported dead, another is listed as missing," he added.

"That's awful," Adele sighed at the report, which depicted photographs of murdered children. "I was hoping to get something on that girl who was killed. Megan—the one Marco knew. I heard they're not releasing the body to her parents yet." She got up and turned off the television.

"Does Radomir have any way to check on that stuff? Or Mr. Winkler?" Ashe asked. "You said Mr. Winkler ran a security company. What about the werewolves in Oklahoma City?"

"I think Marcus and Mr. Winkler are already pulling those strings, but we may not get complete information from them."

"Because it's Pack business." Ashe stared at his plate. Adele had cooked chicken for dinner.

"You have to understand that they're only trying to protect themselves."

"But it isn't only werewolves that are dying, Mom."

"I understand that, honey. That's why Radomir is here."

"Mom, did Dad and Radomir talk to Old Harold before he died?"

"They didn't. Radomir was holding off because he knew it would offend Old Harold if they questioned him. He wanted to gather as much information as he could before going to him. If Harold knew anything, we'll never know it."

"Do they know anything more than they did, Mom? Do they?"

"They have some information. They're not sharing all of it," Adele didn't sound as if she appreciated that. Ashe understood completely.

"I wish it would all go away," Ashe muttered glumly.

"So do I. And I have to stay in town late tomorrow to get the tax papers back from the accountant. April fifteenth is Thursday."

"Is it that late already?" Surprise showed on Ashe's face. The school year was nearly over—only a month was left. "Mom, will Marco bring Sali and me in again tomorrow afternoon?" Ashe worried about his mother staying late in Cordell, especially if she were going to be there alone.

"Denise will take you home with her. I'll manage, stop worrying."

"Mom, somebody is killing people. You don't have anybody in the store with you."

"Hon, I have customers all day long this time of year. I won't be alone." Adele ruffled Ashe's hair, her brown eyes smiling at him.

"Mom," Ashe moaned in despair. Why did adults have to be so difficult at times?

"Denise will feed you dinner and you can stay with Sali until I come home. I should be home around sunset. It shouldn't take much longer than that to get the taxes sorted out. The accountant wants to go over a few things but that's all."

"Please be careful," Ashe muttered as he rose to go do homework.

"Your dad says exactly the same."

"Whatcha gonna do, *empty*, when you're human?" Chad Daniels growled at Ashe as they stood in the hall outside Transformational Arts. Chad, like many werewolves, had dark hair and brown eyes. Chad's sneer, however, was almost a permanent fixture, he wore it so often. Ashe, closely followed by a growling Sali, brushed past the older boy and slipped inside the classroom. Chad always made sure Mrs. Rocklin wasn't anywhere near when he threw insults at Ashe.

"Pig," Wynn snapped at Chad before working her way around the seventeen-year-old werewolf.

"Look, ponytail is getting involved. That *empty* your boyfriend?" Chad taunted Wynn. Jeremy walked up and laughed at Chad's latest comment. Jeremy Booth had lighter hair and hazel eyes, reflecting the colors of his Wildcat, but he followed in Chad's shadow much of the time, allowing Chad to select their targets for bullying.

"Get to your classes," Mr. Harris walked over to warn the older boys. "Before I call Billings."

"Billings is on our side," Chad muttered softly as he walked away. Most of the class didn't hear Chad's last words, but Ashe did. Ashe fumed over it as he sat at his desk. More than anything, he wanted to turn in class, just to show everybody he could. But he'd decided to keep that secret. He couldn't explain why, even to himself.

"Dude," Sali swatted at Ashe, bringing him back to Earth with a jolt. Mrs. Rocklin was asking him to pick up Dori's clothing.

CHAPTER 11

"I'm about to go to the accountant's office," Adele told Ashe. He'd called her cell at five minutes past six. Ashe didn't know why he felt so shaky about his mother being alone in Cordell, but he did. His dad wouldn't wake until eight. *Two hours*. Ashe felt helpless, stuck as he was at the DeLucas' home. Sali was in the kitchen trying to wangle something to eat from his mother while Ashe borrowed the phone.

Cori and Dori had gone home with Wynn's mother, so it was just the two of them in the house with Denise DeLuca. Mr. Winkler was in Oklahoma City on business. Ashe hoped the Dallas Packmaster was getting information from the Medical Examiner's office and from the OSBI Forensics department. Ashe also wondered where Marco was—he hadn't driven home after school. Denise DeLuca seemed annoyed about it but she wasn't going to say anything in front of Ashe.

"Mom, just be careful, all right?" Ashe begged as his mother said good-bye.

"I will. You do the same," she said. Ashe hung up the phone with a sigh.

"How's your mom?" Mrs. DeLuca was putting pot roast together, setting carrots, onions and potatoes around the nearly cooked roast before slipping hand-shaped potholders on and returning the pan to the oven.

"Fine. She's on her way to the accountant's to pick up the taxes."

"I mailed ours off last Monday," Denise said, setting the potholders onto the counter.

"I wish ours were already mailed off," Ashe said. If they were, then his mother would be driving home instead of going to Rory Dalton's office. "I think I'll go work on my essay."

"Dude, you can't be serious," Sali said, coming away from the counter with four crackers spread with peanut butter. It was all his mother would allow him to have.

"You could do the same, since you want to win the contest," Denise reminded him.

"Crumbs," Sali muttered, stuffing a peanut butter-covered cracker into his mouth. "Did you have to mention that?" he said, chewing his food noisily.

"I heard that," his mother shook a wooden spoon in Sali's direction. "And don't talk with your mouth full."

Sali answered by grabbing Ashe's arm and hauling him away from the kitchen and down the hall leading to his bedroom. "What topic did you pick?" Sali asked, stuffing another cracker laden with peanut butter into his mouth.

"I haven't. I've got a lot of possibilities, but none of them look good," Ashe pulled the notebook from his book bag and opened it to the proper page. At least fifteen possible topics were listed, some of those crossed through. A few of them marked through violently.

"Dude, what's wrong with *Living Among Humans*? We all do it, just not all the time."

"It just seems trite," Ashe grumped. It was one of the topics he'd crossed out. "Take it if you want. A better topic might be what the humans would do if they found out we weren't human."

"I don't even want to think about that," Sali shivered. "How different do you think they are from us? Really?"

"Think about it, Sali. Some of them hunt, just not in the same way. Before animals were domesticated, hunting ensured their survival.

You eat vegetables, even though you don't want to sometimes. I hear it's the same with some of them. There are a few with medical conditions that keep them out of sunlight. It can harm those people; just like it can my dad. They just don't grow fangs or claws."

"Or fur on the full moon," Sali nodded. "Mom's keeping my allowance for the next month because I jumped up on the back door last time and put scratches in the varnish."

"Dude, isn't that the sixth time you've done that?" Ashe tore out the page of rejected essay topics and handed it to Sali. He didn't want any of them.

"Maybe," Sali grinned and ducked his head. He couldn't help scratching at the door while he was wolf. He figured it was because he wanted out to run when the Moon was full. "Someday, Ashe, you're gonna buy a convertible and I'm gonna sit in the passenger seat while I'm wolf and let the wind blow through my fur."

"No doubt you'll be leering at all the cars we pass, too," Ashe said dryly.

"Goes without saying," Sali shrugged.

"Dinner's done," Ashe said, closing his notebook half an hour later. He'd heard Mrs. DeLuca pulling the pan out of the oven. Denise DeLuca confirmed it, calling out to them moments later.

"This is really good, Mrs. DeLuca," Ashe said. The pot roast had turned out perfectly and Marcus and Mr. Winkler had come in and sat at the table to eat with everyone else. Marco was still absent. Ashe noticed Mr. DeLuca's frown over Marco's empty seat at the table, but Marcus didn't say anything. Ashe imagined that Marcus wouldn't be silent once Ashe went home. He and Sali helped with the dishes afterward, even as Ashe began to feel strangely uncomfortable. His skin felt itchy-tingly, for some reason. He felt the need to call his mother as he hung up the dishtowel and followed Sali to his bedroom again. Ashe became more and more agitated as he walked until he wanted to crawl out of his own skin.

"Sali," Ashe hissed, once Sali's bedroom door was closed, "you can't tell anybody about this. Promise me!"

"Okay. Uh, tell anybody what?" Sali was confused.

"About this," Ashe whispered and turned to mist. Sali's eyes were huge as Ashe disappeared and flew straight through the ceiling of Sali's bedroom.

Floating above the DeLucas' home, Ashe took a moment to get his bearings before hurtling toward Cordell. His mother was in trouble, he just knew it. Something was happening and Ashe was frightened witless. Mr. Dalton's CPA office was near the bank on East First Street. Ashe was flying so fast as mist that the ground and trees were a blur beneath him, and he was speeding along in a straight line instead of following roads. It was just as Mr. Dawkins, Ashe's Math teacher always said—the shortest distance between two points was a straight line. Ashe arrived above Cordell in a matter of minutes, only to find his mother's old blue Ford speeding westward on Highway 152. There wasn't any reason for her to be going in that direction. None at all. Ashe was following the truck in very little time, worrying that he wasn't going to catch up with it. Fear had him flying faster than ever, and he had no time to concern himself with how swiftly he might be going; he was focused and determined to reach the truck.

"I didn't see that, I didn't see that," Sali drew in the deepest of breaths while he murmured the litany to himself. Ashe had disappeared. Just went invisible, and now Sali couldn't find him. Didn't even know if Ashe was still inside the bedroom with him. "Dude," Sali whined, "please show up again. Please. I didn't see that, I didn't see that," Sali repeated.

"Adele is at the accountant's office, dealing with this year's taxes," Aedan said as he and Radomir walked through the garage. "Ashe is with the DeLucas, and Adele will pick him up. We can check the site Marco found yesterday," Aedan added, clicking the button on the garage door opener to close the steel door.

"He seems sure James Johnson was killed in that wooded area?" Radomir asked.

"Near the Johnson's pond at the back of their property," Aedan nodded. "How the body came to be behind our house afterward is still a mystery, but Marco says there were signs of a conflict on the eastern edge of the pond. He claims there are claw marks there, but the rain and the passage of time have obliterated the scents."

"I doubt we'll find anything to substantiate this claim," Radomir said, climbing into Aedan's SUV. "But we will look anyway."

"We're grasping at straws as it is. I'll follow any lead at this point." Aedan started the vehicle and drove toward the Johnson's wheat farm. "Paul and Jean Johnson are not only devastated at the loss of their son but they'll have to hire someone to help with the harvest."

"I have never had a child, not even a vampire child," Radomir admitted as Aedan drove along. "I think it might destroy me to lose one."

"It might," Aedan agreed, thinking of Ashe.

Ashe was terrified and screaming mentally as he flew through the roof of the old blue Ford. The truck had begun to weave dangerously on the highway as he misted through the metal top, but what he found when he reached the inside frightened him more than that, if it were possible. His mother, unconscious, slumped on the passenger side of the truck while the driver's seat was completely empty. Ashe had less than a blink to do something. Should he attempt to drive the truck himself or pull his mother into his mist and get away? Ashe stared through the windshield and made up his mind quickly.

"Marco could be right," Aedan examined the area carefully, his vampire sight showing him everything as clearly as if the sun had been high overhead. The ground surrounding the pond was covered in grass and newly grown weeds, some nearly a foot tall, except for a spot where the earth looked as if it had been churned up and disturbed. Clumps and clods of dirt, many with dried grasses still clinging to them, were scattered throughout the site.

"Here," Radomir pointed to a spot outside the uneven circle. "This is a wolf's paw print. No doubt about that."

"But what is this?" Aedan indicated another print he couldn't identify. The toes held claws, that much was certain. The print, what there was of it, resembled a human foot in a way; it was long, with a heel and toes. Aedan could see the deep gouges and furrows the attached claws had made in the soil. He was thankful the rain hadn't completely destroyed the prints.

"I've never seen anything like that," Radomir examined the ground carefully. Taking a tiny digital camera from his pocket, he proceeded to record images of the prints and surrounding area.

Marco stood beneath the darkening sky outside the Prairie Harvest Baptist Church in Cordell, with most of the others who resided in the small rural community. They'd come out for a candlelight vigil, to honor Megan Lindley. Each candle shone brightly in a mourner's hand in the deepening night. Marco felt the candles competed with the stars overhead. Were the heavens mourning Megan's passing, too? He liked to think so.

His father refused to allow him to attend Megan's funeral, so Marco hadn't asked about this; he'd just come. Marco was on the outs with his parents anyway; that's why he'd left the message on Aedan's cell phone. He'd visited every possible spot where James might have been lured away and killed. Somehow, Marco had known that James hadn't died behind the Evans' house. He couldn't fathom why his best friend's body had been dumped there, and it didn't matter. All that mattered to Marco was finding who'd killed James and Megan. And then giving the murderer what he deserved.

Marco had known, just as Cori did, that James maintained contact with Randy Smith. Didn't care, either. What harm could it do? His father always said that those were the rules, but sometimes the rules were stupid. And his father wouldn't listen. Marco wanted to turn on the spot, while hundreds of humans stood about him, holding candles to light the night. Wanted to turn and howl out his grief.

Randy Smith was scheduled to die in a matter of days; Marco overheard his father speaking to Mr. Winkler about the Grand Master's trackers, sent out to collect Randy Smith and bring him to Cloud Chief for execution. Marco growled low, but those around him were wrapped in their own grief and didn't hear. He also failed to understand why Megan had been included in the murders. She was human and had no connection to any of it, other than she'd sat and talked with him and James many times.

Ashe barely thought before he acted. The image of the car coming toward them as the truck careened into the oncoming lane had him solid in a moment, dropping into the driver's seat and jerking the steering wheel over, tilting the old Ford dangerously before it righted itself on the proper side of the road. His mother, still unconscious, slid farther down on the seat next to him. Frightened nearly speechless, he hit the brake and pulled over on the side of the road. "Mom?" he shook his mother's shoulder gently. "Mom?"

Adele stirred, moaning softly. Ashe, who had very little driving experience (his father had allowed him to drive on the gravel road that ran through Cloud Chief a time or two) cautiously looked both ways before making a U-turn on the highway and driving slowly back to town. Arguing with himself over whether he should stop at the tiny hospital in Cordell or go home, Ashe's fear of discovery, both for himself and his mother, convinced him to drive to Cloud Chief instead. As the miles were eaten away by the old truck, Ashe formulated his strategy.

Driving into the DeLucas' gravel drive, Ashe checked to make sure nobody watched as he opened the passenger door and helped his mother out. Still unconscious, she was dead weight against Ashe, so he misted her to the front door of Sali's home, became solid long enough to ring the doorbell and then turned to mist again, shooting like a rocket through the walls and straight into Sali's bedroom. Sali, who'd remained unsure about what to do once Ashe disappeared, almost shrieked when Ashe reappeared.

"Hush!" Ashe clapped a hand over Sali's mouth, listening. He heard Denise's shout for Marcus to come and then hauled Sali out of the bedroom with a warning. "You promised," he hissed before breaking into a run, Sali right behind him.

"What's wrong?" Ashe said worriedly as Marcus carried his mother's limp body inside the house.

"Ashe, stay calm, we have to call your father," Denise was nearly in tears, she was so frightened. Ashe fidgeted while Denise did her best to bring his mother around. Marcus had Aedan on the phone quickly, giving Ashe's father the small bit of information he had—that Adele had driven up and then fainted on their doorstep. Aedan was there in less than two minutes, and Ashe knew his father hadn't bothered to drive from wherever he'd been.

"*A rún mo chroí*, what has happened?" Aedan sank to his knees beside the sofa where Marcus had laid Adele. Ashe drew in a breath; Aedan seldom used Gaelic, allowing the accent to slip into his voice.

"I think she's been drugged," Marcus said softly. "I can smell it."

"As can I. Now I wish that physician had stayed," Aedan muttered angrily. "Who could have done this? Who?" Aedan was very close to losing his temper.

"It will be all right, I was in the same situation once," Winkler knelt beside Aedan. "Her metabolism is higher than any human's, so it would take quite a lot to do lasting harm. Let's keep her warm and watch for signs of shock or vomiting. We can bring a physician out if you want, but compulsion will have to be placed afterward." Winkler seemed to know what he was doing.

"We'll monitor her pulse and respiration," Denise said, swallowing nervously and attempting to remain calm. "If things get worse, we'll get somebody out here."

"How did this happen?" Sali whispered. He and Ashe stood against the living- room wall, watching the adults tend to Ashe's mother.

"I think somebody tried to kill her," Ashe muttered angrily.

Radomir walked into the house; Ashe had heard his father's SUV driving up bare moments earlier. Radomir nodded to Aedan and then checked Adele over himself, sighing and saying the same thing Mr. Winkler had.

"Can we try washing her face with a cold cloth?" Denise asked.

"It might work," Radomir agreed. Denise went to get something. Nearly half an hour later, Adele moaned before opening her eyes. Aedan uttered an oath in Gaelic and grabbed his wife's fingers.

"Aedan?" Adele said weakly. "Where am I?"

"You're here at the DeLucas', love."

"I don't remember coming here. Somebody grabbed me outside Rory's office."

"Love, don't worry about that right now," Aedan said, jerking his head at Radomir, who flew from the house so quickly Ashe almost didn't see him move. Likely he was on his way to the accountant's office as quickly as he could get Aedan's SUV started.

"Wait," Winkler said, rushing toward the front door. Ashe heard the SUV start and run while Winkler raced out to climb in with the Enforcer. The second door shut and the vehicle drove away. Ashe thought it best if both went. At that moment, he worried that nobody in Cloud Chief was safe.

"What happened?" Marco walked into the house a few moments later. "I thought you were in your truck, Mr. Evans," he added, puzzled over Aedan's presence. "I saw it turning onto the highway toward Cordell."

"That was Mr. Radomir and Mr. Winkler. Adele was attacked outside the CPA's office tonight and they're going to investigate the scene," Marcus stood and frowned at his oldest son. "Where have you been, Marco?"

"I went to the candlelight service for Megan," Marco growled. Ashe, who'd watched the exchange, knew that Megan was a sore spot between Marco and his father.

"Son, go to your room. We'll discuss this later," Marcus DeLuca ordered. Marco, glad to get away from his father, walked swiftly down the hall leading to the bedrooms.

"I'd like to get Adele home," Aedan stood. "Ashe, will you go out and start the truck? I'll bring your mother out. You can help hold her up while I drive."

"Okay." Ashe walked toward the front door, Sali right behind him.

"Dude, what the bloody H was that?" Sali hissed, once they were outside.

"The disappearance?" Ashe asked. When Sali nodded, Ashe explained. "Dad told me that some really rare vampires can turn to mist," Ashe spoke softly as he walked toward the old Ford. "I turn to mist, Sali. And you have to keep your mouth shut about it. All right? I'll be in hot water up to my neck if some people find out."

"You've been sneaking around, haven't you?"

"Sali, if I hadn't discovered I could do this by accident, I'd have been torn apart by the Pack during the last full moon. I almost got caught in that tree, dude. Now, somebody is trying to kill Mom. You have to keep this secret, Sali. You promised."

"I will, but this will keep you out of Cordell Junior High for sure."

"You think I haven't thought about that?" Ashe climbed into the truck—he'd left the keys in the ignition earlier. Turning the key, the truck started right up. "Go back inside, Sali. Get in the house. We're not dealing with anything that anybody's ever seen before, I think. Don't go anywhere alone, okay?"

"You know more about this than you're telling."

"Sali, Dad's coming. Get in the house. Please."

"All right, but you owe me an explanation."

"And you'll get one. Soon. Go, Sali. It's not safe."

Aedan carried Adele out to the truck and settled her in the middle of the seat. Ashe climbed in on the outside and shut the door while his father slid into the driver's seat. "Ashe?" Adele woke briefly and turned to look at her son.

"Mom? Are you okay?"

"I feel dizzy. Maybe a little sick."

"We're almost home. Can you hang on until then?"

"I think so." Adele closed her eyes again.

Ashe locked the truck and closed the garage door while Aedan carried his mother into the house. Ashe set the alarm, too—listening as his mother was carried down the stairs. His parents' bedroom door opened and closed. Ashe sighed and slumped to the kitchen floor, holding his head in his hands. It had been so close. So close. If he'd waited only a few seconds more...

"Marco, I hope you realize how dangerous it is to be going out alone," Marcus held his temper back. "Your mother and I know how much you cared for that girl, but it's foolish to place yourself in this position. What if the human authorities find out there's someone that knew Megan who they haven't questioned?" Marcus' dark eyes bored into Marco's. "Too many people have seen you spending time with her at the Burger Hut. Don't deny it, son," Marcus flung out a hand. "You and James were in Cordell at least twice a week, talking to her. Mr. Winkler has been trying to find out whether anyone has reported that to the police. The Packmaster in Oklahoma City is in law enforcement. He's trying to get the information. If the OSBI comes looking for you and James, we'll be able to bring you forward, but James is dead. How will we explain his disappearance?"

"Dad, this is so messed up," Marco rubbed his eyes with the heels of his hands.

"Son, I know you lost two that you cared for. But things are different for members of the Pack. During your lifetime, you'll see Packmates fall. It's part of what we are."

"But James was murdered. So was Megan."

"And we're doing everything we can to get to the bottom of this. You have to let us do our jobs, Marco. Stop going off by yourself, son. The last thing I need right now is for someone to tell me that it's not somebody else's son they found dead in a field."

"Dad," Marco wiped wetness from his cheeks.

"Son, your mother and I love you. I ask that you don't forget that." Marcus walked out of Marco's bedroom and closed the door softly behind him.

~

"I don't want your mother going to work tomorrow," Aedan was back and sliding down the kitchen wall to sit beside his son.

"But this is the busiest time," Ashe played with a shoestring on his athletic shoes. The shoes, only a few months old, were already tight on his feet. He'd been thinking of asking his mother for a new pair. That would wait.

"I know. But there's nobody else here who knows the business."

"I do."

"Ashe, you're twelve. While you're more adult than a lot of adults I know, you need someone older there with you."

"Wynn's mom or dad could do it."

"Son, they have their own farm to tend."

"Dad, you, Old Harold and Nathan put up their barn in four days last year. I don't think a couple of days at the store will hurt too much, do you? Mom will really be upset if the store doesn't open."

"She will," Aedan sighed. Pulling his cell phone from a pocket, he dialed a number. Ashe heard Sharon O'Neill's voice quite clearly on the other end when she answered.

"Sharon, this is Aedan Evans," Ashe's father said. "We had a bit of trouble tonight. Adele was attacked outside the CPA's office. We think someone drugged her. She barely made it home before passing out and now she's in no condition to work for a day or two. I was wondering if you or Jonas might be able to help Ashe watch the store."

"Adele was attacked?" Sharon was aghast at the news.

"Yes. She's sleeping the drugs off now. It was dark or nearly so when she was attacked and almost everyone in Cordell was at a memorial service for the girl who was killed."

"Aedan, Jonas says one of us will come. We'll pick Ashe up in the morning around seven-thirty. Does he have keys to the store?"

"He'll have them," Aedan said. "I appreciate this more than I can say."

"Aedan, if you and Nathan hadn't been there for us last year, we'd still be climbing out of that hole. We'll come."

"Thank you, Sharon," Aedan said and terminated the call. "I'll get Marcus to contact Ben Billings and let him know you'll be out of school for a day or two," Aedan ran gentle fingers through Ashe's hair. "We'll get through this, son."

"I don't want any more close calls like this," Ashe muttered, bumping his forehead against his knees.

"I know."

"You were supposed to wait and make sure the job was finished. Not leave at the first opportunity to let things take care of themselves," Wolf growled at his accomplices. The plan was to eliminate the mother, leaving the boy vulnerable during daylight hours.

"It should have been done. I have no idea how she managed to drive home. She was unconscious. I swear it."

"If you expect to get what you want, you're going to have to do better than this!" Wolf's words were hissed in frustration.

"As you did better the first time?" The voice was cool and angry. "You have already gotten most of what you wanted."

"I was operating on the information I was given before. Every bit of that information fit. How should I have known there was more than one? It's your fault for not being more specific."

"Regardless, you must uphold your part of the bargain this time. Should you fail, we will not be merciful."

"If you expect to get what you want from this, you'll have to keep your threats to yourself." Wolf wasn't going to settle for that sort of treatment.

"Fine. Do not fail us."

"Do your job next time and we won't have another conversation like this."

CHAPTER 12

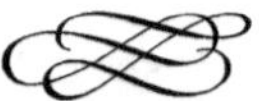

She was very surprised to find that Mr. Winkler had come with Sharon O'Neill early the following morning. "Just to make sure of things," Winkler tousled Ashe's hair as Ashe set the alarm and walked out the kitchen door. The garage door went down next; Ashe watched it close completely before walking with Winkler toward the van that Mr. Winkler drove. Wynn's mother Sharon was waiting inside. Ashe crawled into the back seat, Mr. Winkler put the van in gear and they drove toward Cordell.

"I'm bringing two of mine from Dallas who know a lot about gardening," Winkler informed Ashe later, when Ashe handed a cup of coffee to him. "They'll run the store while your mother recovers. And if she insists on continuing to work here before we get this mystery solved, then at least one will stay to help. She doesn't need to be here alone; that much is obvious."

"Yeah." Ashe knocked the toe of his athletic shoe against a leg of his mother's desk inside her office. Mr. Winkler had already pulled cash from the register and allowed Ashe to slip it inside the safe. With Sharon O'Neill working with them, they'd done pretty well. There were only a few questions Ashe didn't feel comfortable answering on some of the tillers and lawn mowers, but Mr. Winkler had located printed information in the back and went through it with the customers. Ashe learned that Mr. Winkler had an Engineering degree from the University of Texas and was quite adept at starting garden equipment and talking about cost effectiveness and fuel efficiency.

"You know how to do this?" Sharon watched over Ashe's shoulder as he filled out the deposit slip and sorted out the charge slips for the day. Sales had been brisk, although several customers had asked about Adele. Ashe said she was sick and left it at that. A few women made a point to talk with Mr. Winkler, who took it good-naturedly, smiling at them.

"This isn't hard," Ashe grinned. "If we get a lot of checks, I have to go through those at least twice to make sure they were all added correctly, but you can clip them together and put the total amount on one line," he pointed to the figure in question. "It makes things a lot easier. You can't possibly list each check on a line; I'd have to have twenty-five deposit slips, just for today."

"Why did you sort the charge slips?" Sharon asked.

"In case a charge is disputed. We can find the one in question pretty quick if you sort them into the types of card used." Ashe felt like an adult, answering questions about the business end of Cordell Feed and Seed.

"Come along, growing one," Winkler grinned. "Let's pick up dinner and take you home. We'll see how your mother is doing." Ashe locked the door behind him after setting the alarm and they drove to Betsy's Diner, picking up enough food for Ashe, his mother and Sharon O'Neill's family. Winkler phoned Denise DeLuca while Ashe was ordering, asking if she wanted something brought home for her family. Ashe heard her say that she'd already started something. Winkler hung up shortly after that.

"Ashe, how did it go?" Adele asked weakly as he, Sharon O'Neill and Mr. Winkler walked through the kitchen door. Ashe's mother sat at the kitchen table, a tumbler of water at her elbow.

"Sales were good, Mom," Ashe went to hug Adele. "Here's the deposit bag if you want to look. And we have dinner from Betsy's. I ordered chicken and noodles for you."

"That sounds good. Mr. Winkler, we are so grateful for your help. Denise told me that an extra two showed up at her home an hour ago. They're waiting for you now."

"They'll stay in town tonight and I'll take Ashe in tomorrow so he can show them where everything is. They're bonded and trustworthy, Mrs. Evans. They'll run the business for you while you're down." Winkler offered Adele a quick grin.

"I owe you so much," Adele said.

"It's nothing," Winkler waved it off. "They already work for me, so it isn't any trouble."

Adele thanked Sharon, too, who seemed grateful she didn't have to go to Cordell the following day. Ashe saw them out the garage door before closing it and setting the alarm. "Mom, how do you feel?" he asked after walking back into the kitchen.

"Really tired," she said, pulling the Styrofoam container of chicken and noodles toward her. Ashe went to find cutlery and a napkin for both of them before sitting down to meatloaf and mashed potatoes.

"What happened?" Ashe asked after a while.

"Honey, I don't remember much. I was walking out of Rory's office when I was grabbed from behind. They must have injected something; it didn't take long before I was out, I guess. What I can't figure out is why they left me in my truck. I don't remember anything about driving to the DeLucas' house," Adele listlessly picked at her food.

After the meal was finished, Adele was exhausted and unwilling to offer more information, so Ashe helped her down the stairs and got her back in bed before calling Sali. "Any homework?" he asked.

"Dude, we got an English assignment and something in Math," Sali handed out information while Ashe wrote it down. "And when are we gonna talk about what happened last night?"

"Not now, Sali. You know why." Werewolves could hear both sides of a phone conversation, just as well as Ashe could. It wasn't safe to discuss anything over the phone. Sali grumbled but didn't press the issue.

"Ashe?" Denise DeLuca had taken the phone away from Sali. "How's your mother doing?"

"Okay. She looks pale and she said she felt weak. Mr. Winkler got something for us from Betsy's for dinner. She ate but went back to bed."

"If you need something, call the house, all right? Somebody will come over. And I'll cook enough for you tomorrow night, so don't worry about dinner."

"Thanks, Mrs. DeLuca."

"Dad, I found the folder with the tax stuff in the truck," Ashe said later when Aedan and Radomir walked into the kitchen. "It needs to be mailed off tonight."

"I'll take it by the post office," Aedan said, lifting the envelope off the kitchen table. Staying late to take care of taxes was the reason Adele had been attacked; Ashe was sure of it. Somebody had wanted darkness and privacy to do what they'd done, and someone had known she was staying late in Cordell. They'd also known that most of Cordell's population would be at the candlelight service for Megan. Ashe itched to ask if there were any information on Megan's murder but held back.

"Why don't you do your homework in the TV room?" Aedan asked. "That way you can hear your mother if she needs anything. Radomir and I will mail this off and run a few errands." Aedan patted Ashe's shoulder before walking out the kitchen door. Ashe heaved a frustrated sigh as he watched the door close.

He couldn't leave his mother alone; else he'd be out the door with his father, following along as mist. Instead, he set the alarm and clumped down the steps to the lower level, hauling out his English and Math homework, muting the television and setting to work. He didn't look up again until nearly two hours later, when the evening news was on. Something was going on in Fort Myers, Florida; Ashe saw the banner across the bottom of the screen. Flipping on the sound, Ashe listened to the newscast.

"They were only gone for a few minutes," a mother wept on camera as she described the deaths of her twin sons. The journalist took over then, explaining how the two eighth-graders had taken their bicycles to visit a friend down the block. They'd never arrived. Three days after their disappearance, both bodies had been recovered from swampland on nearby Sanibel Island. The murder victims were only a year older than he, Ashe thought, shocked at the news. Someone had killed both of them and they were the only children their parents had. Both parents were extremely upset, Ashe could tell.

"Mom?" Ashe knocked lightly on his parents' bedroom door before going to bed later.

"What is it?" Adele called out.

"Do you need anything before I go to bed? A glass of water or something?"

"I'm all right. Go to bed. Is the alarm set?"

"Yeah. Everything's cool."

"Good. Goodnight, Ashe."

"Goodnight, Mom." Ashe closed the door quietly and walked toward his bedroom.

"Grand Master, Radomir showed me photographs of the site," Winkler spoke quietly on his cell while driving along Cloud Chief's perimeter in the darkness. The van bumped over uneven, grass-covered prairie as Winkler followed the fence line, searching for breaches in the barbed-wire enclosure. After he'd seen the footprint that Radomir photographed, Winkler's suspicions and his hackles had risen. He'd seen something similar twenty years earlier.

"You think they're back? The Dark ones?" Weldon Harper, Grand Master of Werewolves asked.

"I think it's possible. I've talked with our friend in Washington, but he's too concerned with all those child disappearances across the country to investigate."

"All my trackers are out," Weldon Harper sighed. "Or I'd send a few to look. You may have to handle this yourself."

"If the Dark ones are here, the Bright side may be as well—I understand they've been fighting one another for a very long time. I may track down the Bright ones and see whether they'll help with our little problem here."

"If the Dark ones are involved there, the others may certainly be interested, although I can't figure out why the Dark ones would be attacking us or the vampires—they know we can take them down should we band together. Surely they don't want a war with us as well."

"I'm working on this, Grand Master. If the Dark ones killed James Johnson, then someone from this community led them past the witch's shields. We'll have to find the Cloud Chief collaborator as well. I'll keep you updated as things develop." Winkler ended the call and concentrated on driving across the Oklahoma prairie.

"This is Trace Gibson, my Second's younger brother," Winkler's black eyes twinkled as Ashe was introduced to two werewolves the following morning. Ashe should have known they'd be werewolves—Mr. Winkler wouldn't send anyone he couldn't trust. "And this is Jason Landers," Winkler introduced the second werewolf. Trace was tall. Basketball player tall. Nearly seven feet, with brown hair, an easy smile and a slow grace when he moved. Jason Landers had nearly red hair, a square face and was shorter than six feet with a stocky body and powerful build.

"I was raised on my parents' farm outside Denton," Trace said, accepting Ashe's offered hand. "I know a lot about farming."

"I worked for Mr. Gibson, Trace's dad," Jason said, solemnly shaking Ashe's hand next. "So I can still teach muck for brains here a thing or two." Ashe realized then that Jason Landers was much older than Trace Gibson.

"Nice to meet you," Ashe said. He spent the morning showing both werewolves where everything was; Winkler left shortly after dropping Ashe off. Trace and Jason had a van, so they didn't need Winkler's transportation. Trace mastered the register in very little time, but Jason worked best with customers, confidently telling them what each piece of equipment would do, what brands of seeds worked best and which plants to buy. Ashe blinked at how well he knew those things.

"He's nearly a hundred and fifty," Trace leaned down and whispered to Ashe at one point. "He's been a farmer since he was young."

Ashe gulped nervously and nodded. Jason probably knew so much and Ashe wanted to ask so many questions, but felt that might be rude. The day went well, no customer showed up that looked capable of drugging anyone and the werewolves didn't smell anything amiss. Ashe had to sign for shipments, and before the day was over, he and Jason had gone through the inventory so an order could be phoned in to the suppliers.

"You're a pretty good hand," Jason complimented Ashe as he loaded into their van, ready to drive toward Cloud Chief. The two werewolves were going to stay with Micah and Greta Rocklin until they left. Mr. Winkler thought it best that they'd be guarded somehow while they slept. Ashe knew Mr. Winkler was as worried about what was attacking everyone as he was.

"Here's your young man, safe and sound," Jason delivered Ashe into the kitchen. Denise DeLuca and Sali were sitting at the kitchen table, talking with Adele.

"You look better today, Mom," Ashe went to give her a hug.

"I do feel better, but your father and Mr. Radomir don't want me going back to work until we have this mess sorted out. Aedan's afraid I'll be attacked again."

"Me, too," Ashe said, giving an extra hug before letting his mother go.

"I'll go on, Mrs. Evans," Jason said, nodding to Adele. "Mrs. DeLuca," Jason nodded respectfully to her as well, just like a cowboy in the old movies. Ashe was spellbound for a moment, watching Jason walk out the door. He could envision Jason walking around in old jeans and chaps, perhaps, with a cowboy hat on and a nice checkered shirt. Now he wore black jeans and boots, a western belt and a blue polo.

"Good day today," Ashe handed over the bank bag with the deposit inside. They'd drop it off at the bank in the morning on the way to the shop. It would be Saturday and Sali was already asking whether he could help at the store.

"As long as you don't go anywhere alone," Denise DeLuca warned.

"I'll make sure of it," Ashe readily agreed.

"Denise brought dinner," Adele smiled weakly at Ashe.

"It's fried chicken, I was in a hurry tonight," Denise said. "We'll go so you can eat. Call if you need anything."

"I'll be over early in the morning," Sali promised as they walked out the door. Ashe watched them drive away before closing doors and setting the alarm. He then got out plates for the food and opened the plastic container of chicken that Sali's mother brought.

"Want coffee, tea or something else?" Ashe asked, placing a plate of chicken, mashed potatoes and green beans in front of his mother.

"Coffee," Adele said. "This looks good." She began to eat.

Ashe cleaned up later while Adele drank another cup of coffee. "Are you really feeling okay, Mom?" he asked, putting away the clean plates and glasses.

"I'm just tired, honey. I wish I felt better. We don't get sick, you know. I've never felt this bad before. It makes me wonder how humans handle sickness."

"It'll get better," Ashe said, wishing it would happen soon. It frightened him to see his mother like that. Aedan and Radomir found Adele and Ashe at the kitchen table, Adele sipping a fresh cup of coffee and Ashe talking with his mother.

"How are you feeling?" Aedan pulled out a chair next to his wife and placed an arm around her shoulders. Radomir watched, his eyes hooded. Ashe felt bad that he and the vampire Enforcer were intruding on a private moment. "I'll go downstairs and read," he said, heading for the middle door.

"I'll be down in a bit," Adele promised.

"Okay," Ashe called out and shut the door behind him.

Trace drove Sali to Taco Palace to buy lunch for all of them while Ashe and Jason stayed at the store to help customers on Saturday. Dawn Smith came in again while Ashe manned the register, ringing up six bags of fertilizer. Ashe recognized her right away, although she wasn't wearing the green blazer. The weather had turned warm and there wasn't any need for a jacket.

"Is Adele here?" Dawn asked after Ashe finished with the customer.

"Mom's sick," Ashe said softly, wishing Jason would come back from loading the fertilizer for the customer.

"Sick?" Dawn's voice held disbelief.

"Somebody drugged her. Tried to kill her," Ashe muttered.

"Oh, dear God," Dawn had a hand at her mouth. "Do you know what happened?"

"No. Mom can't remember much of it." Ashe imagined that if Dawn had anything to do with his mother's attack, she was doing a good job of covering it up. She seemed genuinely shocked and upset.

"What's going on?" Jason had gotten Dawn's scent the moment he walked inside the store.

"I'm Dawn Smith," Dawn knew Jason was werewolf, too; Ashe had seen her draw in a breath, her nostrils flaring slightly when Jason returned.

"The one with the boy." Jason's words were flat.

"Yes. But I don't recognize you," she said, turning golden-brown eyes on Jason's face and examining him closely.

"From the Dallas Pack," he nodded to her politely. "Brought in to provide security since the attack."

"I understand. Can you tell me anything about it?"

"Nope. Not allowed. If you want to talk to somebody," Jason pulled a business card from a pocket and handed it over.

"William Winkler? The Dallas Packmaster?" Dawn's disbelief was back.

"At the request of the Grand Master," Jason said. "Call that number. I think he'd like to speak with you."

"All right. Thank you." Dawn walked out of the store without another word. Jason went toward the back but Ashe heard Jason's portion of the cell phone conversation afterward. Jason called Winkler as soon as Dawn walked out the door.

"Boss, Dawn Smith just walked into the store, looking for Adele Evans. I handed one of your cards over after we told her Adele was sick. No, I don't know whether she plans to call." Jason listened for a minute or two while Winkler talked. Ashe wished he were close enough to hear both sides of the conversation.

Sali and Trace walked into the store carrying bags of food while Jason snapped his cell phone shut. "Boss has some info on the shootings," Jason said, taking one of the bags from Trace. "Ashe, can you and Sali handle the store while Trace and I talk inside the office?"

"Sure," Ashe shrugged, accepting a bag of food from Sali. "We can eat behind the register."

"Good. We won't be gone long." Trace followed Jason inside Adele's office and shut the door.

"Can you," Sali said before Ashe held up a hand to hush his friend. Sali stepped back, realizing that Ashe was already listening.

"They got word on the shootings, same gun," Jason told Trace amid noises of paper wrapping pulled from tacos. "Registered to somebody local, but the gun is missing from his gun cabinet. Says he hasn't been into it for several weeks and didn't even know it was gone."

"Does he have an alibi?" Trace asked. Ashe heard the crunch as Trace bit into a taco.

"Yep. Rock solid. He was in Weatherford when Terry Smith got hit. And at Betsy's Diner when the girl was shot. Too many witnesses in both places. Somebody stole the gun, but that's the only thing they got. Police are over at his house, checking for fingerprints, but so far they haven't found anything."

"Have you ever heard anything like this before?" Trace asked, taking another bite of his food.

"Nah. Damndest thing, too. "

"Trajan says there might be an explanation, but he can't say anything. I think Winkler is beginning to suspect something, but he's keeping it to himself."

"I sure don't want to end up shot and in a ditch someplace," Jason sighed, crunching into a taco.

"You think they're after just anybody, or do they have a specific target in mind?" Trace asked.

"Don't have the answer to that," Jason replied.

The bell tinkled over the door and Ashe had to leave the conversation behind to help a customer with plants from the greenhouse.

~

"Your mother wants you to stay with us for a little while, Sali," Adele was waiting for Jason and Trace to drop Ashe off later. "The werewolves are having a meeting at Sali's house," she added. "You two are expected as well," she nodded to Trace and Jason.

"Thanks, ma'am," Jason nodded toward Adele. Ashe watched as the van drove out of their yard before he and Sali closed the garage door and Ashe set the alarm.

"I hope you two don't mind sandwiches," Adele said.

"Nope," Sali grinned. He and Ashe put sandwiches together and sat down to eat. When Ashe's father and Radomir woke and walked upstairs, Ashe and Sali went to Ashe's room.

"Sali," Ashe whispered as quietly as he could, "Principal Billings will be in that meeting."

"Yeah. So?" Sali wasn't sure what Ashe was getting at.

"So his house is empty. Nobody there. Now might be a good time to go snooping and see if Randy Smith's essay is there."

"Are you still worrying about that?" Sali grumped.

"I am. What if they've caught Randy already? What if that's why his mom was in the store today? What if they have the wrong person, Sali? What if he never did anything?"

"Dude, you worry too much about that. We have to protect ourselves."

"Sali, I just think this is all wrong, somehow. I can't explain it, I just do." Ashe worried a shoe—it was pinching his toes.

"But what good is it that Billings' house is empty?"

"I can go digging around in it, if you cover for me," Ashe said.

"What?" Sali hissed, forcing Ashe to shush him.

"Just what I said. If you haven't figured out yet that Mom didn't make it home by herself the other night, then you'd better think again."

"You brought her back?" Sali gaped at Ashe in astonishment. "Dude, I don't know whether to say that's the coolest thing or the dumbest thing ever."

"If I hadn't gone, Mom would be dead. I found her passed out in the truck with nobody driving," Ashe hissed. "I had to drive the truck back here. I was scared to death I'd get stopped by the police, and you know what Dad might do if I got caught."

"Eternal grounding," Sali nodded sagely.

"And if your dad's a vampire, eternal takes on a whole new meaning," Ashe agreed. "Come on, cover for me. If Billings comes in, I'll just zip out of there and come right back."

"But what if your mom comes in?" Sali muttered angrily.

"Then tell her I ran outside or something. I'll get in trouble, you won't."

"Fine," Sali sighed.

"Good. I'll be back," Ashe assured Sali and turned to mist.

Principal Billings' house was a mile away from Ashe's, on the western edge of Cloud Chief's boundary. The fence marking the witch's concealment spells stood twenty feet from Benjamin Billing's large house. Since he lived alone, Ashe always wondered why the Principal needed so much room. Mentally shaking himself in order to focus on the task at hand, Ashe steeled his nerves and went right through the roof.

If I'd known it would be this easy—Ashe thought. He didn't have to go into the main part of the house; he found what he wanted in the attic. Each file box was carefully labeled with the word *Essays* written in bold black lettering, along with the year they'd been written. Counting backward, Ashe found the proper box, pulled it inside his mist and hurried away.

"Dude!" Sali's eyes were huge when Ashe and the box landed on Ashe's bed roughly five minutes later.

"Come on, let's see if it's in there," Ashe pulled the lid off the box eagerly and began sifting through the contents.

"Ashe, Sali's mother is here," Adele knocked on the door, making both boys jump in alarm. Ashe shoved what he'd pulled from the box back inside and slapped the lid on it. The container was then stuffed inside his closet while Sali rose to open the bedroom door.

"We'll talk about our essays at school on Monday," Sali gave Ashe a pointed look. Ashe knew what that meant—that Sali would grill him over the whole thing when they were together again.

"Fine," Ashe said. Sali left with his mother only a few moments later.

"Where's Dad?" Ashe asked.

"Out with Mr. Radomir," Adele sighed. "They found out who owned the gun used to kill Megan and Terry, but he'd reported the gun stolen and they can't link him to either crime. So we're no better off than before."

"The same gun was used?" Ashe already knew that, but he didn't want to let it slip that he'd eavesdropped earlier.

"Looks like it," his mother said. "Would you make a cup of coffee for me?"

"Sure, Mom. Sit down; I'll take care of it." Ashe had a cup of hot chocolate while his mother sipped her coffee later.

"Mom, what do Megan and Terry Smith have in common?" Ashe asked.

"I don't really know," she said, puzzled at Ashe's question.

"They do have something in common," Ashe said. "Terry was human and married to a werewolf. Megan was human and either a girlfriend or potential girlfriend, of a werewolf."

"Ashe, what are you saying?" Adele stared at her son.

"I don't know," Ashe shrugged. "If Pat Roberts wasn't dead, I might say he had enough prejudice to do it."

"You think this is a hate crime? That someone is that prejudiced?" Adele was shocked, Ashe could tell. "What about whoever attacked me?"

"Mom, everybody thinks I'm human. I'll be shipped off to the human school next fall if I don't manage to prove them wrong. And Dad's a vampire. Somebody killed Old Harold, probably because he *was* vampire."

"But what about James's death?"

"I'm still working on that," Ashe said, draining his cup of hot chocolate. He wasn't about to tell his mother that James's best friend was human. And not only human, but one who'd been ordered, at risk to his own life, never to contact the community again.

CHAPTER 13

"The kids are getting cabin fever," Denise DeLuca explained when she came to pick Ashe up Sunday afternoon. A beautiful April afternoon enveloped Cloud Chief, the sun was shining brightly and the weather was perfect for outdoor games. "We're gathering on the school grounds so they can play football, basketball or whatever they want," Sali's mother added. Sali grinned mischievously at Ashe, who held his old, tooth-marked Frisbee in his hand—Sali wanted to play as werewolf.

"I think I'll come, too," Adele rose from her seat at the kitchen table. "Maybe some sunlight will do me good. Ashe, will you get those lawn chairs out of the garage?"

"Sure. Come on, Sali." Ashe hauled Sali out the kitchen door. They hadn't gotten to go outside to do anything for *ages*. Denise drove them to the school, where others had already gathered. Most of the older boys were already engaged in a game of football; a few of the younger ones, both boys and girls, were shooting hoops. Sali turned to werewolf before getting out of the car; he was running immediately while Ashe flung the Frisbee in his direction. Ashe laughed as Sali leapt and caught it neatly.

"Look, it's the dog playing with his human," Jeremy Booth hissed the insult behind Ashe's back while Sali was trotting back with the Frisbee in his teeth. Ashe whirled and glared at Jeremy.

"It's about to be the panther playing with the wildcat, and the panther cheats," Cori snarled at Jeremy. Jeremy had been so focused on getting to Ashe he failed to notice that Cori followed him.

"Be careful, *empty*, your friends won't always be around to protect you," Jeremy, his golden-brown eyes filled with hate and anger, snapped before stalking away. He was outnumbered at the moment and he knew it.

"Wonder where his sniveling friend is," Cori muttered, loud enough for Jeremy to hear.

"Cori, don't aggravate him," Ashe said softly. "We have enough trouble as it is."

"How's your mom?" Cori asked, turning back to Ashe and Sali.

"Better. You can ask her yourself if you want. She's sitting with Sali's mom." Ashe nodded at his mother. Adele waved weakly from her lawn chair that sat beside Denise DeLuca's car.

"I will after a bit," Cori said. "How about I go down there and toss the Frisbee back after Sali catches it?" she offered. Sali yipped an enthusiastic agreement, thumping his tail on the ground.

"I think that's a yes," Ashe laughed and tossed the Frisbee, chortling and snorting when Sali took off like a rocket to chase it, paws scrabbling on new grass and fur rippling as he raced away.

"Marco, why didn't you come with the others?" Cori had gotten a ride to the DeLucas when Denise offered everyone something to drink after the get-together. Marco was in the kitchen having a soda when Cori, Sali and Ashe trooped in behind Denise and Adele.

"Didn't feel like it," Marco mumbled, sipping his drink.

"Marco, it'll be okay," Cori gave him an unexpected hug. Marco stared at her in surprise as she moved away and accepted a soft drink from Mrs. DeLuca.

"Would any of you like to stay for dinner and watch a movie?" Denise asked.

"Ashe, if you want to stay," Adele said, "I can go on home and wait for your father to wake."

"Mom, I don't like it if you're there by yourself." Ashe wanted to stay but didn't want his mother to be in the house without anyone else awake and capable of helping her.

"We could go to Ashe's house instead," Marco suggested, surprising his mother greatly.

"That's a great idea. I was going to make burgers anyway; I can do that there," Denise agreed.

"What are we doing?" Marcus walked into the house with Winkler, Jason and Trace.

"Going over to the Evans' to make burgers and watch a movie," Denise said. "Come on, wash up and we'll go." That's how Ashe ended up peeling potatoes while Sali cut up tomatoes and Cori and Marco washed and tore lettuce and sliced onions for the burgers. Adele watched all of them working in her kitchen, a slight smile on her face. Sali teased Ashe about wearing his mother's apron while he worked.

"It's better than wearing tomato juice," Ashe pointed at the red stains and tomato seeds that decorated Sali's old T-shirt.

"Sal, you should be wearing the apron, I don't think potatoes stain," Marco said, chuckling at Sali's predicament.

"Like lettuce is gonna leave a mark," Cori tapped Marco's chest with a finger. Marco's grin widened a fraction.

"It may. I might have lettuce scars," Marco pretended offense. Cori smiled a very pretty smile at Marco and things went well after that. Ashe dumped cut up potatoes into the deep fryer, the burgers were placed on the grill and the meal was served not long afterward.

"We should do this more often," Marcus patted his stomach later. "That was really good, everybody."

"I can't wait until the tomatoes come out of the garden," Ashe said. "And the potatoes are always better than what we can buy at the store."

"Having a bit of a party?" Aedan smiled at the gathered crowd after he and Radomir climbed the stairs to the kitchen.

"I think you should take the night off to spend with your guests," Radomir said to Aedan. "I can get by on my own, I think."

"No, I'll come with you," Winkler volunteered. Both walked out of the house moments later, the dishes were washed and everyone settled into the Evans' media room to watch an old comedy. Ashe grinned and ducked his head when he saw his father's arm slip around his mother's shoulders. They shared the sofa with Marcus and Denise DeLuca. Ashe, Sali, Cori and Marco all settled on the floor and laughed at the antics of the actors on the screen.

~

"Have all your homework?" Adele smiled at Ashe as they loaded into the old blue truck. Adele was going to drop Ashe off and Jason and Trace were going to run the store for a while; Aedan had talked Adele into taking two weeks off.

"I have it," Ashe dumped his backpack onto the floorboard and climbed in.

"Hon, you're definitely growing again," Adele sighed as she slid onto the driver's seat.

"Mom, my shoes are a little tight," Ashe admitted.

"Then we'll have to drive to Clinton or something. I wish I felt up to taking you to Oklahoma City, but that may have to wait."

"Clinton is okay," Ashe said, closing his door. "We can find shoes there."

"Maybe some jeans and cargo pants, too," Adele said. "I'll see if Denise and Sali want to come."

~

"Ashe," Mrs. Rocklin called on him first thing. Ashe found it difficult not to change in front of the class. He could take the teasing over the tiny bat easier than the shame of being called empty. Nevertheless, he kept the promise he'd made to himself. Sali was asked to transform after Ashe sat down again, his face flushed with the effort not to turn.

"I miss Old Harold's cleaning," Sali toed a black streak left on the cafeteria's tiled floor as they stood in line to get a tray.

"I wouldn't care if he never cleaned again if he were still here," Ashe said. "And James and the others, too."

"Yeah. I think we're getting chocolate cake for dessert." Sali craned his neck from their place in line. "Makes up for the potato soup."

"You always complain about potato soup, but you eat it anyway."

"I'm hungry."

"Goes without saying," Ashe agreed, hunching his shoulders.

"*Empty*," Chad whispered as he passed Ashe in line.

"Muck for brains," Ashe hurled back, borrowing one of Jason's insults.

"What did you say to me?" Chad twisted in mid-stride. He'd caught the last of Ashe's insult.

"I called you muck for brains," Ashe said clearly, glowering at Chad. "Go ahead, hit me. Mr. Harris is watching." Ashe jerked his head toward the door where Mr. Harris stood, monitoring the cafeteria. Ashe was completely taken off guard when Chad punched him in the face.

"Ashe, what happened?" his mother bent over him in the tiny teachers' lounge. He'd been stretched out on the sofa, a cloth filled with ice held to his right eye. Ashe had barely seen the punch coming. Feeling embarrassed while three teachers and his mother stared down at him, Ashe attempted to sit up. "No, hon, lie back down," Adele said. "Tell us what happened."

"Chad called me empty, so I called him muck for brains."

"Ashe," his mother sighed.

"I know. Take the high road and all that," Ashe said, trying to nod. Nodding hurt. He stayed still.

"You'll have a nice black eye for a few days," Mr. Harris observed. He, Mrs. Rocklin and Mr. Dodd were the three teachers inside the room. "Chad's been suspended for a week—three people said the same thing you did; that Chad started it and then punched you." Ashe wanted to say that Principal Billings probably wanted it the other way around, but didn't. Billings was a werewolf, just as the three teachers were who stood behind his mother. They thought Ashe completely human. He had no trouble believing that they'd back the werewolf Principal if push came to shove. The comment Chad had made earlier that Principal Billings was on his side still rankled.

"Your father is not going to like this," Adele drove Ashe home as soon as he could sit up without feeling dizzy.

"I know." Ashe hung his head. "I should have kept my mouth shut."

"How long has he been taunting you?"

"Probably three weeks or so. Jeremy, too."

"Those two have no business acting like that," Adele huffed.

"It's just a black eye, Mom. I'll get over it. I should have just let it go."

"We'll put more ice on that when we get home, and we'll postpone the trip into Clinton."

"Mom, my face will get better. My toes hurt all the time." Ashe knew he was whining when the words came out of his mouth.

"Then I won't cancel," Adele said. "We'll get Sali from school this afternoon and go on." Ashe's face hurt when he smiled, but he smiled anyway.

Ashe thought about going through the box of essays he'd stolen from Principal Billings' attic, but his face throbbed so much his mother gave him aspirin and told him to lie down. Ashe fell asleep, waking only when his mother knocked on the bedroom door, telling him it was time to pick up Sali and Denise and head toward Clinton.

Clinton was much larger than Cordell and had two department stores. The variety in number and type of restaurants was also an enticement to Sali, who loved Chinese food. Cordell didn't have a Chinese restaurant.

"Sali, I promise I'll get plenty of egg rolls," Denise said as they climbed out of the SUV. Adele had borrowed Aedan's vehicle for the trip; it was more comfortable and had storage in the back for purchases.

Ashe tried on athletic shoes first. "Dude, I like the blue ones," Sali was pressing his choice.

"I like the brown pair," Ashe turned his foot this way and that in the mirror. He was trying on a men's size eight, a full size larger than his old shoes.

"Try these on," Sali urged, shoving two boxes in Ashe's arms.

"I like these," Ashe said, still looking at the shoes on his feet.

"Honey, those are on sale, so we could get a second pair if you want," Adele said.

"But what if I grow out of these, too?" Ashe blinked at his mother.

"Good point, we'll just take those," she agreed. They went to buy jeans and two pairs of cargo pants after Ashe settled on the shoes he wanted.

"Dude, you'll be taller than your dad if you don't watch out," Sali said as Adele checked the waist and length of the pants Ashe tried on before going to look for more. Denise searched through a nearby sales rack for shirts Marco might wear.

"These are good," Ashe looked in the mirror. "Uh, Sali, I see Principal Billings back there in sporting goods with Georgia Daniels." Ashe had caught a reflection of the two adult werewolves in the mirror.

"What?" Sali swiveled to look quickly. "What is she doing here with *him?*"

"That explains why Chad and Jeremy were saying that Billings was on their side," Ashe hissed. His mother was coming back so he pulled Sali around again.

"Mom, can I get three pairs of jeans and three pairs of cargo pants?" Adele had said four pairs of jeans and two pairs of cargo pants. Ashe was pleading his case, ignoring the Principal for the moment.

"All right," Adele sighed, giving in.

"Dude, your eye is turning green and purple. Do you need a shirt to match?" Sali teased. Ashe examined his bruised right eye in the mirror.

"I think I'll wear yellow tomorrow," Ashe grinned at his reflection.

"That's quite a shiner there, young man," the man at the register remarked as he rang up Ashe's purchases.

"He got it in the school cafeteria," Sali smiled as the clerk scanned clothing tags.

"I had a difference of opinion with a larger adversary," Ashe shrugged.

"I had a few of those too, when I was in school." The man grinned, bagged up the clothing and passed the bags to Ashe and Sali.

"Now, Chinese food," Sali was grinning as they made their way toward the SUV. They had just gotten to the vehicle and Adele hit the button on the fob to unlock the doors when Ashe heard the noise.

"Move!" he shouted, shoving Sali and his mother out of the way. Denise, walking around the front of the car to the other side, was out of the way already when the minivan slammed into the side of Aedan's SUV. Ashe shoved his mother and Sali so hard to push them out of the way they all fell in a heap across the concrete median separating rows of parking spaces. Glass shattered, tires squealed and the impact as the racing vehicle collided with their SUV could be heard from blocks away. The SUV had been shoved halfway down the empty row of spaces and the minivan that hit it was crumpled like an accordion.

"Ashe? Ashe?" Adele was nearly hysterical as she reached for her son, while Denise pulled Sali from the pile and checked him over. People ran toward the scene of the accident to help while others used cell phones to call for an ambulance and the police.

"I'm okay Mom," Ashe said, sitting up and gazing at the two wrecked vehicles. Adele hugged him tightly anyway. Ashe felt shaky, Adele wept and Denise held onto Sali, although he attempted (unsuccessfully) to wriggle away from her grip.

"Mom," Ashe patted Adele's shoulder; she was shaking and too frightened to let him go at the moment. "Mom," Ashe repeated, "I think we need to get Dad here as soon as possible." Ashe had his eye on the western horizon—the sun was slipping below it, leaving them in early twilight.

"Honey, why?" Adele held him away from her.

"Because that's Georgia Daniels' minivan," Ashe replied, nodding toward the vehicle that had crashed into theirs.

Aedan and Radomir arrived quickly, with Marcus and Marco in Marcus' van. Sali and Ashe waited in a small room at the Clinton Police Department later while Adele and Denise answered questions about the incident. Ashe, hearing every word said, learned from another officer working in an office down the hall that Georgia Daniels hadn't survived the accident. What worried Ashe, however, was that she was the only one inside the minivan. Ashe relayed that information to Sali, whose face went pale.

"But," Sali said.

"Hush. We can tell our dads later," Ashe whispered. Sali nodded, his eyes wide. Aedan had slipped into the room earlier to be with Adele, and Ashe knew his father had likely employed compulsion to remain there.

"No, I don't think we need to go to the hospital; my son managed to push us out of the way before the crash," Adele told the officer as they walked out of his office. Ashe noticed the officer's nametag read Goodwin.

"Then he has good reflexes," the officer nodded. "Do you have your bags and things?" Ashe and Sali had unwittingly held onto the shopping bags as they went tumbling.

"I think so. Thank you, Officer Goodwin."

"Call me Eddie," he said, smiling and offering his hand. Ashe knew he was completely ignoring Aedan Evans, because Aedan had likely told him to do so. Adele and Denise shook hands with the officer while Aedan watched both women carefully. Ashe and Sali followed them out the door of the Clinton Police station, surprised to find Winkler, Jason and Trace waiting outside, standing around Mr. Winkler's van and talking with Radomir, Marcus and Marco.

"I'm hungry," Sali complained as he crawled inside Marcus' van.

"We can get something on the way home," Marcus sighed and

climbed into the driver's seat. Trace loaded in with Sali and the others while Aedan, Adele and Ashe climbed into Winkler's van with Radomir and Jason.

"Are you hungry too, son?" Aedan sat on one side of Ashe, his mother on the other. Jason had climbed into the third set of seats. "That's quite the black eye," Aedan added, a slight smile quirking his lips.

"I'm a little hungry," Ashe admitted. "Mrs. Daniels is dead, Dad."

"I know," Aedan sighed wearily. Right then, Ashe wished he had mindspeech, that other rare gift that vampires sometimes had. He'd be telling his dad about seeing Mrs. Daniels with Principal Billings as Winkler drove.

"Will a burger do?" Winkler asked. The Sonic drive-in was the only thing open at the moment. The questioning had taken more than two hours and the other restaurants were closed.

"Yeah. And tater tots," Ashe's appetite was waking up. Adele hugged her son and kissed his cheek.

~

"Ashe, you should get in bed," Adele said later as they walked into the house.

"I know. Dad, can I talk to you for a minute?" Ashe asked, looking up at his father. Winkler had dropped Ashe, his parents and Radomir off at the house before driving toward Marcus and Denise's home.

"What is it, son?" Aedan sat down at the kitchen table. Radomir leaned against the kitchen counter, his arms crossed over his chest.

"I'm going to bed. Ashe, brush your teeth and go to bed too, when you're done," Adele went through the middle door, closing it behind her.

"Dad," Ashe listened while his mother's footsteps faded down the stairs, "Dad," he said again. "I saw Georgia Daniels in Greerson's Department Store while I was trying on clothes. Sali saw her too."

"You think she was watching your mother?"

"I don't know. She wasn't looking at us when I saw her."

"This is confusing, son," Aedan pinched the space above his nose. Ashe knew the gesture was a sign of frustration from his father, who'd never had a headache since becoming vampire.

"Yeah. But Mrs. Daniels wasn't alone." Ashe's statement caused his father's head to jerk upward.

"Who?" he snapped, gray eyes going red and boring into Ashe's blue.

"Principal Billings," Ashe whispered.

"What did you find?" Winkler was waiting for Aedan and Radomir to return from a quick reconnaissance mission.

"Car isn't back yet," Aedan replied. "We didn't get too close to the house in case he's looking for scent."

"I know how Marcus feels about this," Winkler said. "And I've got more information on the Daniels woman."

"What's that?"

"The gun used to kill Terry Smith and Megan Lindley was found in the back of her van, with her fingerprints on it. My contact in Oklahoma City called a few minutes ago to let me know," Winkler said.

"I don't believe for even a moment that she was capable of this." Radomir sounded sure. "I think this is a way to placate the authorities, leading them to believe they have the person responsible."

"Marcus doesn't see it that way," Winkler said. "Georgia Daniels' husband died six years ago in a challenge, and Marcus thinks she went crazy. We've had to use one of the decoy houses outside the property as her home," he added. Citizens in Cloud Chief had a post office box to receive mail, and their license listed an address outside Cloud Chief as a street address. It was necessary to protect the community.

"This needs to be kept quiet," Radomir observed.

"I've already contacted the Grand Master; he feels the same. He's ordered Marcus and his family to keep it quiet while we investigate."

"But if someone else is involved, how did they convince Georgia

Daniels to do this?" Aedan asked. "And what will be done with her son?"

"I'll take Trace and do some questioning tomorrow—Marcus asked Micah and Greta to take Chad in for the night and break the news to him. They'll keep him out of school until this is resolved." Winkler shook his head.

"Are they still planning to execute the Smith boy?" Radomir asked.

"They are, but they have to find him first. The Grand Master has sent two trackers but they haven't located the boy."

"Did his mother ever call you?" Aedan asked.

"No." Winkler sounded disappointed. "I'll let you know what I learn from the Daniels boy tomorrow night. Will you keep an eye on Billings and let me know when he returns?"

"Of course," Radomir agreed.

Ashe, hovering over their heads as mist, zoomed away.

CHAPTER 14

"I've already called Principal Billings and told him that you're staying home today," Adele told Ashe when she woke him Tuesday morning. "He said he'd hand your assignments to Dori and she can bring them. Sali is staying home today as well. Your father says not to discuss the accident with anyone."

"I know," Ashe slid off the bed and searched for clothing. "Want me to make breakfast? I can do scrambled eggs and toast."

"That sounds really good. I'll meet you upstairs."

"Dude, you know how to cook?" Sali and Denise were at the door just as Ashe was scraping a pile of scrambled eggs onto two plates.

"Your confidence in my culinary skills is lacking," Ashe grinned. "Want some? I can make more."

"Sure." Sali settled into a seat at the table while his mother rolled her eyes at his seemingly insatiable appetite.

"How about you, Mrs. DeLuca?" Ashe pulled more eggs from the fridge.

"I'm not hungry, Ashe, we ate breakfast half an hour ago."

"Mom, I'm a growing boy," Sali whined, dipping into eggs and toast while Adele gave him a bright smile before eating her own breakfast.

Denise DeLuca accepted a cup of coffee from Ashe before he sat down to eat.

"Dude, my Aunt Marcie is leaving Uncle Dom early," Sali whispered as he and Ashe walked downstairs later. "Your black eye looks better."

"Yeah, it's purple, green, brown and yellow now," Ashe said. "At least I can see out of it. What do you mean, your aunt is leaving your uncle early?"

"A lot of werewolf marriages are arranged, dude. The males outnumber the females six to one, so not every male werewolf will get to marry a female werewolf. Didn't your mom and dad tell you about that? Female vampires are nearly nonexistent. Dad told me that, too. Anyway, Grampa Sal had Aunt Marcie marry his Second, Dominic Pruitt, who's Packmaster in Phoenix now. 'Course she told him she was leaving him when Cousin Jackson turned eighteen, right after Uncle Dom challenged Grampa Sal and won. Cousin Jackson is fourteen, now, and Cousin Dustin is seventeen. Two kids is the rule, dude, before the Grand Master will allow a divorce. Then the female werewolf is allowed to pick her next mate."

"Dude, do you know how messed up that sounds?" Ashe shook his head. He only knew a little about how the Pack dealt with marriage. "And your uncle challenged your grampa? That sounds awkward."

"I heard Aunt Marcie was really mad at him. He didn't tell her what he was planning. Mom said Grampa was old, but she still gets upset about it, too."

"Did you ever meet your grampa?"

"Mom says I was a baby when he saw me, so I don't remember it." Sali shivered. "Grampa Salidar is the one I'm named after."

"I know werewolves do things differently. I sure hope you don't want the Pack someday."

"Nah. You think I want to deal with some of those guys? They complain to Dad all the time."

"So, your Aunt Marcie is leaving your Uncle Dom, four years earlier than she planned? Where is she going?"

"She's coming here. Mom says Aunt Marcie will be here sometime

Saturday, so she wants to invite people over. Dad said the Cloud Chief Pack will consider her request to join."

"What about your cousins? Cloud Chief will be a big let-down after Phoenix."

"They won't be coming," Sali mumbled. "If the female leaves, the father gets the kids. Werewolf tradition. It's an incentive for the mothers to stay until the kids graduate high school."

"Dude, that is seriously messed up." Ashe flopped against the headboard of his bed.

"Mom and Dad asked to be together, so it wasn't arranged so much. Now, Mom's worried that Marco will think she's going to leave him, too, and that's not the case."

"But Marco's nearly eighteen. You're the one who might be affected most. If it did happen," Ashe amended. He liked Sali's mom and worried that things might not be as stable as he thought.

"Yeah, but Marco's been hit twice," Sali worried a hole in one of his socks.

"Your mom isn't planning to leave, is she?" Ashe voiced his fears aloud.

"Nope. She talked to Marco and me right after she talked to Aunt Marcie. Marco's in a bad mood anyway, so I don't think anybody is getting through to him."

"He was okay when we had the cookout."

"But now he's depressed again. They're having Megan's funeral tomorrow and Marco's still mad that he can't go."

"What if there was a way?" Ashe traced a pattern in his comforter, decorated with green, blue and brown rectangles.

"Dad said he could stay home, but that's all he said," Sali hunched his shoulders.

"But what if there *is* a way?" Ashe persisted.

"He'll be seen. That's what Dad is trying to avoid."

"And if he isn't seen?" Ashe's comment, made with head bowed as he traced a blue rectangle this time, had Sali drawing in a sharp breath.

"You're kidding," Sali gasped. "You can't." He was skeptical immediately.

"Mom told me I was staying home again tomorrow," Ashe said. "Want to go ask Marco if he can get away for an hour or so?" Ashe felt scared and excited at the same time.

"Dude, I don't know," Sali backed up a little, staring at Ashe in disbelief coupled with a healthy bit of fear.

"Come on, try it for five seconds. If you don't like it, I'll put you down."

"Fine," Sali shivered with fear and anticipation, as if Ashe were about to ask him to leap off a tall bridge with only a slender bungee cord attached to his feet.

"All right," Ashe grinned triumphantly and became mist. Once that was accomplished, he touched his mist to Sali, who also became mist. *See, nothing there*, Ashe said silently to his friend as they hovered before the mirror atop Ashe's dresser. No image of either boy was reflected in the glass. Ashe let Sali go and Sali reappeared immediately, staggering to remain upright in the floor.

"Dude," Sali whispered reverently, his dark eyes blinking at Ashe in something akin to worship, "I heard you!"

"What?" Ashe became corporeal, staring at Sali in surprise. "What did you hear?"

"You said *see, nothing there*," Sali replied, grinning hugely. "That was amazing! I could see and hear! Let's go tell Marco."

"He has to promise to keep his mouth shut," Ashe warned, shaking himself. He had mindspeech after all. He had both rare vampire gifts.

"If you take him tomorrow, I think he'd do just about anything," Sali observed.

"Then let's go." Ashe became mist again, gathered Sali up and went straight through the ceiling, through the kitchen floor past his mother, right through the attic and out the roof. Arriving at Sali's home bare moments later, Ashe zipped right past Winkler and Marcus in the DeLucas' kitchen and straight into the hall, where Ashe dropped Sali before changing back to himself. Sali knocked softly on Marco's bedroom door.

"What do you want?" Marco's muffled voice was surly.

"Marco, I think I have the answer to your problem," Sali said softly, leaning against his brother's door.

"What?" Marco almost flung his bedroom door open, halting in half swing when he saw Ashe standing there with his younger brother. "When did you get here?" he demanded.

"Just now," Ashe said. "And we can always leave, if you don't want to go into Cordell with me tomorrow."

"And just how are you going to get me there?" Marco's words were snarled.

"Dude, we're supposed to be at Ashe's house right now, and we may not have much time. Let us in and we'll explain," Sali whispered, his black eyes begging his brother to hear him out. Ashe got the idea that Sali wasn't allowed inside Marco's room very often.

"And this was my idea," Ashe said. "So Sali isn't to blame for any of this."

"Get in," Marco stood aside to allow both boys inside his room. Ashe took in the rumpled bed, scattered clothing and books piled on the dresser. It was an older version of Sali's room. Ashe wasn't about to say that to Sali, though. He bore enough pressure as Marco's younger brother. Marco shut the door and Ashe and Sali moved uncomfortably into the space between Marco's bed and dresser.

"Marco, I can get you into Cordell and inside the church tomorrow, but you have to promise you'll never tell that we went or how it was done," Ashe mumbled, staring at his feet. He'd worn his new shoes; they didn't pinch his toes.

"I don't think that's possible, but go ahead. Tell me how you plan to do this." Marco flopped onto his bed, prepared to be unimpressed.

"All right. Sali, do you want to be the guinea pig?" Ashe turned to his friend.

"Sure. Let's show him impossible," Sali wore a smug smile as he studied his older brother. Ashe nodded, went right to mist and had Sali drawn into his mist and invisible in only a second or two. Marco was backing up on his bed, his feet pushing the bedspread into a puddle as he scrabbled with his feet and hands.

"What the," Marco didn't finish his statement. He stared, hard, as Ashe and Sali became visible again.

"Mom and Dad don't know yet," Ashe said. "You can't tell, Marco, or I'll be in trouble for sure. I found out I could do this on the last full moon. If I come for you right at two tomorrow afternoon, I'll take you to the Prairie Harvest Baptist Church and we'll find somewhere to sit so nobody will see us. We have to come right back after the service, though. If Mom finds me gone, I'll be in hot water for sure."

"Yeah. I know that feeling. You don't feel weird doing this?" Marco slid to the edge of the bed as he asked Sali about riding with Ashe as mist.

"Dude, its flying. Weightless flying. And you can see and hear everything while you're with Ashe. And Ashe can talk to you while he's taking you. In here." Sali tapped his temple.

"I don't know how this is possible," Marco stared at Ashe.

"Dad says there are some really rare vampires who can turn to mist and mindspeak. I think that's all it is, Marco. I get this from Dad, somehow. I'll be here tomorrow at two unless something happens. Be ready to go."

"I'll be ready." Marco still seemed stunned but nodded at Ashe anyway.

"Ready?" Ashe turned to Sali.

"Ready," Sali grinned. Ashe went to mist, turned Sali to mist as well and scooted right through the roof.

"Dude, that is an awesome talent," Sali sighed as Ashe dropped his friend on his bedroom floor moments later. "We should have timed it," Sali added.

"Yeah. I had to be going around sixty or seventy when I caught up with Mom's truck on the highway," Ashe said, flopping onto the bed with a sigh.

"And it was just speeding along without a driver?" Sali asked.

"Yeah."

"Dude, that's just weird. You think somebody started driving and then jumped out?"

"Had to. I guess. How else could it have happened?"

"No idea. Have you started writing your essay yet?"

"Are you kidding? I'm stumped. I don't have a single good idea." Ashe chewed thoughtfully on his lip.

"Me either. And I really want a cell phone."

"A cell phone would be nice." Ashe agreed completely. "But we have to write the essay first, and then it has to be better than anybody else's. Wait—we have a whole box of essays to look through." Ashe stared at Sali.

"Yeah." Sali hauled the box that Ashe had stolen from Principal Billings' attic out of Ashe's closet. Ashe jerked the lid off and lifted out half the papers inside. "I'll take this half, you take the other half. See what you can find, dude."

"Here's Marco's," Sali snickered after a minute of reading. He slapped that one on the bed for future scrutiny and went back to looking.

"If you find Randy Smith's, let me know," Ashe sorted quickly through his pile.

"Not here," Sali had gone through his stack—twice.

"Not here, either," Ashe said, confused. "Here are the other two winners, and a receipt from the post office," Ashe held up copies of the second and third-place essays. The winning essays were clipped together, with copies of two delivery receipts. Ashe pulled those off and stared at them. "Dang," he said nervously.

"What? What is it?"

"What's the Grand Master's name?" Ashe showed Sali one of the receipts.

"Oh." Sali was shocked. "They send the winners to the Grand Master?"

"And to the Vampire Council, I think. This is an address in London," Ashe flipped the other one down so Sali could see. "I don't know who Charles Hoffman is, but I'll bet it's an alias for the Head of the Council or something. I don't know why these essays would go to London for any other reason."

"Dude, that's scary. Those guys are reading our essays?" Sali stared at Ashe.

"Only the winners, but still. And why isn't Randy Smith's essay here?" Ashe flipped through the clipped papers, just to make sure he hadn't missed anything. "Nope, not here," he confirmed. "Where is it?"

"Man, this is weird," Sali said, lifting Marco's essay to read.

"Sali, we have to take this back to Principal Billings' attic. Read that quick and we'll take it back. We sure as heck don't want to get caught using somebody else's ideas if the Grand Master and the Head of the Council are going to read them."

"All right," Sali grumped. Half an hour later, Ashe and Sali dumped the box inside Principal Billings' attic and zoomed back to Ashe's home.

"Sali, it's time to go," Denise DeLuca called out shortly after they returned.

"Be there in a minute," Sali yelled. "Gotta go, dude. Let me know how it goes tomorrow and I'll get your homework assignments," Sali said as both boys walked out of Ashe's bedroom.

"I'll be writing on my essay for a while, call if you need help with dinner later," Ashe said the following afternoon. He'd helped do laundry and clean the house before lunch. Now he was heading toward his bedroom to prepare for the trip into Cordell with Marco.

"All right, honey. I may nap for a while," Adele said. Ashe knew she still wasn't feeling as well as she should, but was afraid to say anything. More than anything, Ashe wanted to find the one or ones who'd done this and hand them straight to his father and Radomir. His father had once been an Enforcer and Radomir still worked for the Council. They'd know what to do with someone like that.

"Okay, Mom." Ashe walked inside his bedroom and shut the door. Just in case, he dressed a little better before misting to Marco's bedroom inside the DeLuca home. Marco was dressed nicely and ready to go when Ashe arrived, his dark hair combed neatly and face freshly shaven.

"Are you ready for this?" Ashe asked.

"Yeah," Marco blew out a sigh. "Let's go." Ashe turned to mist, gathered Marco up and flew toward Cordell.

The Prairie Harvest Baptist Church in Cordell was a sturdy brick building located just off Main Street. Once he was inside, Ashe looked around for a suitable place where he might set Marco down. Marco shouldn't have to remain mist, but he couldn't be seen. A small balcony stretched across the back wall, high enough so they'd be out of sight for the duration of the service. Currently the balcony was filled with paint cans, tools and other items; parts of the church were undergoing renovation.

This is perfect; Ashe sent the message to Marco, setting him down behind the balcony railing. If Marco sat down on a small step stool left there by workmen, then he could remain hidden during the service. Unfortunately, the stool was the only place available to sit; the remaining space was cluttered with supplies.

Marco sat and looked about him, contemplating Ashe's dilemma. "What are you going to do?" he hissed at the air around him.

Don't freak, Ashe mentally told Marco before turning to the bumblebee bat. Ashe's clothing dropped, covering a stack of paint cans. The tiny bat flapped in front of Marco's nose, causing Marco to stare in shock before clapping a hand over his mouth to cover a snicker.

It's not that funny, Ashe grumped.

"Ashe, this is so you," Marco whispered, still struggling not to laugh. "Think about it—your dad's a vampire. Why wouldn't you be a bat?"

Could have been a bigger bat, was all Ashe would say before settling onto Marco's shirt. Clinging tightly to the top of Marco's shirt pocket, Ashe folded his tiny wings and made himself as comfortable as possible while they waited for the service to begin. Ashe pretended not to notice when Marco wiped a tear away. All of Megan's classmates and half the town had shown up for the funeral.

Ready to go? Ashe asked silently as the service ended.

"Yeah," Marco said softly.

Will you grab my clothes?

"Only for you, dude." Marco picked up Ashe's clothing; Ashe turned from bat to mist and hauled Marco toward Cloud Chief.

"Thanks, Ashe," Marco said when Ashe dropped Sali's older brother inside his bedroom later. "I won't forget this." Ashe had remained mist, choosing not to materialize naked inside Marco's bedroom.

You're welcome, Ashe replied. Marco held out Ashe's clothes, Ashe turned them to mist and zoomed away.

Once he was inside his bedroom and dressed again, Ashe spent another hour fretting over an essay he hadn't started. Finally giving up the effort, Ashe clumped upstairs to the kitchen. "We're having stew?" he asked. The scent of it filled the kitchen.

"Yes. I thought you might like some, and we haven't had any for ages," his mother smiled at him. Ashe liked stew, because his mother made cornbread to go with it.

"Thanks, Mom."

"I called down the stairs earlier, didn't you hear me?" Adele said as Ashe settled on a chair at the table.

Working to keep his breathing even, Ashe apologized. "Sorry, mom. I fell asleep for a while." He hated lying to his mother, but he also had no desire to be caught or to let his parents find out he'd been hiding things from them.

"That's all right, hon. I know you were still in the house," Adele said. Ashe hugged himself and stared at the wall.

"I always buy my supplies from Adele. When will she be back?" A customer asked Jason. Trace, standing nearby, watched the exchange covertly. Neither he nor Jason liked the way the man smelled. He didn't look anything other than human, but the scent was off, in Trace's estimation. The man looked to be in his early thirties, with fair skin, blond hair worn to his shoulders and pale-green eyes.

"Don't rightly know," Jason drawled. "She's been sick, so I can't really say. Maybe in a week or two."

"I'll check back, then," the customer said, turning to leave.

"Anything we can get for you today?" Jason asked.

"No." The stranger replied curtly and walked out of the store. Jason exchanged a look with Trace, who walked straight to the back and pulled out his cell to call Winkler.

~

"Ever seen this one before?" Winkler brought the recorded images from the security DVR he'd installed inside Cordell Feed and Seed. Adele, Aedan, Radomir and Marcus watched the recorded image of the blond man who'd walked into Adele's store.

"No." Adele shook her head. "I've never seen him before."

"He knows your name," Winkler said. The machine also recorded sound—Winkler had installed a state-of-the-art system and they could see and hear the man perfectly. Aedan had an arm wrapped around Adele as they watched the images on the television inside the Evans' media room; Adele was shivering as she watched a perfect stranger ask about her by name, inquiring when she'd be back to work.

"Adele, you're not to go back there until we have this sorted out," Aedan insisted, his eyes going red.

"I'm inclined to agree with Aedan," Winkler said. "This is becoming stranger as time goes by."

Ashe hovered over their heads. He was supposed to be in his room—Aedan had asked him to stay there. He hadn't. Ashe might never see freedom again if his father knew how many times he'd disobeyed lately. Ashe couldn't leave it alone, though. He had to know.

~

"We will not fight vampires." The statement was flat and brooked no argument.

"You've said that before. I grow weary of hearing it." Wolf wasn't about to turn his back on these two—he could die easily at their hands, alone as he was.

"Then we shouldn't have to keep repeating it, don't you think?"

"We may have to find a way around this aversion you have with those creatures," Wolf pointed out.

"Creatures they may be in your opinion, but they are among the few that can kill us. We will not fight them unless our lives are at stake."

"You helped with the old one."

"You made it easy. I don't think we might be so lucky with any of the others. Those most certainly will be more dangerous. We cannot force them to our will as we did the female werewolf. And she was not in our original agreement."

"But necessary, to draw attention away, don't you think?"

"Faugh. You worry too much."

"But you have your own method of escape. I don't have that luxury." Wolf had watched them disappear more than once, and that ability baffled him. He was more than curious over how that might be accomplished.

"How unfortunate for you. Get us what we want and soon, or you will very much regret it."

"Ashe!" Cori shocked him by giving him a hug when he walked toward Transformational Arts on Thursday morning. April the twenty-second had dawned stormy and didn't look to let up. Ashe could hear thunder rumbling while Cori hugged him.

"Good to see you, too," Ashe was blushing when Cori let him go.

"Billings is coming," Wynn whispered as she passed Cori and Ashe in the narrow tiled hallway of Cloud Chief Combined.

"I'll talk to you at lunch," Cori promised, giving Ashe a small smile and walking toward her first class. "Your eye looks awful, by the way." Cori's smile as she looked back at Ashe became a full-blown grin.

Ashe didn't need the reminder that his eye was multicolored and looked much worse than it felt. Sali informed him that Chad Daniels would be out of school for the rest of the month following his mother's death. Ashe was sorry Chad had lost his mother, and not sorry that he wouldn't have to face the young werewolf. Jeremy, however, would still be attending class. Ashe hoped to stay out of his way. That hope was very short-lived.

"Empty, was it your fault that Chad's mom died?" Jeremy stood in front of Ashe, blocking the door into Transformational Arts.

"I don't think so," Ashe stared Jeremy in the eye. Jeremy was only an inch or so taller than Ashe, now.

"That is enough." Mrs. Rocklin's voice sounded behind Ashe. "Jeremy, this is not your class. I suggest you get to English before I call the Principal."

Jeremy walked away, muttering that Principal Billings would get rid of the stupid, worthless empty *real soon.*

"Sounds like he needs the English class," Ashe muttered and walked into Transformational Arts.

Ashe sat at the usual table with Sali during lunch, and Cori joined them quickly, sitting beside Ashe. What surprised him almost speechless, however, was that Wynn and Dori sat down next to Cori, and then Marco, followed by Ryan Phillips, another senior werewolf, set their trays down and sat on Sali's side of the table. Sali blinked across the table at Ashe a time or two before getting back to his chicken quesadillas.

"The trackers brought Randy Smith in early this morning," Marco said.

CHAPTER 15

"They're holding him in Pat Roberts' old house," Marco said quietly before dipping the point of a quesadilla into a dollop of sour cream and biting into it. Ashe drew in a breath and lost his appetite. Turning to Cori, he found her staring at him. She looked so sad Ashe was afraid she might cry.

Thanks, Marco, Ashe sent. The only indication that Marco heard Ashe's mindspeech was a flaring of nostrils, nothing more. Ashe figured Principal Billings was dancing with glee somewhere, because he would get to kill Randy Smith come the full moon next Wednesday. "Sali, you want this?" Ashe pushed his tray toward Sali, who nodded. Ashe rose from the table and after only a moment, Cori got up too.

"Cori, this is awful," Ashe fretted as they walked toward the front doors of Cloud Chief Combined.

"Ashe, they can't do this. They just can't," Cori brushed away tears as she held onto Ashe. Ashe carefully steered her outside. Morning rains had drenched the prairie surrounding the school and dark clouds still hovered overhead. A few students had ventured outside, either sitting on benches or leaning against the school building to talk while the rain had let up temporarily. Mr. Harris and Mrs. Patterson were providing supervision to the students outside; none were allowed in the schoolyard unguarded. Mr. Thompson, who'd become a regular sentry at the school during lunchtimes and after classes were dismissed each day, stood nearby in buffalo form, his white coat covered in mist from the earlier rain.

"Look, we'll just put our heads together and come up with something. I hope," Ashe sighed softly, pulling Cori away from listening teachers and students. He didn't want anyone to hear them; nearly all outside were werewolves. Ashe suddenly felt surrounded and threatened by all of them. Even Sali had shrugged callously at Randy Smith's fate.

"What can we do?" Cori sobbed, gripping Ashe's hand tightly.

"The full moon isn't until next Wednesday. We have six days. Come on, stop crying and let's think about this," Ashe awkwardly attempted to console her.

"James would be so upset," Cori wiped her cheeks.

"Yeah."

"Don't leave school grounds," Mrs. Patterson called after Ashe and Cori, who'd walked past the others to keep their conversation private.

Ashe stopped abruptly at Mrs. Patterson's warning, causing Cori to bump into him. "Come on, Cori. Let's go back inside." Steering Cori around gently, Ashe guided her toward the school doors. Marco waited for them, just inside.

"I'll get her to class, Ashe," Marco took Cori's hand and led her down the hall. Ashe watched as they walked away together, his mind whirling with possibilities and consequences.

Sali was unusually silent during the afternoon classes and on the ride home as well. Adele had picked up both boys in her old truck, saying that she'd called Denise and offered to pick Sali up. Ashe had watched Cori climb into Marco's car after school, accepting a ride home with him instead of Wynn's mother, who'd picked up Wynn and Dori. Shaking his head, Ashe hunched down in the front seat as his mother drove toward Sali's home.

"Dude, I'll talk to you later," Sali slid off the old Ford's front seat and gave a half wave to Ashe before closing the door.

"Yeah," Ashe said, scooting over and leaning back against the worn upholstery.

"You heard, didn't you?" Adele put the truck in gear and crunched over gravel as she drove away from the DeLuca's yard.

"I did." Ashe stared out the passenger-side window on the way home.

"It's Pack business," Adele gave a sigh.

"And nobody messes with that. I know," Ashe muttered angrily.

"I have Dawn Smith to thank for you, Ashe," Adele said after a while. "She was the first one to go to a fertility clinic. She wanted another baby with Terry, but they weren't having any luck. A doctor offered her a donated egg. That's how Randy was born, Ashe. He was a miracle, just like you."

"And we all know how well that's turning out," Ashe snapped sarcastically. "Sorry, Mom. It's not your fault."

"Nor yours," his mother pointed out gently. "Your father has made arrangements with a car dealership in Oklahoma City. The salesman is staying late, so we're driving in tonight to pick up his new SUV. I thought about offering to take Sali, too, but after everything else that's happened today, I decided against it. Radomir will be coming with us instead."

"Does Dawn Smith know they have Randy?"

"I don't know, hon. And she didn't call Mr. Winkler. I'm pretty sure of that."

"Mom, what would you do if that was me instead of Randy Smith?"

"Ashe, it's not you."

"But what if it were? There's a story going around that Randy got framed. What if that's true? What if somebody set me up exactly the same way, because they didn't like me for some reason? What would you do?"

"Honey, your father saw the letter Randy Smith wrote. It's in his handwriting and everything. There are still some samples of his writing floating around, you know, so it would be easy to tell."

"When did Dad see it? Where's the letter now?"

"He saw it a few days after Mr. Harris got it—said the envelope was postmarked in Santa Fe and everything. Everything checked out, Ashe. That letter came from Randy Smith."

"Yeah? Did it smell like him?"

"Ashe, stop. Mail gets handled by so many people you can't even tell about things like that once they arrive."

"Fine." The fields of Cloud Chief blurred past Ashe's window as his mother drove, slowing down eventually to turn into their driveway. "I'll go do homework," Ashe said, slouching into the kitchen and leaving his mother to close the door and set the alarm behind them.

～

"Aedan, he's really upset over this Randy Smith thing," Adele had gone down to her husband's bunker when he woke. "Somehow, he's convinced that Randy Smith didn't write that letter."

"The evidence points to the contrary. We might have placed compulsion to ask if we'd found him, but he was already gone by the time we arrived in Santa Fe," Aedan pulled a shirt on. "No doubt Dawn got the warning and sent him away. That didn't keep the Grand Master's trackers from finding him."

"They had more time. You only had two days, Aedan, and no leads."

"Marcus won't allow anyone near the boy now," Aedan grumbled. "I'll arrange to have someone take Ashe away during the full moon next week if you think it will be better for him."

"It won't make any difference. That boy will still be just as dead, and Ashe knows that. It won't matter if Ashe is here or five hundred miles from here."

"I can place compulsion. But I don't want to."

"Ashe will never trust us again if we do that." Adele rubbed her forehead, attempting to ease the accumulating tension.

"I know. Come, love. We must be in Oklahoma City in an hour."

～

"Young man, would you like a soft drink or a bottle of water?" Ashe stared at the salesman, his arms crossed tightly over his chest.

"No, thank you," Ashe said as politely as he could. Surrounded by polished tile floors and shiny new vehicles, Ashe and Radomir remained inside the dealership while his mother and father test-drove the new SUV.

"Young one, I can feel your anger. One must learn how to hide such emotions," Radomir said softly when the salesman walked away.

Ashe blinked at the Enforcer. Perhaps it was easy for someone older than nine hundred years to hide emotions; he'd had plenty of time to learn, Ashe thought. And Radomir had to be older than nine hundred, since someone had been sent that had to be older than Old Harold. Ashe still didn't know why that was. Sure that he wasn't supposed to know for some reason, Ashe wiggled farther into his plastic chair and let his hands drop to his side, settling for a good, hard grip on the edge of his seat instead. When would people think he was old enough to know things? It made him angry that they kept their secrets. A television was still on inside the dealership, and Ashe's attention diverted to it when a newscaster announced that a child had been abducted in Little Rock, Arkansas. An Amber Alert had been issued for the thirteen-year-old.

"Authorities are now becoming concerned, as it has been revealed through an unidentified source that the parents of this child, as well as the parents of murdered children in Saint Louis and Fort Myers, Florida, all went to the same fertility clinic in St. Louis. While authorities have yet to confirm or deny these allegations, it has put many parents on alert," the female anchor said. Hands now in his lap and fingers clenched, Ashe wanted more than anything to have access to a computer and the internet right then. He hadn't gotten the ages of the children in St. Louis, but the twins in Fort Myers had been only a little older than he was. The one from Little Rock had just celebrated a birthday weeks earlier. Ashe would turn thirteen in June. He shivered visibly at the thought.

"It's just what I wanted," Aedan and Adele were back and ready to purchase the SUV. Ashe stared at his mother. Would she answer his questions? She'd never said where the donated egg had come from, or given any other information. Would it be like so many other things? A secret to be kept until Ashe reached some magical age in the future, when the adults thought he might be capable of handling the truth as they saw it?

"Young one, come," Radomir touched Ashe's shoulder gently. Ashe blinked at the tall Enforcer. That's what he was to all of them. *Young one.* Ashe stood and followed Radomir.

Ashe rode home with Radomir in Adele's old Ford while Aedan and Ashe's mother drove the new Escalade. The other one had been totaled in the accident. Aedan liked his comfortable vehicles; Ashe knew that much. Radomir glanced in Ashe's direction at times, but never said anything. His mind on other things, Ashe was perfectly content not to talk.

"Ashe, it's late and you have school tomorrow," Adele said when he and Radomir walked into the kitchen later. Nodding, Ashe went toward the middle door and clumped down the steps, not bothering to wish his parents good night. Dressing in pajamas and brushing his teeth, Ashe turned out his bedroom light, made sure no one was around to see or hear and booted up his computer.

At times like these, the internet was his best friend. Pulling up information on the deaths in St. Louis, Ashe sat back in his chair and stared. The four children ranged in age from fourteen to seventeen. He then began to look up other murders in the area. Someone had already thought the same thing, posting information on two other deaths, one young woman who was nineteen and attending college, and a young man who was twenty and working as an employee for the City of St. Louis. The blogger noted that both sets of parents used the same fertility clinic as the others.

"Where is it?" Ashe was digging through records and other things that he'd filched from the safe inside his father's office. He seldom went inside that small room right off his parents' bedroom. There wasn't any need. *Until now.* Ashe searched for his birth certificate, hoping other information might be there as well. And why, even if Ashe wasn't involved in any way, would someone target children whose parents visited a fertility clinic? It made no sense to him. The folder that held his birth certificate in his hands, Ashe turned to mist and zipped back to his bedroom.

Receipts. That's what he found. Payments made to the clinic and to a physician. In St. Louis. There was information, too, (some of which Ashe had difficulty understanding) about the transfer of a frozen embryo to another facility located in London. A great deal of money surrounded that transfer. Ashe had stared at the number of zeros that followed the one at the bottom of that transaction. Only it was listed as a donation. One hundred thousand dollars his father had paid for the transfer of a fertilized egg—Ashe at one stage of his life—to waiting supernatural scientists in London. Ashe hadn't realized his father had that kind of money. But then Aedan had just written a check for the total price of a new SUV, without waiting for the insurance check to come on the last one.

Disturbed, Ashe misted through the upper floors of his home and settled upon the peak of the roof, staring around him at the ghost town of Cloud Chief.

"Sali, I haven't forgotten that your Aunt Marcie will be here Saturday. I'm sure that Mom and I will be there with cowbells on," Ashe muttered as Sali ran to keep up with Ashe's swift walk toward Transformational Arts. Friday morning had arrived and Ashe suffered the effects of his sleepless night. His eyes felt as if they were filled with sand and he certainly wasn't in the mood to listen to Sali's chatter about his aunt's visit.

"Dude, you're in another funk," Sali's voice held irritation.

"What do you think Randy Smith is in?" Ashe snapped.

"Dude, you don't have to bite my nose," Sali replied, offended.

"More werewolf euphemisms, Sali?" Ashe increased his pace, leaving Sali behind, staring at his friend's retreating back.

Ashe discovered he wasn't the only one upset. Mrs. Rocklin definitely wasn't herself and called on Dori twice. Dori didn't argue, she merely turned a second time and Ashe gathered her clothing both times, following her to the changing room without being asked. Thankful that he hadn't been called on, Ashe escaped Transformational Arts and headed straight for English class without waiting for Sali.

"What is wrong with you?" Sali huffed, sliding into his seat next to Ashe.

"Sali, if I had an hour or two, I might be able to make a dent in what's wrong with me. In the meantime, you'll just have to settle for everything, all right? *Everything* is wrong with me."

"Well, let me know when everything *isn't* wrong with you." Sali turned in his chair and faced the front of the class. Mr. Harris gave the class a reading assignment and told them to start on it right away while he walked out of the classroom at least twice. Ashe glanced furtively at Mr. Harris, who seemed just as distracted as Mrs. Rocklin did. The rest of the day went much the same. Even Principal Billings didn't look happy. Figuring it was because his teachers weren't in a good mood, Ashe ignored the Principal of Cloud Chief Combined.

"Ashe, are you going to say anything?" his mother had driven the new SUV to pick Ashe up at school. Now she watched him as he wordlessly sat on the passenger seat of the new vehicle.

"Do you know what I have in common with Randy Smith? What Randy and I have in common with those kids that got killed in St. Louis and Fort Myers and Little Rock? Do you, Mom?" turning away after his outburst, Ashe stared out the window, watching green fields rush past. Spring had come and the hot weather that gripped western Oklahoma every summer wouldn't be far behind. Wheat would be harvested soon, and hay and straw baled. None of that mattered to Ashe at the moment.

"Ashe, what are you talking about?" Adele pulled over and stopped the SUV, putting it in park and letting it run.

"Didn't you see the news? Somebody let it slip that all those dead kids' parents went to the same fertility clinic in St. Louis, just like you and Dawn Smith did. Those kids are getting killed, Mom. Somebody is looking for them. Tell me why that is." Ashe's breath was ragged and he rushed through the words before he lost his courage to say them.

"Oh, dear God," Adele muttered. "Ashe, I don't know how you found that out, but you are protected, here. Do you think your father will allow anyone near you?"

"They didn't have to get close to Randy Smith, did they? They just found a different way to do him in. They're gonna let the werewolves do it," Ashe snapped angrily.

"We will not discuss this here in the car. I'm taking you home and you will go to your room and stay there until I talk to your father about this. Do you hear me?"

Ashe didn't say anything. He'd heard, all right. Of all the residents of Cloud Chief, Ashe had the best hearing.

❧

"Ashe, what's this I hear about an argument with your mother?" Aedan's eyes hadn't gone red yet, but Ashe figured that wasn't far off.

"I can put two and two together, Dad."

"And that's because you went digging through things without asking," Aedan pointed out judiciously. "Didn't you?"

"Because nobody tells me anything." Ashe huddled into his seat on the living room sofa. He didn't want to fight with his parents. Didn't want to fight with anyone, if the truth were known. It made him feel nauseous. But this—this was too important to ignore.

"Son, we're trying to protect you. Granted we didn't put this together until you mentioned it, but every adult in Cloud Chief is committed to protecting the children."

"Like Randy Smith?"

"Son, do not bring that up with me. Radomir and I spent more time on that than we should have. The boy will pay the price for a few careless words and a letter afterward. That's Pack business. You know that just as well as anyone here."

"But what if he's innocent? Doesn't that bother you? That could be me, Dad. It could." Ashe was trying to make his point, but the look on his father's face told Ashe what he needed to know—that his father wouldn't interfere with Randy's execution. "Never mind." Ashe said helplessly. "I can see nobody would interfere if it was me, either."

"Son, that's enough. You'll do without dinner tonight, and stay in your room." Aedan rose and stalked from the room, his eyes red.

"He refused breakfast," Adele said. "And lunch." Did his mother think he didn't hear? Ashe heard his mother talking with Denise DeLuca. He'd been introduced to Denise's sister, Marcella, but everybody called her Marcie. She had a haunted look in her eyes, in Ashe's estimation. Likely from leaving her two sons behind in Phoenix. Denise sent him to Sali's room, saying Sali was waiting for him there. Ashe wasn't sure he wanted to talk to Sali either.

"Dude, come look at this!" Sali held what looked like an old family album on his lap as he sat cross-legged on his rumpled bed. "These cars are cool. Grampa had a convertible. Look, Ashe. This is the one we need to get!"

Unwillingly, Ashe piled onto the bed to look at the car Sali pointed at in an old photograph. An ancient Cadillac convertible, with fins and taillights that reminded Ashe of old movies he'd seen, was depicted in the creased photo. The photograph was so old, it was in black and white. "That's Grampa, sitting in it," Sali said reverently. "Mom told me." Sali tapped the photo. "It was red—the car, that is."

"It is a nice car," Ashe reluctantly agreed.

"There's more," Sali flipped a page or two, showing Ashe other vehicles from a bygone era. A few were in color; many were not. The photographs were filled with people Ashe didn't recognize. Sliding against Sali's headboard, Ashe settled in to look at pages of photographs, painstakingly affixed to heavy, yellowed paper by small black wedges holding corners of photos. "Aunt Marcie says that nobody's looked at this in a long time," Sali said, turning another page.

"I don't think we have any old photographs," Ashe sighed, staring at members of Sali's family, many of whom were deceased.

"Here, keep our place, I'm going to see if Mom will let me have something to eat," Sali hopped off the bed after shoving the album into Ashe's lap. Ashe sighed and watched as his friend disappeared through the bedroom door, holding their place with a thumb while he looked ahead. On the next to the last page, his eyes opened wide. Then, glancing furtively around, Ashe carefully removed a photograph and slipped it inside a pocket of his cargo pants.

"Wow, there's one missing," Sali said when they reached that spot later. Sali had been careful with the small bowl filled with potato chips, letting Ashe turn the pages while they searched for more cars. Several photographs of people on horseback were displayed toward the back of the album. Ashe liked those more than Sali did.

"Could have fallen out," Ashe shrugged, not meeting Sali's eyes.

"I guess. This is neat, huh? Aunt Marcie said she found this in Grampa's things," Sali said.

"You never know what you might find when you go looking," Ashe replied enigmatically. "Will the Pack approve her membership?"

"Probably. Dad said she could take over Pat Roberts' house, if she wanted it and the Pack approves her application."

"Will she have to marry somebody here?"

"She gets to pick this time. Most female werewolves don't stay single long unless they want to. Anyway, that's what Dad says."

"Hey, squirts. Wanna go outside and play football or something?" Marco stood in the doorway, a football in his hands. Ryan Phillips was standing right behind him. "Come on, tapeworm. Let's get some sun while Mom and Dad say it's okay." Marco was tossing the football from one hand to the other and grinning.

"He called you tapeworm," Ashe grinned at Sali.

"Yeah. Let's go." Sali closed the album and left it on the bed as he and Ashe slipped their shoes on and followed Marco and Ryan.

"Ashe!" Cori hugged him the moment he'd walked outside—Dori and Wynn, with classmates Hayes, Jeff, Larry and a few others were all in the yard. Ashe looked around and saw Mr. Dodd, Micah Rocklin and Mr. Harris, all in the yard, talking quietly together.

"Ashe, everybody's on alert because Dawn Smith made some threats," Cori whispered in Ashe's ear as she hugged him.

"What?" Ashe stared into Cori's green eyes, a worried frown plastered on his face. "What kind of threats?" he asked softly.

"She said Randy might not be the only kid killed," Cori muttered. "Come on, let's go play Frisbee or something."

Ashe knew it was after six when Winkler, Trace and Jason drove up in Winkler's van. Trace and Jason were still running the store for his mother, and Mr. Winkler must have gone with them. Ashe leapt to catch the Frisbee Sali tossed in his direction, playing in human form this time. Ashe flipped it toward Cori, who laughed and went chasing it. "Dinner will be ready in fifteen," Marcus DeLuca stuck his head out the door and then stood back to allow Winkler, Trace and Jason inside.

"Heads up!" Sali shouted, hurling the Frisbee in Ashe's direction. Sali's aim was off, forcing Ashe to leap to the side in order to catch the flying disc. The sudden movement saved Ashe's life. A sharp crack sounded and Ashe felt the sting in his right shoulder as his hand stretched out to grab the plastic toy flying toward him. The Frisbee grazed the tips of his fingers as Ashe fell, things going dark around him while shouts and screams sounded. Ashe was unconscious by the time he landed across the new grass in Sali's front yard.

CHAPTER 16

"*A*she, honey, please wake up." His mother was crying and his right shoulder ached.

"He's coming around," Radomir's voice was close. Ashe blinked at the Enforcer, who stood behind his mother. Adele Evans sat on the edge of Ashe's bed, his fingers gripped tightly in her hand.

"What happened?" Ashe croaked. His mouth was so dry he almost couldn't speak.

"Somebody shot you. Your dad, Nathan and most of the werewolves are out looking for the gunman. Or woman."

"Mom, it wasn't Dawn Smith. You have to believe me," Ashe squeezed his mother's fingers. Right then, he felt as weak as a newborn lamb.

"Baby, I want to believe you. I do. But what if you're wrong?" Adele choked back a sob.

"I'm not."

"Ashe, do you need something for pain?" Radomir asked. "I should go help your father while I can."

"Mom, do we have ibuprofen?" Ashe's pain was waking. "Who got the bullet out?"

"It went all the way through, young one," Radomir almost smiled at

Ashe. "While I have some experience removing bullets from a vampire's flesh, I would have been afraid to take one from your shoulder. Thankfully, that was not necessary, although you have wounds on both sides, now." He pointed to Ashe's shoulder. "We have bandaged the wounds as well as we could, but you must rest after your mother brings the medicine."

"Mom, they were aiming for my heart. I jumped to catch the Frisbee. Sali's terrible aim saved my life." Adele wiped away more tears at Ashe's explanation.

"We'll buy Sali a nice dinner soon," she said, and rose to go find the bottle of pain reliever.

"I will go now, since the young one is awake," Radomir did smile this time. He nodded at Ashe and left the room.

Ashe discovered he still wore the cargo pants he'd had on earlier, although his shirt had been removed and a thick pad of gauze showing a bit of red was taped to his right shoulder. Reaching down, Ashe patted the large pocket on the side of his pants. The photograph was still there. Now he had to make careful plans, and having a bullet wound in his shoulder certainly limited what he might be able to do. Pulling the photograph out, although it shot shards of pain through his shoulder to do it, Ashe placed it in the drawer of his bedside table and shut it as quietly as he could.

"Here, baby," Adele handed two ibuprofen to Ashe and helped him sit up so he could take them with the glass of water his mother held for him. Ashe discovered how shaky he was when he sat up.

"What time is it?" Ashe whispered, once he was settled back in the bed and the awful pain of sitting up had subsided.

"It's after two in the morning," his mother replied.

"Mom, I don't think Dad and the others are going to find anything," Ashe sighed. Already his eyes wanted to close again. Sleep might take away the pain if the ibuprofen didn't.

"Honey, why do you say that?" Adele brushed hair away from Ashe's forehead.

"Because they don't know what to look for," Ashe mumbled and fell asleep.

~

"Nothing," Aedan shook his head as he and Radomir walked into the house half an hour before dawn. Sunday, April twenty-fifth had arrived, three days before the full moon. "How's Ashe doing?"

"Sleeping. I gave him ibuprofen and he went back to sleep, but he may be waking soon and need more." Adele hugged herself and stared out the kitchen window. Light would come soon, and Aedan would have to go to his bunker.

"Perhaps you should petition the Council for a physician to live in the community," Radomir said. "If a vampire physician cannot be found, then perhaps one of the humans the Council employs might be willing."

"We'll see," Aedan agreed. "I want to see my boy before dawn comes." Aedan followed Adele to Ashe's bedroom.

~

"Son?" Aedan touched Ashe's face carefully, waking Ashe.

"Dad?" Ashe thought his voice sounded as rough as bark on a pine tree. "Mom?" Adele was standing right behind Aedan. "Can I have some water?"

"Sure, honey. Do you need more ibuprofen?"

"Yeah." Ashe's shoulder felt as if it was on fire. Aedan lifted him up this time, and with his strength, it wasn't as difficult. Ashe swallowed pills and gulped water thirstily.

"Take it slow, son." Aedan's hand rubbed Ashe's back gently as Ashe did as his father asked. "Done?" at Ashe's nod, Aedan lowered Ashe into the bed. "I think Denise and Sali may come over after a bit so your mother can get some sleep," Aedan smiled. "Ask for medication if it's needed, all right?"

"I will." Ashe closed his eyes, hoping the pain would go away soon.

~

"I got him here as quickly as I could," Winkler brought a werewolf Adele and Denise didn't know two hours later. "He works as a paramedic for the Denton Fire Department," Winkler added. "I asked him to come and take a look at our young man."

"Thank you," Adele wiped tears away. "We've been giving him ibuprofen; that's all we had."

"I have something a little stronger," the werewolf said. "I'm David Lang," he added, holding a hand out to Adele. His other hand gripped what looked to be a case filled with medical supplies.

"We'll redress the wounds," David introduced himself to Ashe and sat down to examine Ashe's injuries. Sali had come in initially, but the room had become too crowded, so he'd backed out to wait until the adults were finished.

Ashe watched with trepidation as David produced a syringe wrapped in plastic, peeled the plastic away and expertly stuck the needle into Ashe's left arm after swiping the area with an alcohol wipe.

"What's that?" Ashe asked.

"Something for pain, young man. You'll feel sleepy in no time. That way it won't hurt so much when we rip off the tape and gauze. I reckon it's stuck to the wound already."

"Great," Ashe muttered. It wasn't long before Ashe's eyes did close, and he was asleep while David removed both dressings, cleaned out the wounds and bandaged them again. Then Winkler lifted Ashe off the bed and held him while Denise and Adele changed sheets.

"He'll sleep for three or four hours, I hope," David said, handing bottles of medication to Adele. "One of these every four to six hours for pain if he asks. This is an antibiotic," David held up another bottle. "Chances are he won't really need it, but we want to cover all the bases. Give it to him every eight hours. Clear liquids at first, but let him eat a little solid food tomorrow if he's up to it. Don't send him to school or let him do anything strenuous for two weeks. Longer if it looks like he's not healing as fast. Change the dressing every day and use those tubes of ointment with the bandages." David handed over a bag filled with bandages and medication to Adele.

"I can't thank you enough for this," Adele said.

"Don't worry about it. Just catch those idiots that did this." David smiled at Adele before following Winkler out of the house.

～

"Dude, your blood was everywhere, and I don't ever want to see that look on your dad's face again," Sali whispered.

"Now you know why I don't like getting in trouble," Ashe murmured. He felt nicely numb. Whatever the paramedic had given was working; the pain in his shoulder didn't even bother him.

"Mr. Radomir found the bullet in the dark," Sali sounded impressed. "I mean, we can see great in the dark, but I don't think we could have found that."

"They haven't found anybody. Have they?"

"No." Sali shook his head. "And everybody's in an uproar about it."

"They're not targets. At least most of them aren't. Sali, what happened to James's cell phone?"

"Nobody found it," Sali said. "Dad and Micah looked everywhere, and even upset Mr. and Mrs. Johnson when they searched James's room and stuff. But they never found it."

"Too bad," Ashe sighed, closing his eyes. Sleep was threatening and Ashe allowed it to claim him.

"Why does he want to know that?" Sali muttered to himself before leaving Ashe alone to sleep.

～

"He's asleep," Sali grumped, sitting at the table with his mother. Adele had agreed, after much coaxing, to lie down for a while.

"Sali, neither of you has been sick before. It doesn't happen with our kind. But a bullet will pull one of us down, or drugs, sometimes, if they're strong enough. You saw what happened with Adele." His mother ruffled Sali's black hair affectionately.

"Yeah." Sali drew invisible patterns on the Evans' kitchen table. "They're trying to kill the whole family," Sali said.

~

"I'm not sure how you knew to contact us," the woman eyed Winkler with distaste. Her kind didn't associate with werewolves. Nasty creatures, in her opinion. And *mortal*, never forget that.

"That doesn't matter. What does matter is that your Dark cousins have discovered your attempt to increase your numbers and they're picking them off, one at a time."

"What? That isn't true," she huffed.

"Proof." Winkler handed over a folder full of information. Not wishing to dirty her hands on what the werewolf offered, her subordinate took it instead. He didn't seem to mind where the folder came from; he leafed through it quickly and drew in a sharp breath.

"It's true," he gazed at his queen.

"There are two of your cousins in Oklahoma, and who knows how many more in all these other places, killing children or attempting to do so. Did you think to do as the cuckoos and leave your eggs in another's nest, allowing them to raise your children? And then, when the time was right, were you prepared to swoop in and gather them up? When you needed more soldiers for your army, perhaps?" Winkler gave the queen a hard stare.

"It is none of your business," the queen snatched the folder from her servant's grasp. "We will deal with this. Immediately. I'll have someone at this place," she scanned the folder to find a name.

"Cordell. And do it quickly. There isn't much time."

"Very well. We'll have someone there in two days."

"And I want bodies afterward."

"You'll have them. Feel free to do whatever you want with what's left of them."

Ashe slept through most of Sunday, waking for a short while when his mother brought chicken broth, water and more medication. Ashe ate as much as he could. Sali and Denise left as soon as Adele was awake and prepared to take over Ashe's care. "How do you feel, honey?" Adele asked.

"All right," Ashe said. "The medication keeps the pain away."

"Good. Sali tried to talk his mother into letting him stay with you tomorrow, but she refused."

"He'd just be restless," Ashe observed.

"I know. That child can't stay still for very long," Adele smiled.

"And he has to eat constantly or he'll become a black hole, sucking every bit of sustenance in his direction," Ashe joked weakly.

"Go back to sleep, hon. Your dad will probably check on you when he wakes." Adele patted Ashe's knee, picked up the bowl and walked out of Ashe's bedroom. Ashe waited for the door to close before pulling the photograph out of his bedside table and staring at it.

"Tomorrow," he promised the image. "I have to be awake enough tomorrow."

"Looks like more stormy weather's moving in," Ashe's father said later, as he sat on the side of Ashe's bed. "How are you feeling?"

"I'm okay, Dad. The medication works great. I sleep most of the time."

"That's good," Aedan said. "Go back to sleep, son."

What was he looking for? In Ashe's drugged state, he wasn't quite sure. Hadn't been when he'd set out. Now he flipped through papers, receipts and other scraps of this or that. This file box had been left in what looked to be a home office, with records and school papers littering the desktop. What if there wasn't anything to find? Ashe, feeling sick and in pain, desperately resumed his search. Wait, what was that? A receipt, with an address? Yes. That's what it was. Ashe jerked it from the box. Here was proof—if he could get anyone to listen to him. Ashe misted right through the roof after putting everything back as well as he could. Now there was only one more errand, and Ashe hoped he might stay conscious long enough to accomplish it.

"I made scrambled eggs and toast. I hope that won't upset your stomach."

"Rather have pancakes," Ashe mumbled, pushing himself up with his left elbow. The whole right arm shook, shivered and pained him if he jogged it even a little.

"I don't think that would be good for you right now," Adele said, setting the tray over Ashe's lap. "When you're better, I'll make all the pancakes you want."

"Maybe Sali should pretend to be sick if it'll get him what he wants to eat," Ashe smiled weakly at his mother.

"You look a little flushed. Are you sure you're not feverish?"

"No, I was thinking cold and clammy. When can I take a bath?" Ashe asked.

"I have some of those waterproof bandages that David left for you. We can cover up the wound with those. Do you think you can stand up long enough?"

"We have that plastic stool in the kitchen," Ashe pointed out. "It's a good thing I'm left-handed. I can wash myself."

"Then I'll get the stool and we'll see about getting you cleaned up."

Ashe was exhausted but feeling better after the shower. He'd been embarrassed that his mother had to help him, but eventually let her shampoo his hair because he couldn't do it very well one-handed. He got a good look at his wound, too, the front one, anyway. His mother said the one on the back was worse, since it was the exit wound. The phone rang while Ashe was settling back in bed. Adele went to answer it. Ashe heard every word when Denise DeLuca explained that somehow, Randy Smith had managed to escape. Ashe smiled and closed his eyes.

~

Something was pounding on the roof in Ashe's dream. Hard. He reminded himself that he was underground and safe, but the pounding continued. Eyes popping open, Ashe heard the rush of wind.

"Ashe, I think it's another tornado," Adele rushed in and knelt next to Ashe's bed. "That's hail hitting the roof, and it's almost the size of baseballs."

"Mom, it's okay, we're underground," Ashe tried to soothe his mother; she was shaking. She'd been through so much, lately, and this wasn't going to help.

"But what about the others?" Adele was worried for the rest of Cloud Chief. Not all of them had underground rooms or storm shelters.

"The electricity is still on," Ashe said, just before it blinked and went out. "We're okay," Ashe spoke into the darkness.

~

"Into the hallway, everyone!" Mrs. Rocklin shouted as the winds rose outside. Sali, glancing through a window, saw the trees at the edge of the school grounds whipping wildly. He scooted toward the door.

"Sali!" Marco grabbed his younger brother and shoved him into the floor against a cinderblock wall. Marco dropped on top of Sali, holding him, Cori and Wynn as tightly as he could; they'd all knelt down beside Sali. Others were doing the same, older ones hunching over the younger, teachers included.

"It's coming!" Mr. Dodd shouted as the roof of Cloud Chief Combined lifted away and was ground to bits by whirling winds.

~

"Ashe, I have to check on the others," Adele was still frightened but prepared to go help the others if help was needed.

"Go on, Mom, I'll be okay here," Ashe assured her. "Make sure Sali's okay. And Cori and everybody else."

"I will. Don't try to get up by yourself, Ashe. I'll be back as quick as I can."

Ashe nodded as his mother hurried out of his bedroom. Listening carefully, Ashe knew when his mother reached the kitchen, and moments later heard the kitchen door shut and the garage door lift up. Their house was still intact, it seemed. Normally, Adele would have set the alarm for the upper floor, but she was likely too distracted. Ashe wasn't sure he could climb the stairs to do it himself. It likely wouldn't matter anyway; his mother would be back soon. Ashe closed his eyes to sleep.

~

"No!" Denise DeLuca screamed as she flung herself out of the small car. The school was nearly gone, many classrooms had collapsed and she could find no immediate signs of life. Adele drove up moments later and nearly fell when she climbed out of Aedan's new SUV.

"Denise, we have to go look. We have to," Adele grabbed her friend's arm and led her toward the school building. Denise had stood, petrified at what the damage might mean. Both her boys had been inside. Other vehicles were arriving as Adele found the front steps of the school amid the rubble. More than anything, Adele wished that her vampire husband were there. Lifting walls and sections of heavy brick would be nothing to his strength. Instead, they had to make do with what they had.

"Any signs of life?" Mr. Winkler arrived with Marcus and Micah, heaving away concrete blocks and other debris, flinging it aside. "Hello!" he shouted. "Can anyone hear us?"

"Help!" Marcus recognized Greta Rocklin's voice. More people came, including two Adele didn't recognized.

"Not to fear, we will deal with this," one of them said. Adele stared in shock as the two of them, slightly pointed ears and all, held out their hands, lifting debris up with considerable power and sliding it through the air as if it were dandelion fluff. It fell with a crashing thump onto a deserted portion of the schoolyard.

"What the?" Marcus stared.

"Elemaiya," Mr. Winkler grunted, lifting away one of the heavy front doors and tossing it aside. There in the hallway, lined up along a section of cinderblock walls that still stood, was every student from Cloud Chief Combined, alive and unhurt.

"Thank God," Denise DeLuca muttered before falling to the ground in a faint.

The door beeped when it opened, just as it always did. His mother was home. The sound woke Ashe, and he was just about to settle into a doze again when he heard the voices.

"Perfect opportunity," one of the voices said. Ashe recognized it, all right. Had heard it every one of his seven years at Cloud Chief Combined. "Set the charges, and we'll still have time to get Nathan Anderson while the rest of them are at the school."

Charges? Ashe was sitting up and frightened in the space of a blink. They were setting charges? They were going to kill him and his father. And Radomir, and Nathan Anderson. Ashe heard them walking above his head. Three of them. Terrified, Ashe gathered clothing and a few other items before he went to mist, rushing through the underground portion of his home and diving downward once he reached his parents' bedroom.

Ashe hurtled away from his home as three men walked out of it and climbed into a vehicle Ashe recognized. *Mom!* He shouted mentally. *Mr. Winkler! Mr. DeLuca! They're about to blow up the house, and then they're going to blow up the Andersons!* Ashe was flying as swiftly as he could toward Nathan Anderson's home, hoping with everything in him that his mist would protect vampires in sunlight.

Nathan was gathered inside Ashe's mist and he was already flying skyward when the vehicle arrived in the Anderson's driveway. Ashe heard the boom behind him as his home was destroyed. Afraid to look back, Ashe flew high over the school and saw the devastation there while people were milling about it like ants. After the explosion marking the destruction of his home, some of those ants were loading into trucks and cars and skidding away from the school, driving swiftly toward his and Nathan Anderson's homes. Ashe hoped they'd catch the ones responsible before they got away.

CHAPTER 17

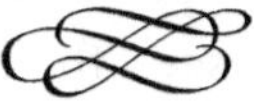

arcus was driving like a madman, with Winkler beside
him in the locksmith's van. Two others that Marcus
still had difficulty coming to terms with were sitting in the back. They
had nearly reached Nathan's house when the second explosion rocked
the ground beneath them, almost causing the van to slide off the
graveled path. Mr. Winkler uttered a curse when Marcus skidded to a
stop in the Anderson's front yard and jumped from the van.

"No," Marcus whispered, falling to his knees. The house had been
blown apart, the lower levels, including Nathan's underground
bunker were exposed to daylight, and the rest of the house was on
fire. Lavonna Anderson, who'd driven up right behind Marcus, was
screaming Nathan's name the moment she flung herself from the car.
Dori and Cori, both in tears and looking frightened, were hugging
against their mother.

"Is Ashe dead, too?" Sali had come with his mother and Marco.
Now, they all stared at the smoldering remains of the Anderson's
house as more rain began to fall.

"That first blast was probably the Evans' home," Winkler muttered
grimly. "Come," he grabbed both of the strange men by the scruff,

dragging them toward Marcus' van. "We'll be back," he said. Marcus, no longer paying attention to anything Winkler did, failed to respond.

∽

"I had to sedate her." David Lang was back and talking to Denise DeLuca inside the DeLuca's kitchen. Adele Evans was lying on the sofa inside Denise's living room. She'd been screaming and crying, almost from the moment she'd seen the ruins of her home.

"Did we really hear Ashe's voice, just before?" Marcus raked fingers through his dark hair.

"Yeah, Dad. You did. And that's not all Ashe could do, either." Marco had an untouched bottle of soda in front of him at the kitchen table. "Dad, where are Cori and her family right now?"

"At the O'Neill's, with Sharon and Jonas. Sharon says they're not doing very well, either."

"Can I go see them?"

"Son, whoever did this is still out there. I talked to Winkler half an hour ago. They're still looking, but they haven't found anything yet. I don't want anyone leaving the house. We could all be targets."

"Then I'll call over there and see if Cori is all right."

"Use my cell, the land-lines are still out of service from the tornado," Marcus handed the phone to his oldest son.

"Ashe, you can't be dead," Sali stroked the edges of his Frisbee, the round disk bearing tooth marks from too many games with his friend to count. Sali was huddled in his bed, shoes and all, feeling numb. For the first time in a very long time, he felt sick instead of hungry.

∽

"I'll notify the Council." Weldon Harper, Grand Master of the werewolves, spoke with Marcus DeLuca over the phone. Marco and Sali heard both sides of the conversation when Marcus called to inform the Grand Master of the day's events. "I'll wait until I hear from Winkler, though. I hope he'll capture those responsible, so I can at least tell the Head of the Council that. Radomir is his vampire child, you know."

"Oh, no," Marcus moaned.

~

"I'm still trying to figure out how you did this." Randy Smith sat in a corner of Old Harold's hidden bunker. Ashe, exhausted, had slept most of the day after dropping three vampires in the floor and passing out immediately after. Now, Ashe was awake and Randy was asking questions.

"I'm not really sure. Dad told me once that some really rare vampires can turn to mist and mindspeak. I can do that somehow without being vampire."

"You don't shapeshift?" Randy asked.

"No, I do that too, but it's embarrassing," Ashe mumbled. He still felt tired and his wound had bled again; there was a patch of red that had soaked through the front bandage. Ashe was afraid of what the wound on his back might look like.

"Has to be better than not doing anything," Randy sighed.

"Yeah. Sorry," Ashe apologized.

"Not your fault," Randy said. "I'm just glad you can do what you do. Otherwise I'd be dead meat, come tomorrow night."

"I couldn't let that happen," Ashe said. "Now, all I have to do is try to explain all this to Dad before he removes my head when he wakes."

"Then start explaining now," Aedan Evans said, startling Ashe. "Immediately."

~

"Cori, I hope he's not dead," Marco said. He'd called Cori earlier, but promised to call back when he had more privacy. He and Sali were sitting in the floor of Marco's room, Denise DeLuca's cell phone held between them so both could hear.

"Marco, if their house looks anything like ours," Cori wept.

"Cori, sweetheart, don't cry," Marco begged. "Just give it a little time, all right? If we don't hear anything by tomorrow, then we'll know the worst has happened with Ashe." Sali stared at Marco—he'd called Cori sweetheart. When did that happen?

"Daddy's dead," Cori wept. "And there's nothing left to bury."

"Cori, don't cry, please?" Marco was pleading with Cori over the phone. Sali's mouth dropped open in surprise.

⮧

"Your proof?" Aedan sounded skeptical at Ashe's story. Ashe was thankful that Old Harold had thought to place a lamp inside his bunker. Not for his father, but for him and Randy. Ashe handed an old photograph over, with a receipt from a gas station in Santa Fe. Aedan stared at both in surprise.

"I think I know where we need to go now," Nathan Anderson was staring at the two items over Aedan's shoulder. Radomir, who'd listened silently the entire time, nodded his head in agreement.

"You two, wait here, we'll come back for you," Aedan ordered, pointing at Ashe and Randy. "Don't leave this bunker for anyone else, do you understand?" Aedan pulled out his cell phone and made a call. "Winkler?" he said.

⮧

"Nice to know you're still among the living," Winkler said, answering the call.

"No time to talk pleasantries now," Aedan's voice came through the cell. "We know who's behind this, and we know where they might be." Aedan gave the location to Winkler, who whistled, agreed with Aedan and ended the call.

"Come on," Winkler jerked his head at Trace, Jason and the two Elemaiya. "We've got our targets. Let's go get them."

⮧

"Come on, son, let's get you out of here," Aedan was back and lifting a dozing Ashe.

"Did you get them, Dad?" Ashe asked sleepily.

"We did. Two are dead and the other one will spill everything he knows to Marcus DeLuca. Marcus can decide what to do with him after that. Randy, you come, too. You're in the clear, now." Randy Smith, captured and condemned to death only a few days earlier, breathed the fresh air of an Oklahoma night as he stepped outside Old Harold's home. "I'm free," he whispered, feeling as if the greatest weight in the universe had been lifted from his shoulders.

"You," he spat at Winkler and Radomir's prisoner, who sat between the Enforcer and the Dallas Packmaster in the back of Winkler's van. "Did you kill my dad or did you have somebody else do it?"

"One of the others," the prisoner replied, his voice robot-like.

"He's under compulsion to tell the truth," Radomir said. "I placed it myself. But save your questions for when we reach Mr. DeLuca's home. That way we will not be repeating ourselves."

"All right," Randy sighed. "How's Ashe doing?"

"He's fine, breathing evenly and his heart rate is good," Aedan replied. Ashe's father held the sleeping boy in his lap on the passenger side of Winkler's van while Nathan Anderson climbed into the driver's seat and started the vehicle. He didn't even use the lights to navigate his way through Cloud Chief.

"Dad, it's Winkler's van!" Marco shouted, looking out the kitchen window.

"Come on," Marcus led the way outside, followed by Marco, Sali and Micah Rocklin. They all stood in shocked surprise as Winkler and all three missing vampires piled out, followed by Randy Smith, Ashe Evans and Paul Harris, Cloud Chief's English teacher. Mr. Harris was held firmly between Radomir and Winkler.

"Here's your culprit, and there are two dead collaborators in the back of the van," Winkler said.

"What the hell?" Marcus stared in dismay at Paul Harris.

"Come along, he has a story to tell and I don't want you to miss a single word," Aedan said, carrying Ashe, who was now awake.

"Hey, dude," Ashe gave Sali a weak smile. Sali was whooping and punching the sky immediately.

~

"This is what Ashe used to solve what we couldn't," Aedan handed over the photograph and the receipt. The photograph showed Paul Harris, standing next to Dawn Smith, his hands on the shoulders of two small boys. Twins, actually.

"Dawn and Paul were married?" Denise was shocked by what she saw.

"Long ago," Aedan nodded. "You only knew Dawn after she left Paul Harris behind. Ashe filched that photograph from your father's album," he added. "It's yours, when Marcus is done with it, that is."

"But how?" Denise still didn't understand.

"My boys are dead, and she went off and married that human," spittle flew from Mr. Harris' mouth as he hissed the word *human*. "I wanted both of them to die. The boy and his father. My boys died in a fire and she went off and married *him*."

"How did you hook up with those others?" Marcus growled at Mr. Harris. He'd seen both bodies in the back of Winkler's van. One looked human, except for the pointed ear tips. The other was something out of myth. It carried a jackal's head atop an eight-foot human body, except for the claws it bore on hands and feet. One of the two that had come to help Winkler said he was misshapen—an aberration from the normal. Not knowing exactly what normal was for that particular race, Winkler had refrained from asking questions.

"I went looking for someone who could help me," Paul Harris replied, his eyes unfocused. "I caught them spying on the New Mexico community one night, and when I learned they were looking for a boy who appeared human and whose mother had gone to a certain clinic in St. Louis, I'd found the perfect collaborators." Paul Harris blinked at Marcus—his words were forced. He wanted to fight Radomir's compulsion, but it was much too strong. He couldn't deny it.

"Randy fit the description; they just needed to get him away from Dawn and Terry," Mr. Harris went on. "They don't have any desire to start a race war with the vampires and the werewolves; they've had a war going with some of their own kind for thousands of years. But the numbers are dwindling on both sides. When the Bright side came up with the idea of farming out the births by donating eggs, it was an ideal situation. Their half-children are nearly as capable as the full-blood ones, and make good soldiers in the army. When the Dark side got a whiff of what the Bright side was doing, they sent out some of their own to kill the children."

"This is worse than I ever imagined it could be," Radomir sighed. "In my experience with the Elemaiya, even though they call themselves Dark and Bright, in my opinion there's not much difference between the two. They only see an enemy and will stop at nothing to kill one another. Put them side by side and they look exactly the same."

"I've never heard of them before," Marcus said. "Paul, how did you manage to get Randy to say what he did, to get him expelled from the community?"

"Not hard. Those things have their own version of compulsion. They told him what to say and when to say it. Convenient, don't you think, that Ben happened to be in the same restaurant when Randy let that slip?"

"You arranged it," Marcus said flatly.

"I certainly did. I fooled every one of you. Didn't I?" he grinned widely, leering at Marcus. "It would have been easy to kill Randy afterward, except my collaborators discovered he wasn't the one they were after. Ashe was."

"But what about James? Why was he killed?" Denise asked. The Johnsons would want to know.

"He saw the Elemaiya that night. Was going straight to you, Marcus, with the information. We had to stop him, you see. One of the others dumped his body behind the Evans' house. We thought it would implicate Aedan. We didn't know he wasn't at home."

"And you wrote the letter that Randy was supposed to have written," Marcus was now beginning to see how it was all done.

"I did. I have plenty of papers from all the students over the years. Wasn't hard to reproduce Randy's handwriting, now was it? I drove to Santa Fe the weekend before the letter was delivered here and mailed it from there."

"Hence the receipt," Radomir tapped the receipt for fuel that bore the Santa Fe address. "He then attempted to place the blame on Harold for James's death, beheaded Harold and killed Pat Roberts, only Pat's body wasn't supposed to be found so we'd think Pat killed Harold and fled afterward. And then had his cronies place more compulsion on the Daniels woman to kill herself and attempt to kill Ashe at the same time, to account for the human deaths. When he was standing in your yard, Mr. DeLuca, pretending to help guard the children, one of his partners tried to kill Ashe with another stolen gun."

"But what about Megan?" Marco had listened silently while Paul Harris confessed, but no mention had been made of Megan.

"We don't need humans infiltrating Cloud Chief," Mr. Harris focused on Marco. "You would have brought her in; don't try to deny it. So I had her killed. It was convenient, too, after we killed Terry Smith, to make it look like a human serial killer was on the loose. The Daniels woman was a perfect choice for my plan." Marco cursed at Paul Harris' words.

"Unbelievable," Marcus said, shaking his head and hauling out his cell phone. "Grand Master?" Marcus said when the call was picked up on the other end. "I have a new development."

~

"I'm not sure I've ever heard of a high school graduation held in a barn," Sali grumped, fanning himself with the folded leaflet listing names of the graduating class. Marco's name was one of seven.

"Come on, it's fun," Ashe grinned at his friend.

"Ashe," Marco, dressed in a black graduation robe and mortarboard hat with a silver tassel, leaned over Ashe's shoulder and whispered his name.

"Huh?" Ashe stared up at Marco. Marco tapped his left shoulder. Ashe stared for a moment before grinning and nodding his head. "I'll be back," Ashe said and rose to follow Marco.

Fifteen minutes later, Sali was still sitting by himself in front of the small stage Aedan and Nathan had built for the graduation ceremony. They were only waiting for night to fall before the lights would come on, the vampires could appear and the graduation would commence. Sali watched as the sun set moments later and lights winked on inside the O'Neill's barn. Each year, the graduating seniors all made a speech when they accepted their diplomas. They were warned every time to keep them short and polite.

"Salidar," Aedan smiled and sat next to Sali, with Adele sitting on the other side. Sali had chosen seats in the second row, right behind the ones his parents would occupy when they came in. Graduation was quite a ceremony for the community.

"Here come Mom and Dad," Sali whispered, causing Aedan to chuckle. All the parents of the graduating seniors were led in behind the school faculty and seated in the front row. Once that was accomplished, Melody Patterson, the science teacher, moved to a piano and began to play *Pomp and Circumstance*. The crowd hushed and the seniors marched in. Sali looked across the aisle where Dawn and Randy Smith sat. Cori, Dori, Nathan and Lavonna sat with them. Cori smiled at Sali before turning her attention back to the seniors, her eyes mostly on Marco.

Principal Billings gave the usual address to the crowd before calling the seniors forward, one by one. Marco had asked to be last. "Where's Ashe? He's missing this," Adele whispered to Sali, who shrugged. Some of the seniors' speeches were funny, some fumbled, some poignant. And then it was Marco's turn. He walked to the podium and gripped the edges lightly, surveying the community before him.

"My friend James was supposed to be here tonight," Marco said. Many heads bobbed in the seats before him. "All I can do is honor him and his memory, in a ceremony that he was supposed to share with us," Marco added. "I haven't ever been good with words and as a senior, I know I'm supposed to say something profound," Marco went on, grinning suddenly at the crowd. "But my dad always told me actions speak louder than words. I think James would appreciate my actions tonight. Principal Billings, this is for you."

Marco stood back and tapped his shoulder. What looked to be a tiny brown spot dislodged and flew away from Marco, only to hover and flap in Principal Billings' face for several seconds. The frightened Principal flailed his arms, screeched loudly and did his best to fend off the tiny creature. When the miniature bat sent out his piercing call, every werewolf, vampire and shapeshifter in the crowd heard it and winced. As if by magic, Ashe appeared on stage before a stunned and terrified Principal Billings, while Marco whipped off his graduation robe and settled it over Ashe's bare shoulders.

"Guess I won't have to go to Cordell Junior High after all," Ashe announced with a grin. Principal Billings scowled angrily as the crowd stood and cheered.

EPILOGUE

The Grand Master turned the envelope over in his hand. It had been mailed from Cordell, Oklahoma, and the sender had only placed initials instead of a name in the upper left corner. It was properly addressed, however. Someone had gotten his name and post office box. Slitting the envelope open, two pieces of paper dropped out. The Grand Master opened the smaller of the two.

I know you didn't get this the first time, so I'm sending it to you now—A. E. The second, longer piece was then unfolded and read thus:

Amputation
by
Randall Smith

Every year we plant a community vegetable garden. Ground is plowed, tilled, sowed. I walk behind a shapeshifting lioness as she drops seeds into the moist, turned earth, watching as the corn kernels fall from her hands. Most land in the furrow. I see one that falls outside it, blown by the wind perhaps, or by fate. I am that seed. The one that fell beyond the accepted trough of soil. The one to be culled as soon as it sprouts away from conventional parameters. It doesn't belong. Will never belong. Neither to the community that birthed it nor to those who surround it. That is my fate—to live, unaccepted by two worlds and not just the one.

I am half werewolf, but that half lies dormant within me, a seed that never grew. A siren that taunts and teases and remains forever out of reach. How many others like me are there? Taught from birth that they will never truly belong anywhere? Sighing, I carefully rake soil over the row of planted corn and when the others aren't watching, I tip the errant kernel into the furrow with my boot and cover it, too. Unlike me and others like me, it will have a chance, now. An opportunity to belong to only one world. A chance to be accepted by the neighbors around it. That opportunity will never come for me. Even now, those around me distance themselves. I will be outcast soon. Oh, I will still come home every day to my parents. For a few years, at least. But the friends I grew up with will drift away, when we no longer have the bonds of common interest to pull us together. The knot has been untied. No, severed. Once broken, it will never repair itself. Cannot repair itself.

I am the wound that will not heal. The scar to be removed, the weed to be pulled. An injured limb that will fester and infect the rest of the body if it isn't cut away. Perhaps I will stand before the Grand Master someday and argue for the rights of the half-children. The ones cast away after the age of twelve, sent to learn among humans.

My mother says she loves me, but she is werewolf. My father says the same, and he is human. Yet neither of their worlds accepts me as their own. Neither will step forward and claim the misshapen child they produced together. No, the deformity is not on the outside. It is inside and hidden. Can never be brought into the sunlight and examined. Talked of. Explained. This will be my life from now on. Shunned. Forced to walk apart.

Other.

The End